THE
RUGGED
AND THE
Refined

THE
RUGGED
AND THE
Refined

WYOMING TERRITORY

RUTH TRIPPY

HOLLAND PRESS

The Rugged and the Refined
© 2021 by Ruth Trippy

Holland Press
Auburn, Georgia

Printed in the United States of America

1. Women Teachers—the West—19th century—Fiction. 2. Cowboys—19th century—Fiction. 3. Wyoming Territory—Big Horns—Fiction. 4. Buffalo—Occidental Hotel & Saloon—Fiction. 5. Cattle Barons vs. Homesteaders—Johnson County—19th century—Fiction. 6. Hole-in-the-Wall—Rustlers—Fiction. 7. Romance—Fiction. 8. Christian—Fiction.

Cover Design by Sean Allen
seanallencreative@gmail.com

ISBN

Jesus saw Nathanael coming to Him,
and saith of him,
'Behold an Israelite indeed, in whom is no guile!'

John 1:47

HISTORIC PHOTOS

1883 Sketch of Buffalo, Wyoming Territory

Lord Moreton Frewen

Charming youngest son of a wealthy Englishman, came to Wyoming in 1878. Established the huge 76 Ranch. Ran up debts involving others and earned the nickname, "Mortal Ruin."

Major Frank Wolcott

Received his military title in the Civil War. Early 1870s appointed U.S. Marshall for Wyoming, but removed from office by the governor for offensive behavior. Later led the infamous Johnson County War.

Occidental Hotel Saloon - Yesteryear

Occidental Hotel Saloon – Present Day

BOOKS BY RUTH TRIPPY

ACKNOWLEDGMENTS

Ah! That broken wheel on the stagecoach journey, the way "trouble" began in my story. However, during my research trip in the West, I took a stagecoach ride and the driver told me that a broken axle was more likely. So I rewrote the scene. Before sending the book off for publication, I had an uneasy feeling about my description of axle repair on the desolate Wyoming plains. I finally got up the gumption to call the curator of Cheyenne Frontier Days Old West Museum, Mike Kassel. He answered by saying he didn't think a broken axle was possible. After Mike consulted with an associate who builds stagecoaches from the bottom, up, Mike told me that axles were made of iron, and in order to damage one, the stage would have to go off a cliff. Well, I thought, there's nothing like main characters suffering an early demise! These Cheyenne experts had me back to writing in a broken wheel. But who would have guessed a lodgepole pine log would be the temporary fix to get the stage to civilization?

My heartfelt thanks go to my Critique Group: Donna Lott, Peggy Moore and Carol James who gave input on the entire book, including those rewrites of Chapter One. Thanks also to those who critiqued part of the novel: Hope Welborn, Bette Noble and Laura Petherbridge.

The Occidental Hotel in Buffalo, Wyoming, was wonderful in directing my husband and me to the Crazy Woman Canyon, the site for Margaret and Nat's adventure (including ours!). And our sojourn at this famous Western motel was an adventure in itself, the two nights we slept in the Herbert Hoover suite, where this President had lodged for two weeks.

Appreciation goes to the Jim Gatchell Museum in Buffalo and Sharon Miller who sent me the picture labels I was unable to copy in the museum. I saw the note near the piano owned by the charismatic Lord Frewen, learning of his dastardly intentions toward a homesteader supposedly settled on Frewen range. Also, a big thanks to Nancy Tabb of the Buffalo Public Library who sat with me and guided me to historic documents for both the town of Buffalo and Johnson County.

Then there's my chauffeur: husband Ernie, who drove to Wyoming and beyond for "adventure." He has found his way into each male protagonist in my novels, but this time he outdid himself. My colorful husband shared Nat's athleticism, his sense of humor, his poetic turn of phrase despite a lack of advanced formal education, and yes, also his wild past.

A big thanks likewise goes to my son Matt who assisted me numerous times with computer problems, helping me navigate through what still seems foreign territory.

My editor Gloria Spencer caught all sorts of little things I thought I had already taken care of with my many rewrites. Thank you, Gloria. And, I appreciate the fine formatting Allison Smith did for this book.

Another talented person is Sean Allen who created my book cover. Whenever I suggested something, he came through immediately, often with an idea to top mine.

With each of my novels I try to highlight a spiritual truth. So, I am grateful for the prayers, not only of my Critique Group, but especially the faithful prayers and love of my Aunt Anita Van Wyk and my friend Candy Menedis. I'm also mindful of my responsibility to keep a writer's heart right before the Lord, and to spend meaningful time with Him, keeping sensitive to that next inspirational thought or insight He gives me for the book.

This story, readers, is my gift to you.

Blessings,
Ruth Trippy

1

Margaret Arnell gazed out the stagecoach window, lulled into a half drowsy state by the heat and constantly bumping coach. The trail was rough. She felt cooped up and tired, not having realized the stage would travel day and night, stopping only for meals.

Long ago she had shed her jacket and gently, without anyone noticing, she hoped, loosened the top of her blouse so that her neck would catch any wind. She'd not admit to thinking of the cooler rooms in her parents' home in Chicago. It was her own decision to travel to Wyoming, hunting a little adventure to escape her very sheltered and predictable life at home. She had to make good, or she'd feel ashamed of taking a stand to come here.

Tall, waving grasses stretched mile after mile as the stage headed for the newly formed town of Buffalo, and to its west, Fort McKinney and the Big Horn Mountains. She was a teacher, or about to become one, so she had investigated all this before leaving home.

To relieve the tedium of the trip from Rock Creek, a banker Mr. Richard Norland, had been telling stories about his experiences in the West. Sitting next to her, he'd been most attentive.

On the opposite seat, Mrs. Lumpkin, with her baby, and a very young cowboy next to her, seemed to appreciate the stories as well.

Some miles back a couple of other passengers had alighted at an isolated ranch, so now they had more room—and air—in the coach. But hot air, Margaret observed. Her interest had quickened a while ago when she spied mountains out the window of the coach, but then the heat and dust had overtaken her.

Now the rocks seemed to have become larger as the coach started uphill and the ride became bumpier.

Suddenly, she heard a sharp crack and felt a horrible jolt as the coach lurched. She fell heavily against the banker. The young cowboy threw his arm over the mother and baby to stop them from flying off the seat.

The driver was shouting, swearing to high heaven, trying to bring the horses to a stop. The coach dragged, bumping along terribly.

What had happened?

The coach halted, but rocked unsteadily. Mr. Norland held Margaret firmly. She tried to straighten herself and looked up. "Excuse me, sir!" She hadn't meant to grab him like that.

Inside the coach the baby was screaming, the mother talking over him, trying to calm things. The young cowboy, who'd been swearing right along with the driver up top, apologized, then tried to soothe the mother and baby.

Everyone strained to right himself in the lopsided coach.

The driver jumped down from his perch and appeared at a door. "We're getting out, folks. 'Course first class passengers are allowed to stay inside."

"What happened?" the banker asked.

"Front wheel broke."

Margaret and Mr. Norland were first class passengers, their tickets assured them of remaining inside in comfort during any emergency, but she was eager to get out and stretch her legs.

THE RUGGED AND THE REFINED

Besides, she wanted to see what had happened.

She joined the men at the front of the stagecoach. The man who had been riding shotgun gave her a sideways glance as if questioning her presence there. He couldn't know about her innate curiosity. Gracious, that's one reason she'd left Chicago.

"We need to cut a tree for a pole," the driver said, turning to the banker. "The trouble is—" his gaze swept the grass-covered plains "—trees are downright scarce around here. 'Course there'd be plenty of cottonwood along a river." He jerked his head back the way they'd traveled. "There was a small stream a couple mile back, but as I remember, a larger one's farther on. We'd have better luck there." He spat on the ground. "What I wouldn't give for a lodgepole pine 'bout now."

"Why's that?" the banker asked.

"You won't find a nicer, straighter log in creation."

"Where can you find them?" Margaret asked.

The driver jerked his head to the west. "On the side of them mountains, 'bout fifteen mile away."

Margaret left the men to figure out how to handle the problem.

Searching for a place to sit, she noted a fine film of dust had settled over the rocks and bushes. How she longed to wash her face with water. But because that refreshing commodity was scarce, she dared not.

The shotgun rider, squatting near the broken wheel, now stood and straightened up. He walked over to Margaret.

"Will it be much longer?" she asked.

"Ma'am, I'm 'fraid this is goin' to be a slow business. We need a straight, hefty tree branch. I'm goin' up that rise to see if I can spot some cottonwood. Would you like to stretch your legs a bit?" He motioned up the incline. "Just a hundred feet or so up there, and we'll come on back."

She hesitated a moment, then decided to join him. Her mother had cautioned her before she'd left home. "I hear

Western men are gentlemen toward women, but there will be exceptions. There are plenty of roughnecks and cowboys—so you be careful. Have your wits about you." Her mother had sighed. "I don't know why you want to teach out west anyway. Even if that family sponsoring you in Wyoming sounds perfectly proper, you had a good offer here in the Ladies' Seminary."

It felt like the scoldings she'd been given as a child.

That was precisely one of the reasons she'd decided to come West—to be on her own, to be treated as an adult. She had begun to feel as if she hadn't room to breathe.

The train ride west had been delightful. Mile after mile of wide-open country to Cheyenne. Yes, here she could breathe freely.

And it had been perfectly safe. The Union Pacific Railroad saw to that.

Afterward, from Cheyenne to Rock Creek, the long miles on the stagecoach traveling north to Buffalo, the West no longer seemed so romantic. Rolling plain upon rolling plain of dry grassland had become tedious. The trail was dusty. Dirt blew into the coach. Then came the feeling of isolation. After that last small ranch, this looked like no man's land. Not a dwelling in sight, but plenty of rolling hills, grass, rocks. And dust.

Margaret and the shotgun rider reached the top of the rise. Both were silent, scanning the horizon, "I know it seems desolate out here. And dry."

"Yes, it does." She looked west and pointed. "The Big Horns?"

"Yes, ma'am."

"Is that where Custer was killed?"

"No. That was a ways up north in the *Little* Big Horns. But yup, in '76 Custer and his whole outfit got wiped out, just seven years ago. Those Sioux were smarter than he thought. Too bad."

She'd read accounts of it in the paper. Everyone had. She could hardly believe she was in the very country where that massacre had occurred.

"Ah-h!" A curse burst out of him. "Sorry, ma'am. Was studyin' that column of dust out yonder and all but forgot I had a lady with me."

"Is something wrong?"

"Don't rightly know. That much dust might be a number of riders…and out there with no trail…." His voice sounded worried. He tipped his hat. "'Excuse me."

Margaret watched him shamble down the rise and disappear around the other side of the stagecoach. Had he gone to see the driver? She decided to follow.

Obviously, he'd been concerned about something, and she wanted to know what it was. She had a lively interest in situations and people. Even as a young girl, she'd gotten into trouble, and been rescued more than once.

"Curiosity killed the cat," Margaret's governess had often warned, even though she applauded the girl's inquisitiveness. After all, there was such a thing as recklessness.

Margaret stopped at the near side of the coach and listened to the men talking on the other side.

"Don't like that dust," the shotgun rider said. "Not that much of it, anyway. Likely it's several riders." He spat into the dirt. "Now, you tell me what they're doin' comin' across country that way, no road or trail out there…and this here place we're stranded, you can't see 'til somebody's right on top of you."

"Trouble is," the driver agreed, "we got that Hole-in-the-Wall gang somewhere in this territory. And a few renegade Injuns roamin' off their reservation causin' mischief." The driver paused, as if assessing their next move. "Go up there again and keep a lookout. First we'll see who's comin,' then we'll tackle this wheel."

A twinge of fear struck Margaret. She'd heard and read about outlaws and Indians, and this country was pretty wild. She backed away from the coach and bumped into the banker. He'd come to stand behind her, listening as well.

His hand steadied her.

"Thank you. I'm so sorry, I didn't realize you were here." But she felt uncomfortable with him so close. She stepped away and his hand dropped.

"I know you're worried, listening to that stage driver. But don't be afraid, Miss Arnell." He patted the side of his coat with one hand. "My friend and I can protect you."

Did he have a concealed gun? It must be small. No bulge could be detected where he indicated. She instinctively drew back another step. "I think I'll go see how Mrs. Lumpkin and her baby are doing."

It was the best excuse she could think of to move away. He'd accompanied her from Cheyenne, introduced by the elderly couple who'd chaperoned her from Chicago, old friends of her parents. This couple had been instructed to find someone to go with her from Cheyenne to Buffalo. During the long miles, he had entertained them all, but now she remembered, again, the way he'd kept glancing at her. Of course, she was the only single woman on the stage. But once again, she felt the need to show her independence. Leaving her parents as she had, she wasn't about to tie herself to a man. No matter how handsome or attentive. Was he handsome? Not exactly. But he was well-dressed and polished—as much as one could be in this heat and dust.

Mrs. Lumpkin had found a large boulder and she sat with her back against it, her baby crooked in her arm. Margaret chose a flat rock nearby. The baby was fussy and the mother tired. Margaret had never handled babies, so hesitated to help hold him. However, she could offer to get whatever the mother might need. And she'd sit and talk awhile; it would help pass the time for them both.

As an only child growing up, she'd longed to be with other children. Her wealthy family had provided her with a private tutor for years, and finally the last twelve months of schooling she'd been placed in a class with other students her own age. And loved it. They were the brothers and sisters she lacked, and thus, had birthed her love of the classroom—and teaching.

As Margaret talked, Mrs. Lumpkin rocked the child in her arms. Finally, the fretful boy fell asleep. The mother sighed. "If you don't mind, I'm goin' to nap, too."

Margaret repositioned herself. Dared she lift her skirts to get some air? It was so hot.

She looked around and saw the shotgun rider, still standing on that rise. She decided to join him once again.

Now looking in the direction where he'd spotted that dust, she could see nothing. "You think they're still coming?"

"Sure do."

"Where?"

"See that pile of rocks in the distance? Off behind it is a dip, with a little dust lingerin' in the air."

She squinted. "I see it!"

"Don't sound so happy, ma'am. Might be trouble. That bunch ain't takin' no trouble to hide its comin'. Must be awful confident."

"You think there are several men?"

"Likely so, with that much dust." He turned to leave. "We'd better get ready for company. Good or bad."

He glanced in Mrs. Lumpkin's direction. "Ma'am, maybe you better stay with her."

Margaret stood, undecided, but when she noticed the shotgun rider join the driver near the horses' heads, she quietly walked to the protected side of the stagecoach. She positioned herself so she could look through the coach windows to see what was happening toward the rise. The sun beat down where she stood, the air stifling.

Mr. Norland stepped near her. "Stay out of sight, away from these windows." He took her elbow and positioned her where she was better protected. But now she couldn't see. He took up the place where she had just been standing.

A slight irritation rose in Margaret. Even though she was afraid, curiosity welled up in her. She wanted to know what was happening.

The driver instructed the shotgun rider to station himself on one end of the stagecoach, the young cowboy, a lad of about fifteen, to stand on the other end, both using the coach as cover. The driver took his stance near the horses.

Margaret waited, alert, tense. She could hear no sounds from the baby. Thankfully, he still slept. And probably, the mother, too.

The silence was palpable. No one dared breathe.

Suddenly, birds flew up from beyond the rise. Something had startled them. Margaret's muscles tightened.

She heard movement. Hooves hitting rock. It was difficult to tell exactly how far away they were. Living in the East, she'd never listened to horse hooves to gauge distance.

She closed her eyes a few moments, to calm the tension. Then she could hear the sound of multiple hooves hitting rocks and stones. Near her, the hammers of one gun after another clicked back.

"Ho, there!" a forceful voice called out. Saddle leather creaked and stones crunched underfoot as someone dismounted.

The driver called out, "Hello! What's your business?"

"Headin' out to a neighbor's homestead." There was a pause. "You got trouble?"

The coach driver stepped from behind the horses. "Yup. Broken wheel."

The newcomer cleared his throat. "Well, I'm draggin' a couple of lodgepoles behind my mule. And I've got tools."

"Be much obliged for your help, mister. The next stand of cottonwood is a far piece from here."

Margaret's breathing steadied. This stranger apparently posed no threat. She stepped near Mr. Norland to see through the coach's far window.

"Ma'am," he whispered. "Let's hear a little more before we make ourselves known."

Taking his advice, Margaret quietly studied the scene on the other side of the coach. A tall fellow had paused beside his horse, taking off his wide-brimmed, black hat. He ran the sleeve of his rough brown shirt around the inside rim. Then he stretched broad shoulders, set his hat back on his head, and pulled it well down over his forehead. As the cowhand walked over to inspect the broken wheel, the driver joined him.

"You're lucky," he said to the driver, "that I happen to be draggin' lodgepole pine. Neighbor ran short for his lean-to. So, you know 'bout makin' a travois?"

"Yup. We got enough men to put that back wheel up front."

"Good. I'll go 'n cut off a length." He motioned to the young cowboy. "Son, if you'll give me a hand."

The man sauntered over to a mule and extricated an axe from the pack. The mule had been dragging logs behind the cowhand's horse. Margaret smiled. The mule explained the multiple rider theory, plus all that dust raised by the logs.

The cowhand untied a pine and let it drop to the ground, then dragged it off a few feet. "Needs shortenin' a bit. Here, take my gloves," he offered the boy. "Hold the trunk steady, this'll jar some."

The man spread his feet and tapped a spot on the trunk. Lifting his arms high, his whole torso strained with the blow. The axe hit the tree with a resounding *thwack*, jarring the boy, but he held on.

In short order, the needed length was cut. The cowhand retied the remains of the tree to the mule.

He carried the log to the rear of the coach. The other men had already put the rear wheel onto the front. "Now," he said, "if you'll help me wedge this log up under the undercarriage—"

Margaret stood a way off, watching intently. The men

positioned themselves. They angled the log, then grunted and heaved.

Margaret had seen a picture of an Indian travois, but how strange this looked. Whoever thought a log could replace a back wheel?

The men gave one last heave. "That's it!" the driver shouted.

The baby awoke and began to cry. From where Margaret stood, she heard the mother try to sooth him.

The men stepped away to inspect their work. The log dragged behind the stagecoach in the same manner as an Indian travois. But now the stagecoach was all lopsided.

The cowhand stretched, locked his hands behind his neck, and took a deep breath.

The driver thrust out his hand. "Want to thank you, mister."

"You're welcome." The cowhand grasped the driver's hand.

As his hand dropped, he glanced where Margaret stood. His gaze lingered, his eyes holding hers. The banker stepped to her side.

From behind the boulder, Mrs. Lumpkin appeared with her baby. "Well, now…" she began.

Startled, the cowhand turned.

Without another word, he tipped his hat, then walked briskly to his horse and stepped into the saddle. Touching the horse's flank, he was off.

He didn't look back.

2

Nat Logan lifted the saddle off his horse and flung it on top of the stall's wall. The pack mule he'd see to in a few minutes. Despite the fact he felt all in, his animals got first consideration. He was grimy with sweat and trail dust, but he ignored the discomfort.

The boss had told him to "take five." He'd do just that after rubbing down his horse. His mind drifted to what the boss had said.

He'd come off the plain past the house, when Mr. Walker stepped out the office, asking him to come inside. He tied the horse and mule to the rail. The office felt cool compared to the heat outside.

"Sit down, Nat. This will just take a minute." Mr. Walker sat opposite. "I appreciate you taking those lodgepole pines to our neighbor. What did you think of our cattle numbers in the west pasture?"

"Hard to tell, they were so spread out. But there weren't as many as I expected."

"I was afraid of that. The cattle on the eastern range seem to be keeping up their numbers fine. So what do you think's wrong?"

"You've mentioned some of the neighbors missing steers. Now it looks like we've been hit, too. Rustlers?"

"I hope not. With Hole-in-the-Wall some thirty miles from here, I'd hoped those gangs wouldn't bother with us."

"Well, we got some good stock," Nat said. "And there's always a few Sioux raidin' parties on the loose."

"They're supposed to be on their reservation."

"Those young bucks occasionally like some fresh beef. Can't blame 'em. Just happy they haven't stolen any horses."

"Those corrals being near the house makes 'em a bit safer. But those first years, I had a cowhand set out nights, guarding against road agents. Those thieves always like the best horses, and you know I try for superior stock. And thanks to you," he nodded for emphasis, "that stallion you brought in last year for my mares has turned out some dandy colts. You have a way with horses."

"I love them, that's the first and the last of it, sir." Nat felt a smile come on. "They know it."

"Good. Back to this other—I want you to keep an eye on that western herd. And keep your ear to the ground on talk going around. Especially what cowboys from other spreads are saying."

"They've already mentioned Hole-in-the-Wall. The trouble is, no one knows exactly where that hideout is or how to get into it. You got to know it's well guarded. Probably with a narrow entrance that's easily watched."

"Rustlers and Indians aren't the only possibilities." Mr. Walker leaned forward over his desk. "The last time the big ranchers met, there was talk of homesteaders conveniently taking unbranded calves for their own. Or any stray cattle."

"Huh! 'Bout the same as rustlin' wouldn't you say?"

"Sure would, and I'll tell you something. The big ranchers won't stand for it. That, and those fences the homesteaders are putting up. The big spreads won't have their open range fenced off right before their eyes. Why, Harry over to the Bar-Q said a homesteader north of him just fenced off acreage the Bar-Q has been using. Ask me if Harry was upset. But he wasn't sure what to do except warn them off the property." The boss straightened in his chair. "You know once those homesteaders get established, they don't move. I'm afraid there's going to be violence in this territory if Harry's attitude is any indication."

After that bit of speculation, Nat had left the office. He hadn't said much. Well, his business was with that western herd.

He hauled the load off the pack mule and rubbed him down, determined to put any trouble out of his mind. Tired didn't describe how he felt.

With the animals fixed up, he headed for the water trough. He scooped up the liquid, dousing his face and neck. The wet felt good sloshing over him. He wondered why he hadn't done it before. His brain, that's what. It was all in.

He headed back to the barn, chose an empty stall and slumped down against one wall. He'd better be quick about taking a break before that dang Colburn came around. Ever since Nat had come to the ranch, the foreman had had it in for him. If he saw Nat napping now, he'd kick him and be glad of it.

From the first, he'd been suspicious of Nat, maybe because of Nat's brother. Usually, a rancher or foreman didn't care about your background as long as you were a good hand.

But the foreman suspected Nat's brother belonged to one of those gangs hiding out in Hole-in-the-Wall. Years before, Nat had hung out with his brother, and it had toughened him up. But when Lem started robbing—after that one time when Nat held the gang's horses—he'd called it quits.

That didn't explain enough about Colburn's sour attitude though. Could it be Sally? They'd both been sweet on her. Now, that was a thought.

Seeing her on the stagecoach today was something of a shock. But right now Nat was so tired, he didn't really care. Dang it, he'd take more than "five." Only when he woke up, would he get going. He was in no mood anyone telling him what to do. After all, he'd reported in to the boss...and before anything else crossed his mind, he'd nodded off.

"Logan!" The foreman yelled, standing over him. "What you lazyin' around for? You got another hour's work before supper." Colburn kicked at him. "Now git up!"

Nat fought down a curse. "Boss told me to take five. But I'm goin' now." He dragged himself up. He wasn't about to give the foreman another excuse to fire him.

Josephine Walker bent over the garden. She liked feeling the earth in her hands. The soil in these parts wasn't terribly good, but with the manure they'd worked into it over the years, it had improved considerably.

Looking up, she spotted Nat crossing the yard. Early on, she'd wanted him fired. Told her husband so, in no uncertain terms. Nat was too rough, and she'd listened to their foreman complain about the cowboy's reputation. But her husband said he worked hard and had a way with horses, so there was no way he'd let him go.

However, he said she was free to let Logan know the ropes, referring to the talk on manners and deportment she gave each cowboy who came to work the first time. Her husband gave her free rein as long as she granted the cowboys some latitude.

"You have to be realistic," he said. "Otherwise, we won't have anyone stay and work for us."

Of course, as rough as cowboys could be, they showed respect toward "the missus." Whenever one of them addressed her, it was always respectful, in a voice almost hushed. To western men, chivalry was real. And nothing could make them give it up.

With Nat, she'd instinctively felt he was different. She prayed before she tackled him, not knowing if she could break through to him. But afterward, thinking about it, she realized he'd taken her "talking to" rather well. They'd been like two bulls, sizing each other up. He hadn't said much, but something—maybe it was a change in the way he held his shoulders—made him look less belligerent. And then as the months went on, he'd unexpectedly gone out of his way to say hello. Tip his hat with a smile and say, "Mrs. Walker." Gentle and slow, like he was savoring it. It had made her heart melt. And, then recently, after they talked some, he jokingly called her "Ma." Why, she almost dropped. Once again, tenderness swept over her.

Now she saw Nat turn into the spring house. Apparently, he was running an errand for the cook. He did make a fine figure of a man, if still a little wild. He'd probably never lose that devil-may-care air—not completely. But he'd mellowed out compared to when he'd first come to the ranch.

She was glad of that, because in a few days their young grandson would arrive to spend some months with them. The Walkers had only the one daughter, and she'd married and moved to California. Jason's coming had been the impetus to send off for a teacher from Chicago. Besides, this part of Wyoming needed a school. Most of the women had their hands full keeping their ranches going, both the big ones and the smaller homesteads.

The homesteaders, even if not intending to, had spelled trouble in this part of Wyoming. They fenced off the parcel of land they worked, land the big ranches considered their own. Of course, most of the big ranchers had never bought that land or claimed it in court. They'd purchase a strip land along a river, have their cowhands claim the next sections up that same river, then also sections on a nearby river. Afterward they'd run their cattle on the land between the rivers, never bothering to pay for it or legally claim it. And now homesteaders were fencing off some of that land and using the water the big ranchers considered theirs.

Mrs. Walker considered the homesteaders decent folk, but

the big ranchers thought them a plague, and most of these big ranchers were her friends.

It was a problem, and she could see it becoming an even bigger one. Maybe having a school where the youngsters could be educated together would bring the big ranchers and the homesteaders more into sympathy with each other. She'd thought to wait to build the school until things were more settled, but suddenly she'd decided to get it started as soon as possible.

She rose when she saw Nat walking back from the spring house. "Nat!"

He stopped and turned, a pleased look on his face. For the umpteenth time, she was glad the initial trouble between them had blown over. He carried two overflowing buckets of water. With ease. Those big shoulders were the reason, she was sure.

"What can I do for ya, Mrs. Walker?"

"Nat, I've noticed you have a way with wood. You did a fine job constructing that springhouse. Cook has said time and again how it keeps the spring protected from debris. She can take water out of there for drinking and not worry about animals getting in. And the shade helps keep it cool. She's appreciated it most decidedly."

"Glad to hear that, ma'am."

"Which brings up my proposition." She smiled up at him. "Our grandson is traveling here from California, and I want schooling for him. Learning some practical things around the ranch would be good, but I don't want him falling behind in his reading, writing and arithmetic. Now, ordinarily I could help him, but I've got a vision for something bigger. We need a school for children in this area. And to do that properly, we need a teacher. Someone from the East, like I've heard other places have.

"With that in mind, I sent off to Chicago, and she'll be arriving in Buffalo by stage this afternoon. I'd have had you fetch her, but Mr. Walker already had you doing something else, so I sent one of the other boys."

She noticed an odd look in Nat's eye, but didn't comment. Instead, she barreled ahead. "I want you to start looking around for materials for the schoolhouse. Maybe we'll have something like a barn raising, the neighbors participating, with a big feed and all. But someone needs to plan the building, organize the materials and such, and I'm thinking you're the man to do it. So, if you'd start looking over the area where we got the logs for this house…."

⸻

Nat's mind ran to the slope just off the Big Horns with that particularly good stand of lodgepole pine. Maybe he could ride over tomorrow and case it out. He'd ask Mr. Walker—not the foreman. That man would find him something to do, like digging holes and putting in posts.

Mr. Walker had taken the idea of fencing in one of his pastures from his homestead neighbors. But putting up fence posts was one thing Nat didn't cotton to. No, he'd try to see the boss tonight after supper and set up that trip to the Big Horns.

That settled, his mind turned to what Mrs. Walker had said. A teacher arriving by stage? By any chance, that wouldn't be the woman he'd gotten a glimpse of earlier? He hadn't seen much of her. She'd been in some kind of dark traveling dress. And she was pretty. He'd noticed that man standing close to her. That banker they'd heard coming to Buffalo? He'd stood near like she belonged to him.

Nat didn't think of himself as a lady's man, but there was something about that teacher he'd particularly noticed. A trim figure and those green eyes. But warm eyes. They'd held his for a good two seconds. Or maybe he'd held hers.

Then he'd seen Sally. Sally with a baby? He'd turned away before she saw him, or he hoped so.

He'd had the edge over the foreman, had even considered proposing marriage to Sally, but then she'd run off with that traveling salesman.

This afternoon, he thought the best thing was not to be noticed—and got on his horse quick.

Man, he hoped she wasn't coming here, but with Cook being her aunt, that likelihood was all too plain, even though Mrs. Walker hadn't mentioned it. Maybe the Missus didn't know.

Sally would be a complication in his life right now. He hoped he'd gotten over her. Then he told himself sternly, he *had* gotten over her.

3

Margaret stepped down from the ranch wagon and looked at her new home. It was a long, single-story, well-proportioned log house. A wide porch fronted the house. Shallow steps led up to a large central door. The driver reached for her bag.

"Ma'am," he said, "I'll tell Mrs. Walker you're here. Then I'll take your things to your room." He walked up to the main door and disappeared inside. In the intervening moments, Margaret noticed comfortable chairs on the porch and two other doors leading into the house. At that moment a woman exited the main entrance, someone probably in her fifties with lovely silver hair. It shone where the sun fell on it. She was attractive in a buxom, motherly way. A ready smile came to her lips.

"Miss Arnell! So nice to have you here." The woman gave her a long, warm embrace. Margaret's own mother couldn't have been more welcoming. The long, dusty ride began fading into the past.

"Come inside and have something cool to drink. You must be all in. Then I'll show you to your room so you can rest before supper."

Margaret followed the older woman and stepped into the main room. It had surprisingly high ceilings with floor to ceiling windows. "…for my tall husband," Mrs. Walker was saying. Several large chairs and a couch grouped around a colorful rug. The room was rich with soft earth-tones. Margaret noticed a pot-bellied stove to warm the place in cold weather.

"This is such a friendly room," Margaret said. "And quite a large house compared to the others I've seen."

"Thank you. This was one of four rooms when we first built the house, large for its time. We've expanded it since. The cattle business has done well for us." Mrs. Walker gestured to her right. "On this side of the house are the family quarters with my husband's office directly off the porch. To our left is a short hallway leading to your room, the kitchen and dining area." She gestured for Margaret to sit in one of the arm chairs. "And here's Cook with your cool drink."

Nat hesitantly entered the kitchen, but saw only Cook stirring a big pot for supper.

"You wanted me?" he asked.

Cook turned around. "Yes! She was here a moment ago, an old friend to see you."

He might have known. It'd been a good while since Sally had left the ranch with that ne'er-do-well. Leastways, that's how Nat had sized him up.

Steps alerted him to someone entering the kitchen from the main part of the house.

"Hi, Nat!" Sally rushed up to him and threw her arms around him. "Good to see you again."

He put his arms carefully around her, the occasion seeming to call for it, but he stood like a tree and kept himself about as unresponsive.

Sally looked up at him. "How long has it been? A year? Well, it'd almost have to be over a year now, hadn't it?" She giggled.

It didn't look like she was going to mention seeing him at the stagecoach. Or him seeing her baby. He was relieved when she drew her arms off his neck. He quickly stepped back.

"You here for a visit?" he blurted out. God knew he hoped it was only that, and not to settle in. But with her own mother being dead, and Cook always looking out for her—

"I'm not sure. Depends. I'm here for a while anyways. Mrs. Walker said I can stay as long as I make myself useful. And there's that little area we curtained off in the storage room. Used to be mine. Remember?"

Fool question. He felt heat rise up his face. Was she suggesting anything? But she had a child now. And the child would have a father. Where was he?

Cook interrupted his thoughts. "Sally, would you give this stew a stir now and then? I don't want it to scald. Just remembered I've got something else to attend to."

"Of course, Auntie."

Sally drifted over to the stove, picked up the large spoon and stirred. "This looks so good. Smells it, too." She lifted the wooden spoon with a sample. "How 'bout we try it?" She looked at him, a sly little smile on her face. "My aunt won't mind. And you can tell the boys how good it tastes." She held out the spoon. "Here, you first." When he hesitated, she said, "Come on! You're not afraid of me, are you? We used to be such friends." Reluctantly, he stepped near. "And we still *can* be."

He let the stew roll around his mouth. "Sure's good." That's all he'd say.

But Sally chattered away. "A lot has happened to me since we saw each other last...."

Nat stood on first one foot then the other, not knowing quite how to extricate himself. He couldn't tell where Sally was leading, but he didn't want to be drawn back into her net. Not like before. She still hadn't said anything about her baby—or husband. She rattled on, told the latest happenings down Cheyenne way where she'd been living.

Her fluttering hands kept drawing his eyes. She *could* be terribly entertaining. And, she looked awful pretty. Suddenly, he drew himself up smart. "Wal, Sally, that's all interestin'. But I gotta go. Promised Mr. Walker I'd check out that new mare he brought in last night."

"Oh! Will I see you later? We're just gettin' reacquainted."

"Maybe. I'll be sure to tell the boys how good the stew is." He nodded and stepped out the door hightailing it to the barn.

Margaret walked into the dining room. She had hoped to be early, but at the last minute had redone her hair into a French twist. She had taken extra care choosing her second-best dark dress, adding a white collar and a broach—wanting to look like a teacher, yet with the refinement of someone acquainted with the best society.

Now she was afraid she was a little late. Everyone was standing at table, Mr. Walker at one end, Mrs. Walker the other. Six chairs on each side claimed by cowboys—hair slicked down— now quiet, for as soon as she entered conversation ceased, all heads turned in her direction.

Mrs. Walker motioned Margaret to an empty chair at her side. "We girls need to stick together," she whispered. "You can see we're outnumbered."

Margaret was introduced and one of the cowboys helped seat her. After grace was said, Mrs. Walker indicated the man on her left as the ranch foreman, Mr. Colburn. He was a big, burly sort of man. When a young woman came in with platters of beef, Margaret saw the foreman startle and his eyes follow the woman as she set the dishes down at each end of the table. Margaret, also surprised, recognized the young mother from the stagecoach. Thinking back on their time on the stage, she realized both of them had spoken in general terms as to their destinations: Mrs. Lumpkin said she was joining her aunt, a cook on a ranch, and Margaret had said she was going to teach in an area that had no school.

Mrs. Lumpkin didn't address Margaret, apparently not wanting to be noticed. Bringing in other bowls of food, she served in a business-like way, then left the room without returning.

The food was passed around. Platters and bowls that had been heaped high quickly emptied, and before long, Margaret saw how serious these men were about eating. The room remained quiet.

When dessert was served, Mrs. Walker began talking with the foreman and drew Margaret into the conversation. Margaret noticed Mr. Walker did the same with the men on his end of the table.

"Miss Arnell, I'm sure you don't know we have an English lord in these parts. Mr. Colburn, didn't you recently visit Lord Frewen?"

"Yes, ma'am." The foreman looked across the table at Margaret. "You should see his log house. More like a castle. In fact, locals call it Frewen Castle."

"Imagine, Miss Arnell! Such a large home out here on the prairie," Mrs. Walker exclaimed. "Lord Frewen is very charming and *quite* the character."

The foreman harrumphed. "Charmin', maybe. But a good manager? Don't you believe it. Ma'am, just to show you—his headquarters are more than 200 miles to that Rock Creek station north of the Union Pacific line. And those are difficult miles. I don't size him up as much of a businessman."

Mrs. Walker put down her fork. "That may be." She turned to Miss Arnell. "His ranch is huge, measuring eighty miles from north to south and fifty miles east to west. Mr. Colburn already mentioned how large the house is."

The foreman jerked his head in the general direction of the

ranch in question. "Lord Frewen said he's thinkin' of buyin' out his brother and callin' his ranch the Powder River Cattle Company. We'll see."

"Well," Mrs. Walker said, "I have to say he's unusual in these parts. When his new wife was with him, they gave the most extravagant parties. A long list of lords and ladies came for hunting, scouted by Buffalo Bill Cody no less. Mr. Walker and I were kindly invited once, probably because we're among the oldest—and biggest—land owners in these parts. But Miss Arnell, you should see their home. Mr. Colburn said it was a log cabin. Some say it's like an European hunting lodge. What an exquisite two-story one with every luxury. English hunting parties and high teas filled their social calendar. Ladies who visited were treated to hothouse bouquets delivered on horseback. Really! It was enchanting."

"Do you think you'll be invited to another party?" Margaret couldn't help asking.

"Well...unfortunately, Lord Frewen's wife Clara became ill and suffered a miscarriage when she joined one of the hunting groups in the fall. She returned to New York City, and we haven't seen her since. I take it she went back to live with her family—her father's the financier Leonard Jerome, and her sister is Jennie, Lord Randolph Churchill's wife. So you can't blame her for finding life out here rugged. My, the winters alone!"

"Wal, last winter was a mild one," the foreman commented. He and Mrs. Walker drifted off into a discussion of the winters, and Margaret found herself glancing down the row of cowboys. Earlier, one had caught her attention. He looked familiar, sitting at Mr. Walker's right. Suddenly, it came to her. She believed he was the man who had helped with the stagecoach that afternoons. All cleaned up, he seemed quite different and his brown hair darker, still wet from an obvious dunking. As she was looking at him, he glanced her way and their eyes met. She was conscious of a lingering interest in his. Would she be able to thank him after the meal? He certainly had gotten them out of a fix.

The meal completed, the cowboys quietly set their chairs under the table, trying not to scrape the legs against the floor. Mrs. Walker smiled, saying in an undertone to Margaret that she'd asked the cowboys to be more careful with her furniture—and her ears.

Arising from her chair, Margaret excused herself and walked to the other end of the table just as the cowboy she was curious about was leaving. "Sir," she said, "could I have a few words with you?"

On his nod, she asked, "Were you the gentleman who fixed our stagecoach earlier today?"

"Yes, ma'am."

"I don't believe I'd have made it to this meal tonight if you hadn't helped so ably. You left before we could properly thank you. We were all most grateful." Margaret tried to convey with a smile the gratitude she felt.

At that moment, Mrs. Lumpkin walked out of the kitchen with an empty tray and made straight for Margaret and the cowboy she was talking with. Immediately, Margaret sensed the woman's prickliness.

"We've met before," Margaret offered. "I didn't realize you were coming here. I almost didn't recognize you. Did you arrive later?"

"Oh, yes! I feel like I've come home, havin' lived here before. Know pretty much everyone on the ranch except for a few new cowhands. Isn't that right, Nat?"

Nat nodded, but was silent.

"Yes, Nat and I are old friends. And now that I'm back, hope to become better ones." She smiled up at him.

Margaret looked at them. It seemed there was something special between these two. And a certain warning of *hands off* from the woman. Margaret was tempted to say another quiet *thank you* to the cowboy and turn away. Yet she'd hardly expressed her gratitude sufficiently.

Mrs. Lumpkin widened her smile at Nat, then nodded to the other cowboy who had stayed to help clear the table.

Margaret decided she'd stay a moment longer, and *then* turn gracefully away.

"I'm sorry, I didn't get your whole name," Margaret said. "There were so many of you at table and Mrs. Walker went through the introductions rather quickly."

"It's Nat Logan, ma'am."

"Nat. Is that short for Nathanael...or Nathan?"

"Nathanael. But it's been Nat most of my life. Nathanael was too much to live up to." Humor was mixed with a self-deprecating smile. Margaret appreciated the subtlety. This man might be interesting.

"Did you always live in these parts?" she asked.

"No ma'am. I hale from Kansas. Before that the family came from Ohio. Always itchin' to move on, I guess."

"In a way, I understand. I came out west to get a bit of freedom, to see what was beyond Chicago."

"Chicago? Were you there in that big fire in '71?"

"Yes! Thankfully, our house was located outside what became the fire district. At the time, no one knew how far it would spread. It was terrible! So many people lost everything."

She smiled ruefully. "My family, on the other hand, benefited. Father was in the building business, so you can imagine how busy he's been. Now, you wouldn't recognize the city. It's built up again, bigger and better than ever."

"That's where the boss ships his beef to be slaughtered. First we drive the cattle to the railhead near Cheyenne. Then the Union Pacific cattle cars take them on to the big city. Some of the cowboys ride along to make sure everything's okay."

It felt good to talk about her hometown, even though Margaret had been gone such a short time. But just as she was about to say something, Mrs. Lumpkin came over to them once again.

Margaret turned to see a peculiar look in the woman's eyes. As a female, she could see the signs. But this other woman was already married. My gracious, she herself was a more likely candidate for this man.

She could see the woman wanted to talk with this cowboy, so she excused herself.

As she walked down the table's length to rejoin Mrs. Walker, Margaret took herself to task.

What had she been thinking? She was already taking the measure of this man. Even though she'd enjoyed talking with him, she was a teacher. *Educated*. Had she come out here to teach or to get a man? She inwardly grimaced. If it was a man, surely not this one. He was only a cowboy and probably poorly educated at that.

4

On the slope of the Big Horns, Nat considered the lodgepole pines. He liked seeing trees so straight and tall, smelling their sharp fragrance. Just what was needed for the schoolhouse.

He thought of his talk with Miss Arnell, how her father had helped rebuild Chicago. She was used to seeing some pretty fancy building, he guessed. And thinking how Mrs. Walker had complimented his work on the spring house, made him want to do something really fine for the school.

It wouldn't be what Miss Arnell was used to in Chicago. But he'd do something out of the common.

Thinking what that could be, he suddenly remembered a building he'd been to in Cheyenne. Before stepping into the main room, there'd been a small room leading in from the outside. They called it a vestibule.

That's what he'd do. Have a small room at the front of the school where students could hang their coats and things. Like a fancy lean-to in the front of the school. Acting as a buffer to keep the cold from the classroom.

He could see it now. People would talk of it for miles around, this schoolhouse. And Miss Arnell would appreciate it.

He wanted to see approval in those warm, green eyes of hers.

Last night, when he'd told Mr. Walker about this trip, the boss said they'd use a few of the ranch hands to cut down the trees. Then transport them to the place Mrs. Walker had in mind for the school. In the meantime, he'd ask some other ranchers to send men to help square off the logs. That'd get the job done in no time.

To raise the schoolhouse, they'd give a special invite to any ranches with kids and get up that building in one day.

Nat took time to mark the best trees for cutting.

That accomplished, he got into the saddle and started down the incline. While here, he might as well check the western range down south a way to see how their cows were doing. He'd spotted a few cattle on the way so guessed where most of them had stopped to graze.

Part of the herd should be over that next ridge. The boss was concerned about their numbers. Nat decided to cross the ridge where rock outcroppings offered cover. Caution from his less-than-law-abiding days wouldn't allow him to skyline himself.

That rock pile not only offered cover, but gave something interesting to look at in a prairie where grass waved mile after mile in the wind.

He helped his horse pick his way up the ridge and heard cattle lowing in the distance.

Suddenly, a shouted, "Yip!" then others rent the air. Was the herd moving? He quickly kneed his horse back of the taller rocks and, leaning in the saddle, peered around the outcropping.

Two men on horseback, maybe more out of view, were driving cattle south. He rummaged in his saddlebag and grabbed his field glasses. Yes, those were their cows. But round-up time was over.

He didn't recognize the horsemen either. One of them rode an appaloosa with a half-moon on its left rump. A strange sensation hit him. His brother's horse had that distinctive marking.

And no one rode that horse but Lem.

Rustlers?

He jumped down from his horse and slipped his Winchester from its scabbard. Then knelt to position it on a nearby rock.

He took careful aim and fired a little above the head of the horseman on the appaloosa. The man startled and crouched in the saddle. Nat quickly got off another close shot, then aimed for another of the rustlers.

He kept the bullets high, not meaning to kill man or horse. These were meant as a warning, but a warning with guts. He got off a few more carefully placed shots. The horsemen scrambled right, then left, making difficult targets. Out in the open with no cover, they rode hard, intending to put distance between themselves and the shooters.

Nat kept the bullets flying, reloading rapidly, making it seem as if more than one man was firing. The fact that he was hidden was enough to spook anyone—even a wild gang like this. They didn't take time to fire back at unseen, unknown targets.

Nat kept reloading and firing until the rustlers rode out of range and disappeared.

The cattle they'd been herding south still moved, but now did so more slowly. Nat mounted his horse. Hopefully, the thieves wouldn't be back anytime soon.

He descended the ridge and rode a good mile to catch up with the cattle, then worked them until they headed in the right direction. The work was hard and dusty.

After the cattle regrouped farther north, Nat nudged his tired horse up a ridge. He'd watch this area for a while in case those men came back. He no longer wanted to make himself a sitting duck by being out in the open. Picking his way up the ridge, he kept to trees and scrub for cover.

He spotted a place near large rocks with a couple of trees for shade. Stepping off his horse, he chose a tree to sit against. Cook had made him a sandwich with the fixins knowing he'd be on the range all day.

He put together a small fire for coffee, careful to gather dry wood so the smoke would filter through the tree branches and be lost in the wind. The food hit the spot.

What were the chances that gang of thieves was one of those hiding out in Hole-in-the-Wall? It was within riding distance south of here.

Sipping the hot coffee, his thoughts turned to that appaloosa. Surely Lem wouldn't have sold his horse. It was an uncommonly good one, if still a little wild. It had speed and endurance. Had one of those gang members stolen it? He couldn't imagine his brother lending that horse, even if he was a member of one of the gangs. Did that mean Lem was injured? Or dead?

Nat remained most of the afternoon, scouting some. None of the gang had come back so far.

He could trail them, but at this point he made too good of a target riding out in the open, especially for anyone hiding in the rocks and trees. Nat looked over the herd that now grazed quietly on the prairie.

The risk wasn't worth it. He'd just go back to the ranch and report to the boss.

—————————◦◦◦◦◦—————————

Josephine Walker looked up from her stitchery. The three of them sat cozily in the sitting room. After a day's hard work and the evening meal spent with the cowboys, she sat with her preferred people: her husband smoking his pipe meditatively and Margaret reading by the kerosene lamp. Every once in a while, one of them would say something, and the other two would stop and make a few comments, maybe followed by a short discussion, then go back to whatever they were doing.

It was amazing how easily Margaret had fit in with their family life, the few days she'd been here. Such a pretty young lady.

Dark lashes framed her eyes. Her brown hair looked silky glowing in the lamplight with a sheen of reddish gold. All the cowboys on the ranch had more than noticed her.

But here, in the bosom of the family so to speak, she fit in easily, ready to add to the conversation, yet unobtrusive in the sense that Josephine didn't feel annoyed having her around at this time which she ordinarily spent with just her husband. George didn't seem to mind either. Of course, she made it a point to see he got special attention afterward. Even if he was tired and ready to drop off to sleep, she made sure his feet were rubbed, that he had cuddle time. Something. And, she needed the private time with him as well.

She studied her husband now. His thick gray hair was neatly combed. His tall, still straight frame relaxed into the curve of the comfortable chair. Those same shoulders could ease around her in one of his comfy hugs, the kind that took tension out of a hard day.

Those early years establishing the ranch, they'd worked so hard they'd fall into bed, not caring about anything else. How long had that lasted? Josephine remembered it as the time she felt most distant from her husband. And neither of them had done anything about it. They hadn't had the sense to know something was wrong. But as the weeks went on, their words became sharper and sharper to each other. Or duller and duller. And when they did talk, they talked *at* each other. Not *with*.

It wasn't until that first cold snap bringing freezing weather—when they *had* to cuddle in bed—that things started to thaw between them. Funny how extreme cold had brought back warmth to their relationship. She hadn't known how important the physical was—between a husband and a wife—until they'd gone through that famine in their marriage. For months she'd felt so terribly distant from George, wondering if they were even married. Had started to think they'd formed only a partnership to establish a ranch.

During that long season, they'd erected a house. But a *home* was sadly lacking. She'd been a fool. And hoped she'd never be that kind of fool again.

"Josey," her husband began, "when are you going to town?"

Her woolgathering came to a sudden halt. She smiled at her husband, knowing something was on his mind. What did he need that he didn't want to go into town himself? He *had* been very busy of late. "Funny you should ask. Besides a little shopping, I'd like to go and advertise for the new school. Have the ranchers in town meet Margaret."

George looked over at their guest. "My wife's an unusual woman. Spotted that right off and claimed her for myself." He grinned at Josephine. "Sometimes she needs time away from the ranch, and I do want to keep her happy."

He turned to Margaret once again. "But most days, I don't have time to do what I'd like for her. There's so much to get done on the ranch that I'm gone from early morning until suppertime. Usually, I take my noon meal with me, or the Missus here sends it out with one of the ranch hands."

"That's all right, dear," Josephine said. Her husband's words made her feel all warm and glowing. "This time of year, I understand you being gone so much. Margaret is a gift, though. There's nothing like having a like-minded woman around to talk with."

"I'm pleased the two of you get along so well." George tamped more tobacco into his pipe. "With Margaret here, it helps me feel better being away so much."

He winked at Margaret. "Early on, I knew you filled the bill, and nothing, but *nothing* is too good for my Josey."

Just then a horse snorted.

"Someone's out there." He rose from his easy chair. "Don't bother getting up, honey. I'll see to it."

He flung open the door, and as soon as he saw who it was, glanced back over his shoulder. "It's Major Wolcott. He'll be here on business." He closed the door behind him, and Josephine and Margaret could faintly hear him hail the man on horseback.

"My husband always has a hearty greeting for anyone who comes. Besides, ranch hospitality is a given, considering the distances between spreads."

"Won't they come in?' Margaret asked. "Maybe I should go to my room."

"Oh, no. Mr. Walker will take him into his office, through that door from the porch. We won't be bothered." She smiled mischievously at Margaret. "But sometimes I like to be bothered. It's hard to keep my curiosity at bay. Especially considering who this guest is."

She saw Margaret's eyebrows rise in question.

"Major Wolcott and my husband go back a way. We both arrived here in '76 when there were only trappers and traders. You know, this was just a territory to pass through to California or Oregon. People just hadn't settled here.

"Major Wolcott served in the Union Army. Then he was appointed US Marshall for Wyoming Territory. However, the governor removed him three years later because of 'offensive' behavior.

"He's something of a big noise in these parts, owns the VR Ranch, is a member of the WSGA"—she leaned closer to Margaret—"that's Wyoming Stock Growers Association. They have a beautiful building in Cheyenne, a hotel and restaurant with meeting rooms. It's quite something. Maybe we'll go there this year.

"Like I said, Major Wolcott is influential, and because of his background in the war and as US Marshall, I can see him taking charge when trouble threatens. I think that's what my husband is protecting us from hearing. Trouble is 'men talk,' my dear."

She rose from the couch. "But I'm going to see if they need some refreshment. Major Wolcott will surely need something, coming all this way on horseback."

Josephine walked to the door that led to her husband's office, paused a moment, then opened it. "...having trouble with rustlers or with those d—m homesteaders," Major Wolcott was saying, his voice hard and forceful. "I'm sure those nesters are branding my mavericks." He stopped when he noticed a woman's presence.

"I wondered if you men want some refreshment. Coffee?"

"Yes, Josey. Bring us some coffee, please. And something to eat. The Major has a long ride after this."

"Would you like to stay the night, Major? We have room."

"Thanks, ma'am, but I need to get to Buffalo."

She was about to close the door when her husband added, "And send Colburn and Nat here, will you?"

Josey smiled her assent and shut the door.

"I'll be just a few minutes, Margaret. Go back to your reading."

Minutes later, Josephine entered with a tray. Margaret crossed the room to open the office door for her.

"Don't knock," Josephine said quietly. "I want to see what I can hear." She smiled in a conspiratorial way.

Quietly, Margaret opened the door. "Someone needs to hire a gunman!" Major Wolcott all but shouted.

"Here you are, men." She nodded in Colburn's direction who had already arrived, then looked at her husband. "I had to send off for Nat. He's in that north pasture, but he'll be here in a few minutes."

She didn't apologize for overhearing the outburst. She might hear it from her husband afterward, but that didn't bother her. She was trying to start a school to mitigate the growing antipathy between the big ranchers and homesteaders. At least, the ones in their immediate area. This was her concern, too.

Depositing the tray on her husband's desk, she adroitly left the room and closed the door, returning to her place on the couch.

Ten minutes later, Josephine heard boots with spurs jingling march across the porch to the office door. "That'll be Nat."

"Sounds as if he has plenty of energy and determination," Margaret observed.

"Yes, it's such a masculine sound, isn't it?" Josephine found herself inwardly smiling. Nat had that effect on her. She glanced at Margaret, wondering if she might feel at all the same. Those two were very different—but her sense of the romantic was surfacing.

She got back to the subject at hand. "I wonder why Nat was sent for. You know, this whole business of Major Wolcott's visit tonight bothers me. That man can be such a firebrand."

Once in a while they heard raised voices from the room next door but could rarely distinguish words. However, the next hour she and Margaret continued to sit quietly.

Later, she heard her husband say good-bye to the Major, but then he returned to his office and talked with Colburn and Nat a bit longer.

Josephine put down her needlework. She needed to share her thoughts with someone. "You know, Margaret. It's strange my husband sent for Nat as well as the foreman. I hope there'll be no trouble, real trouble with the rustlers—or homesteaders—or whoever's involved." She picked up her needlework again. "My husband thinks a great deal of Nat's take-charge attitude. And fighting spirit," she added, almost as an afterthought. "Maybe that's why he was included."

After about ten more minutes, Nat exited the office through the porch door, crossed the porch with spurs jangling, and ran down the steps and onto the yard. Colburn left more quietly.

Shortly afterward, George entered the sitting room and announced he was ready for bed. Josephine could tell her husband had something on his mind and rose quickly from the couch. She turned to say goodnight to Margaret who had already arisen with her book.

As Margaret left the room, Josephine extinguished the

lamps. Her husband banked the fire. A glow from the logs lit the room like moonlight. Smiling, her husband reached around and gave her a decided pat to hurry her toward their bedroom.

5

The ranch wagon bumped on toward town, Margaret hanging onto the board where she sat. What would her friends say if they saw her now? The buckboard had been turned into a carriage of sorts, with a canvas top to protect her and Mrs. Walker from the sun. As they traveled north, the Big Horn Mountains rose to their left. The wide open, grassy plains stretched to the right.

Margaret had been looking forward to this trip, ever since Mr. and Mrs. Walker had talked about it a few days ago.

She smiled. Another memory suddenly surfaced.

That night, after she'd said goodnight to them and started down the hallway to her room, she suddenly remembered she needed to ask Mrs. Walker something. She retraced her steps to the sitting room. She gained the open archway when she saw Mr. Walker encourage his wife to move faster to their bedroom by giving her a decided pat on her backside. It was one of those "husband and wife" things, not meant for other eyes. Margaret smiled, realizing it nourished a desire for the same kind of playfulness with the man she married. Would that day ever come? The banker had been attentive on the stagecoach....

Now riding toward Buffalo, the distance seemed shorter

than when she'd first traveled to the ranch. Today she had a sense of where they were going. Approaching the fledging town, she saw it as quite a significant place after living at the ranch on the vast, empty plains. Buffalo represented civilization.

"Nat, would you drop us at Myers Hotel?" Mrs. Walker asked. "We'll eat in the diner. After you take the horses to the livery stable, why don't you join us?"

Nat tipped his black hat. "Thank you, ma'am. You go ahead and eat. I don't know how long my business will take, but I'll at least look in on you."

"You be sure and do that."

Margaret nodded her appreciation as Nat handed her down from the buckboard. She hadn't had much opportunity to speak with him since that first night. He was always at evening meals, but he sat at the other end of the table, and she'd had no reason to go the length of the room to talk with him.

Mrs. Walker led the way into the diner, and it seemed everyone either greeted her pleasantly or nodded to her from across the room.

The table she chose was situated near the door, but off to one side. When the waitress brought them menus, Margaret looked down the offerings and noticed beef entrees ruled the day. No wonder, this being cattle country.

She settled into her chair, grateful to be seated on a firm, comfortable seat, and not on a jostling buckboard. However, she was thankful for today. It was to be her introduction to the town as well as to some of its residents. Mrs. Walker wanted to parade her around as the new teacher. And it gave them both an opportunity to do necessary shopping. Margaret discovered she needed a hat with a wider brim to protect her face from the sun. And ties to keep the wind from blowing it off. Mrs. Walker said there was a store where she might find something suitable.

Mrs. Walker looked up from her menu and said in a low tone, "I sit here because I like to keep abreast of who's in town and greet them when they come in, even if it's only with a nod or smile. It's important to keep on the best terms possible with the other ranchers. My husband, you might have realized, has one of the largest spreads around, and something like that can breed jealousy, even though we were among the earliest settlers and worked hard for what we acquired." A gentle sigh escaped her. "I'll never forget the times when we wondered if we'd make it. So, I want the smaller, newer ranchers and their wives to feel welcome. Both to visit us and to ask for help or advice."

Mrs. Walker looked again at her menu. "All right. I know what I'm ordering. This is on me, so choose what you want. When Nat comes, I'll have him do the same."

Before long the waitress brought two plates of steaming beef on bread smothered in gravy. The aroma made Margaret realize how very hungry she was. She'd ordered the same as Mrs. Walker and as both started on their food, they glanced up at each other, amused. They mixed hearty eating with as much ladylikeness as possible.

They'd just about finished when a man approached their table. Margaret recognized him as the banker from the stagecoach. "Nice to see you again, Mr. Norland."

"The pleasure is mine, Miss Arnell." He smiled broadly. "Have you recovered from your stage ride to Buffalo? That was quite an ordeal with the axle breaking."

"Yes, I'm quite well, thank you."

"I'm glad to see the incident didn't scare you back East. We don't have so many lovely ladies that we can afford to lose any."

"I hope I'm made of sterner stuff, Mr. Norland."

"I'm glad to hear that. With you making the decision to come out here in the first place, I should have deduced that." He turned to her companion.

Margaret took the hint. "Let me introduce Mrs. George Walker. She and her husband own a ranch south of Buffalo. She asked me to come to Wyoming to teach and I'm living with them."

"Nice to meet you, ma'am." He nodded as if tipping his hat. "I'm making the rounds of the ranches, telling them about the bank we'll be establishing in Buffalo. I understand there's already an informal setup, but with all the Eastern and British syndicates forming cattle companies, I'm here to institute a formal bank."

"I'm sure my husband will be interested. You're welcome to visit us anytime."

"Thank you." He turned, once again, to Margaret. "I've noticed some fine countryside for riding. Do you ride, Miss Arnell?"

"I haven't done so yet, but I would like to—with Mr. and Mrs. Walkers' permission."

"When I travel to the Walker Ranch, I'd be honored to escort you. Would that be all right, Mrs. Walker?"

"That would be very nice."

"Even though I'm a banker," he responded genially, "I don't like to stay cooped up too long. I enjoy riding, and with Miss Arnell at a destination, I'd be more than compensated for the effort."

"Then we'd be honored if you'd stay for a meal," Mrs. Walker said.

"Now you'll have me over to your place in no time. Thank you."

He excused himself to return to his table. When the door opened, Margaret noticed Nat enter. He looked over the room, his gaze settling on the banker. Then he approached their table.

"Sit down, Nat. You are my guest, order whatever you want." Mrs. Walker looked pointedly at Margaret. "I want our driver to be able to get us home and not pass out from hunger."

"We often go for hours without food on the trail, ma'am. I'm used to doin' without."

"Well, you're not going to do without while I head up this

expedition. Besides, we Walkers are known for our hospitality."

"I know that, ma'am." He nodded at one of the chairs. "Mind if I take this one so I can see the door?"

"Of course. As you observe, I already have a good view of it. But I'm thinking you have different reasons."

"Yes, ma'am. I promised your husband I would take care of you and Miss Arnell."

She looked at him with a warm smile. "Thank you, Nat." She paused, then leaned toward Margaret. "We needed a driver today, but in my husband's estimation, not just anyone would do. Mr. Walker knows this man will look out for us, no matter what. I don't think Nat has a fearful bone in his body. My husband admires a man with courage."

Nat grinned. "Or someone who's tomfool enough to stick his neck out in a tricky situation."

"Well, I hope such an occasion doesn't arise. In any case, you make us feel perfectly safe. And with our school teacher, you are also safeguarding the future education of our youngsters." She directed her gaze back to Margaret. "That's another reason I want to sit here. If any ranchers out our way happen through that door, I want to encourage them to send their children to our new school. In fact, I noticed one of our ranch ladies in the far corner with her two children." She cut her final piece of meat and raised her fork to her mouth. "In another minute, I'll go and talk with her. Now, order your food, Nat."

Mrs. Walker signaled the waitress and made sure Nat requested enough to eat.

"Excuse me now. I'm going to step over to our neighbor." Mrs. Walker rose, and added, "Why don't you come with me, Margaret—just to be introduced. Then come back and keep Nat company. You two can get to know each other. By the way, Nat, Mr. Walker wants you and the other cowboys accompanying Miss Arnell anytime she rides out from the ranch."

Margaret followed Mrs. Walker to the table where a mother

with two children sat. She judged the boy and girl to be about seven and nine years of age, old enough to attend school. The mother seemed genuinely glad to meet her, and they chatted a minute, then Margaret returned to Nat as Mrs. Walker wanted to talk longer with her neighbor.

"So, you ride, Miss Arnell?" Margaret noticed Nat immediately took up where Mrs. Walker had left off.

"My father kept a couple of horses and insisted we learn. I enjoyed it, although most of my time was spent with books. I imagine your life was quite different."

"Well, when Ma lived, she encouraged book learnin'. She especially liked poetry. But when she died I was nine or so, and after that I wasn't much of a student."

"So you didn't keep up your studies?"

"A little here and there. But mostly, my brother and I had too much to do takin' care of ourselves."

"I'm sorry."

"Thanks. But things have worked out. Mr. Walker is a good man to work for."

The cowboy's food arrived, and as he was obviously hungry, Margaret let him eat for a while before broaching another topic.

"I take it you're very familiar with the Walkers' ranch. I've heard it's large."

"Yes, one of the biggest in these parts. 'Course, you need a good amount of acres to raise cattle, to have enough grazin'. Since '75, ranchers have been bringin' up cattle from Texas, a lot of it. The grass in Wyoming is better. And it's open range."

"What does that mean, open range?"

"No fences. Our cattle just roam wherever, mostly on our range, then some get on over to one of the neighbors. We get them back roundup time when we separate them by brand." He took another bite of food, and after swallowing, said, "So when you ride, you can pretty much go wherever you want. No fences to worry about. Exactly what I like."

43

"Wouldn't it be safe enough for me to ride alone? I wouldn't want to take you from your work."

"Safe enough if you stay near the ranch." He grinned. "But it's been rumored you like a little adventure, so might take off where you could get into trouble."

"People have been talking about me?" Margaret didn't know whether to feel flattered or affronted.

"Well, you got to know cowboys. There's not much excitement in our lives. And very few single females. So, when a new woman appears on the scene, especially one like yourself—pretty and all—it creates quite a stir. Naturally, the cowboys want to know all about you. If Mr. or Mrs. Walker drops a little somethin' about you, we can make that somethin' into quite a tale." He looked at her, a glint in his eyes. "Why, I'm sure most of us have rescued you from some type of danger already. Want to play the hero, you know."

"Oh!"

"You're perfectly safe with us. A cowboy wouldn't let you come to no harm—or disrespect you in any way. They just like to imagine things and spin a few yarns. Keeps them entertained."

"I see."

He chuckled. "You can be a woman of few words, like some of us cowboys."

She choked back a laugh. This Nat could be amusing. It might be kind of fun to go riding with him as escort.

Just then the door to the restaurant opened and closed with a decided slam.

Nat looked up, and Margaret's gaze followed his. Two men entered, roughly dressed, their clothes dusty. Neither bothered removing their broad brimmed hats.

The apparent leader of the two looked over the room and spotted Nat. He motioned his companion to follow and stopped in front of their table.

"Hello. Logan, isn't it? Haven't seen you in a coon's age.

Where's your brother, we're lookin' for him."

"Lem and I parted company some time ago. Don't know where he is."

"Heard he'd come into these parts. Knew he'd find a place where business was good."

Nat remained poker faced. "Haven't seen him—or heard from him."

"Huh…figured you two be hooked up—like the ol' days."

"I'm on my own now."

The leader glanced at Margaret. "I can see that. This your girl—or missus?"

"Neither. We're both guests of the lady talkin' over there." There was a distinct pause. Margaret noticed he was letting the topic drop. He didn't seem eager to impart information.

"I git you!" The man gave Nat a knowing look. "And I can see you're not about to introduce this lady here to some old friends."

Margaret felt an underlying threat in his voice. She wondered why. They *did* seem rough.

Nat pursed his lips, not saying anything. Just stared them down.

The lead cowboy continued. "Yeah, we're up from western Colorado, here into Wyoming Territory. Parted ways from some good men. They thought your brother was up this way…." He let his sentence fall away, looking at Nat expectantly.

"Sorry. Can't help you."

"Been lookin' over the cattle in these parts. Good business, I'd say." The leader looked at Nat more closely. "So…what you doin' now?"

"Workin' on a ranch."

"They need some hands?"

"No! We're all filled up."

"Wal then." He touched his hat to Margaret. "Guess we'll mosey on to a table and get us some grub."

Nat escorted Mrs. Walker and Miss Arnell out of the Myers Hotel. He glanced at Mrs. Walker. She'd take the lead in planning the rest of this excursion.

"Nat," Mrs. Walker began, "Miss Arnell and I are going to do a bit of shopping. I want to talk with a few people as well." She smiled up at him. "You know, this is my big outing, so I'm going to make the most of it. And being with Miss Arnell is so much fun." She lifted the watch hanging from the front of her dress. "Let's meet in two hours."

"Back here?" he asked.

"Yes, and let's have a cup of coffee. With a piece of pie." She gave a conspiratorial smile. "We need to fortify ourselves before the trip home."

"Couldn't agree more, ma'am." He liked the way Mrs. Walker thought. He and she had come to think alike on a lot of things. Almost as if they was kin, like she was his mother. Well, in one way she was. He thought back on that talk they'd had a month or so ago, about religious things. He'd never forget *that*.

"Okay, then. We'll see you in a couple of hours. If for some reason we get caught up in shopping or talking, give us a little leeway, won't you? I don't want to feel like I've got to rush."

"Sure 'nough, ma'am." He touched his hand to his hat.

Nat stood looking at the two ladies as they walked away. Miss Arnell had a little swing to her walk. It was downright pretty to watch. What would the boys say when he told them 'bout that?

He adjusted his hat, pulling the brim down a little against the bright sun. But maybe he wouldn't say anything.

He suddenly realized he'd changed a bit. Ordinarily, he wouldn't have hesitated telling his story and embellishing it some. Now, he hesitated. He felt like he wanted to protect Miss Arnell. Protect from what?

He considered that. Maybe from indecent thoughts the other cowboys might have. Oh, they'd always treat her with respect.

But suddenly he wanted that respect to go deep down. Not colored by any questionable remarks of his.

This was new. He wondered…and shifted from one foot to the other.

Yes, this sure was because of that talk he'd had with Mrs. Walker. She'd told him that he would start to think, even act different.

Yes, that spiritual talk had been more than just talk.

Of course, he had noticed that kicky little sway Miss Arnell had to her walk. He was still a man. And Miss Arnell a mighty attractive woman.

Still, this change was a puzzle. Sometimes he was his old self, and sometimes this new one. He'd have to ask Mrs. Walker about that.

The two women disappeared into the general store.

Nat looked across the street at the Occidental Saloon. That would be his next stop. Not to drink. He didn't want that on his breath for Mrs. Walker. But he'd find out the latest news. The two rough necks in the restaurant had brought Lem front and center to mind. If they'd seen his brother in western Colorado, more than likely he'd been in Brown's Hole, hiding out on the Outlaw Trail.

Crossing the street, Nat wondered why those fellas in the restaurant hadn't gone right to Hole-in-the-Wall. Maybe they didn't know the way in. Few did. Certainly no lawman ever entered. At least, never to come out again to tell the tale.

His brother might have gone there. That half-moon horse in these parts almost proved it.

But again, his brother didn't let anyone ride that horse. Was his brother in trouble?

Was he his brother's keeper? He doubted it. They'd left it that each would find his own way. Still…Nat let it drop and jerked open the saloon door.

6

Logan!" The foreman shouted. "I thought I gave orders to clean those two stalls next to the ranch wagon. And thoroughly!"

Nat looked up from splitting wood. "Must've told someone else. Didn't hear 'bout that."

"Gave the order through Shorty."

"Haven't seen him all day."

"Well, git to it, anyway." The foreman turned to walk away, then looked back. "Now!"

When the foreman was out of sight, Nat threw the axe hard into the log. Dang that Colburn! What was sticking in his craw?

Nat started for the barn. Was it because Sally talked with him last night, singling him out after supper, and Colburn saw it? But what did the foreman expect? Nat was assigned to help her clear table.

Of course, Sally had a way of drifting near. It was hard to avoid close contact with her. Now that he remembered it, just when he was putting a stack of dirty plates in the kitchen, Colburn had *happened* into the room as Sally put a tray of cups next to Nat. "Now, don't drop those plates, Mr. Logan," she'd said playfully and bumped her hip against his. And Colburn had seen it.

Nat was sure cleaning stalls was his punishment. This was not his job. It was Shorty's. He spit on the ground. And Shorty was slipshod on thoroughness.

Nat entered the barn and headed to the stalls at its rear. They weren't being used and had gotten only a slapdash cleaning weeks, maybe months ago. Dirt piled in the corners, a dirty rag and scattered hay littered one stall. The other was just as bad.

His irritation mounted at the foreman and Shorty. He should be out on the range with cattle or horses. In fact, he'd planned on that after splitting those logs. Under the open sky.

That was the thing about Wyoming. He'd been other places, but never under such wide-open sky. About took his breath away sometimes.

He leaned against a stall. Pure and simple, he loved that sky. And the mountains in the west anchoring it. He liked seeing a storm come over those Big Horns. Huge thunderheads, building up. Wind whipping over the plain, rippling the long grass. Then those big thunderclouds breaking up, loosening the rains.

Least, that's the way he saw it. The landscape was simple, but never the same. Something was always happening, changing. Hard to put it into words, but to his eye, it had a kind of poetry. The kind of poetry his mother loved.

Nat heard the foreman shout just outside the barn. Dang him! He grabbed the shovel and started on the first stall.

Scooping up dirt in the corner, his eye caught a glimmer of red. He bent down, pushing dust aside. A ring! Now what in tarnation—? Then he remembered. Mrs. Walker had lost a ring.

One with a ruby stone in the center. Her husband had given it to her, and she prized it. She'd worn it to that big Frewen getup, dressed in her best for the English gentry.

But with all the hard work these last years, the ring had become loose on her finger and she would take it off in order not to lose it. But then she'd gone and lost it. Had it somehow slipped off her finger or out of her purse when they'd returned home?

There was no way of knowing. But here it was. He blew off dust and carried it outside to the trough. Dunked it under the water and swished it around. When he took it out, he unloosed his shirttail to dry it. Held it up to the sun.

The sun caught the red glow in the stone's center. What a beauty! He wondered how much it was worth. His mind drifted to that ranch he wanted some day. And the wild horses he wanted to break to halter.

Aw—drat! That was how he'd react months ago. He must git rid of that thinking.

Instead, he'd think on the Missus, how pleased she'd be, gettin' her ring back. He started for the house then remembered she'd gone to Buffalo to collect her daughter and grandson.

"Logan, what you doin' out here?" the foreman growled as he walked up to Nat. "Finished those stalls yet?"

Nat jammed the ring into his pocket. "Just gettin' back to 'em."

"Well, git a goin'! We ain't got all day." The foreman stopped in front of him. "What's that ya got?"

"Ah, nothin'." Had Colburn seen the ring? Nat turned back to the barn. "Another few minutes and I'll be done."

"Well, hurry up! The Missus be back from Buffalo before we knows it. I want those stalls lookin' clean as a whistle." He spit chewing tobacco. "You boys are all the same with takin' your breaks."

A well of fury rose in Nat. He wasn't one to laze around. And the foreman knew it.

———◦◦◦———

Nat's stomach growled, he'd worked hard all afternoon and hadn't taken time to eat anything. Now he was famished, but he had one thing he wanted to do. After giving himself a quick wash-up and putting on a clean shirt, he snuck out of the bunkhouse before the other cowboys left for supper. He was determined to see Miss Arnell alone for a few minutes.

Last night he'd asked Mrs. Walker if he could meet the teacher beforehand in the family sitting room. He wanted to arrange a time for that first ride. Mrs. Walker said to go ahead, but he didn't want to do this with other cowboys around. Boy, he knew he'd hear about it afterward.

Just keep things nice and easy, he told himself. Nice and simple.

He climbed the porch steps. He had no way of knowing if she'd be early, but he'd be there in case.

Opening the door and stepping into the sitting room, he had to let his eyes adjust from the bright sunlight outside.

He glanced in the direction of Miss Arnell's room. He sure hoped she'd come. As he stood there, his mind wandered; he wondered what her room was like. Mrs. Walker was sure to make it comfortable. And Miss Arnell would add all her little things from home.

Strange him thinking that. Before he'd seen Sally's room, he'd never wondered about it. To tell the truth, he'd never *had* to, 'cause she'd invited him right in. And he'd gone.

In hindsight, he saw he shouldn't have, and she shouldn't have invited him. One thing led to another and, after a while, things got a little too cozy between them.

He guessed that was why she took for granted they'd take up where they left off. Except she now had a husband. Least, that's what she said. He was somewhere farther out west. Nat wondered when he'd put in an appearance. Didn't seem like Sally was pining for him. Fact was, she was her old flirty self.

Just then, his eye caught a trim figure entering the sitting room. Miss Arnell held out her hand.

"Mr. Logan. Nice to see you again."

He liked the feel of her hand and was tempted to hold on a little longer. But Mrs. Walker had told him how to greet a lady. Let her call the shots, she'd said. And this lady let her hand drop right away. Boy, she sure wasn't Sally.

For some reason, that made him all the more determined—as cowboys said—to get a piece of the action. And he could do *something*. He caught her eyes and held them. Then smiled his slow smile.

"Nice to see you again, Miss Arnell. Did you recover from our long trip to Buffalo?"

"Yes. But to tell the truth, I was grateful for a padded chair on my return home. It was the constant bumping on that board seat that finally did it. It wasn't so bad on the way to town, but on the return, I'll admit my human frailty asserted itself."

He laughed. "You weren't the only one saddlesore. Not in those words exactly, but you know what I'm sayin'. I'm used to bein' in the saddle and it's a sight more comfortable than the board they call a seat on that ranch wagon."

She joined his laughter.

He suddenly felt comfortable with her. Their ride together should come off just fine.

"Speaking of saddles and such, Mrs. Walker said you like to ride, and I'm your designated escort the first time out from the ranch. I came a little early tonight because I wanted to ask you before everyone gits here for supper. Thought it'd be easier to arrange a time without a lot of nosy ears around." He couldn't help grinning ear to ear. "Forgive my mixed-up talk. Nosy ears don't exactly go together."

"A mixed metaphor! On the contrary, I think it's a most colorful way of expressing oneself."

Pleasure rose up in him. "Kind of you to say so, ma'am." He felt a little embarrassed; after all, she was a teacher. Then he barreled ahead. "Would tomorrow or the next day suit?"

"How about tomorrow? Early afternoon, say, one or two o'clock? I need to spend some time in the morning with Mrs. Walker's grandson, to determine where he is in his studies."

"Let's do two o'clock." That'd give him time to clean up

after morning chores and have lunch—and extra time in case he ran late.

"That would be fine."

"Wait, Jason!" Josephine saw her grandson yank open the door to the sitting room and quickly followed, not wanting him to unceremoniously interrupt a conversation. Nat was supposed to be there, making arrangements to escort Margaret on her ride.

Through the doorway, she saw Margaret turn from Nat to her grandson. Josephine knew her dark-haired, blue-eyed boy would win the teacher's heart. And she wasn't wrong, seeing the look in the teacher's eyes as her attention centered on Jason.

She glanced at Nat. He was looking at both the teacher and boy. Was there yearning in his face? Then his eyes quickly shuttered.

Josephine crossed the room to join them, and placed her hand on her grandson's shoulder. "Jason, I want you to meet your new teacher, Miss Arnell. And Mr. Logan. He is one of the cowboys on our ranch. If grandfather agrees, Mr. Logan will teach you to ride." She saw the quick look Nat shot her way. She had forgotten to mention this to him, but there was no one she'd trust more, other than her husband. Unfortunately, George was too busy right now.

She smiled at both Margaret and Nat. "And this, you have guessed, is my grandson Jason." She looked down at the boy, loving pride catching at her.

Just then her daughter Allison walked into the room, dark-haired like her son and elegant.

Josephine made the proper introductions. When she introduced Nat, he nodded respectfully just like she'd instructed him. He stood with his hat in his hands, his shoulders back, standing straight and tall, yet not arrogantly.

She was proud of him, as if he'd been a son. This man held a special place in her heart. She hoped her daughter could see that. For all his rough ways, he also displayed gentleness and strength, and a willingness to learn that she hadn't seen in other men.

Josephine was glad to see Allison chatting with both Nat and Margaret, treating them as equals. Could Margaret and Nat ever be on a par with each other? They were so different. The more a person got to know them, the more this was evident. But what a handsome couple they made.

Yet doubt crept in. They *were* so terribly different. That little urge she'd had last week to see them together, in a closer way, seemed outside the realm of possibility. Was it even desirable?

Nat was letting Margaret do most of the talking. Josephine was pleased. He'd taken to heart that verse in Proverbs about how any fool who keeps quiet is deemed wise. She could see he was determined to make a good impression on Allison. He wanted to fit in.

"Shall we go in to supper?" she suggested.

The smell of food was in the air. She knew her cowboys, and she was sure Nat was hungry.

He turned and started for the doorway, leaving the others to follow, then suddenly stopped. He stepped to the side, his face flushed. "Ladies," he said, "Why don't you go first," and he indicated the doorway.

Josephine motioned the others to precede her. When she passed Nat, she looked up. One corner of his mouth was raised in a pleased smirk.

"Well done," she whispered.

His eyes flashed a thank you.

As she preceded him through the door, she thought, *he is learning*. Even though he'd been embarrassed by his bad manners, he'd realized it and brought himself up short. That bit of gentlemanly conduct sat him well.

7

Nat bent down, cupping his hands to hold Miss Arnell's foot while she lifted herself onto the sidesaddle. What a slim boot. Of course, even though she was slender, that didn't mean she didn't have a figure. He'd noticed that from the start.

She was the kind that looked dainty, and might need some protection out on the trail, but she didn't seem some defenseless little thing. She probably held a few aces up her sleeve. He didn't know if she knew how to shoot, but if she did, he thought he could depend on her to fight. There was that strength in her. So he could relax some, and not be looking out for every small thing that might bother her.

"Glad to see you have a new hat, ma'am. Somethin' that ties up firm. You'll need it with this wind on the range."

"Mrs. Walker warned me." From her vantage point on the mare, she looked down at him with a smile. "And I appreciate your escorting me."

"My pleasure, ma'am." At least he now knew what to say. Mrs. Walker had coached him on how to address the teacher. For some reason, his boss's wife wanted him to know what to say and do regarding Miss Arnell. Probably nothing special to impress this teacher with…Mrs. Walker just wanted him to learn what was nice in general.

"Someday," she had said, "you will want to know how to court a woman, a real lady, and you might as well start with the females on our ranch."

So, she'd insisted he start with herself, even though she was old enough to be his mother. This all reminded him of his own mother, now dead, and made him want to treat Mrs. Walker with respect. Times were when he missed his mother something powerful, even at his age.

Ma had tried to teach him about God, but he'd been a hardheaded, rebellious sort. He was sorry about that and wondered if she could look down from heaven and see him now. He'd changed, that's for sure. Thank God, he had Mrs. Walker.

All this passed through his mind in a matter of seconds before he mounted his horse and leaned over to open the corral gate, nodding Miss Arnell to pass on through. With ease, he shut it, quickly coming alongside her. He had to admit, he liked the feel of her at his side. A couple of other ranch hands looked up from their work, watching them pass. He felt his chest swell a little—couldn't help feeling proud escorting the teacher.

He headed their horses south. "We'll head this way over the grassland, then turn west toward the mountains."

"I'd like that."

He noticed she rode easy in the saddle.

Mrs. Walker had told him escorting Miss Arnell would be a favor extended to a number of cowboys. Well then, he'd make sure to become the favorite so Miss Arnell asked for him special. This escorting was easy compared to driving cows.

At least, he hoped so. This lady here was a sparky thing, especially in her conversation. He tried to keep up with what she said, and add in a few interesting things himself. He was sure he'd be one of the few cowboys that could. He wasn't as quiet as some. There were cowboys so silent you hardly knew they were there.

He supposed that's why men of their type took to the range. It meant long hours alone. If you didn't like it, you could figure that kind of life wasn't for you.

Well, he liked both. To be by himself, just looking over the wide-open spaces, and liked someone to speak to. Like talking with Mrs. Walker. Why, he could spend hours with her. One side of his mouth quirked up. He was sure Mr. Walker would like that a *whole* lot.

"You're smiling, Mr. Logan. Anything you care to share?"

"Oh, just thinkin' about the Walkers. That Mr. Walker, he likes the missus an awful lot. On her word alone, if we misbehave too much, we'll get ourselves fired." He remembered the time he about got the boot. "Yeah. He likes her a whole lot."

"They do value each other." Miss Arnell sat a little straighter in the saddle. "I've noticed they haven't let their marriage get old and stale the way some do. I like that."

He studied the woman riding at his side. He doubted a man married to her would ever find her stale. She had spunk. She liked to *do* things. Had curiosity. He liked that, too.

Right now, he could see she liked to ride and look at the countryside. She liked a little adventure, too. He wondered if she'd like that canyon trail. Some pretty spectacular rocks there. Piles of them.

Suddenly, his mind saw a rock falling down the side of the canyon, and he pictured himself grabbing her from her saddle and holding her tight with the boulder missing them by inches.

Now that was pure foolishness. Here he was already thinking of rescuing her. His imagination tended on the wild side. That sure was jumping ahead. He'd better watch himself.

But he did wonder about that trail....

"There's a canyon in these parts, one with a lot of rocks out of the ordinary. Formations, some call 'em. Maybe you'd like to go there some day."

"That sounds interesting. Is it far?"

"Well, a little. A person would need to take some lunch—have themselves a picnic before ridin' back." He wouldn't mind spending more time with her. Why, he could think up all kinds of adventure. Those pulp magazines he'd seen, why, he could come up with stories just as good. Shoot—maybe he could be a writer.

He glanced sideways at the teacher again. Who knows, maybe she could teach him a little. He saw them sitting cozy together, shoulder to shoulder. Her patiently teaching him to write, him trying his darndest. Last night, he'd seen the way she took to Jason. He wondered if she'd show as much interest in him if he were a student.

But he'd have trouble concentrating with her so near. And probably she wouldn't be sitting so close. Wouldn't allow it. After all, she was a proper young lady.

But that made her all the more appealing. Most men liked a little challenge. Then the conquest was all that sweeter.

She would be real sweet. Real sweet to hold close.

He felt himself redden. Boy, he needed to watch himself. He wasn't only jumping ahead, he was galloping!

He needed to get the ants out of his pants. Galloping—that was a thought. Miss Arnell seemed a good rider, and the ground was level enough here.

"Care to let the horses have their heads, ma'am? Mine has some ginger to get out. What'd you say?"

"Yes! I'd like to race a little." And without warning, she took off.

He heard her laugh. *Now that was too much.*

He spurred his horse.

But he let her have the lead—for a while. She was too much fun watching from the rear. She made quite a horse woman. He wondered where she'd learned to ride like that.

He would encourage her to go out every day. And if he didn't get to escort her because those other cowboys needed a turn, least this would up the number of times he did.

After a minute of her ahead of him, he spurred his horse once again and came abreast. He pointed to a small group of trees in the distance, signaling to stop there. She nodded a yes. He gave a last spur to his horse and pulled ahead.

At the trees, he stopped and rested his hands on the pommel as she drew up beside him.

"I think you were playing with me, Mr. Logan. I'm a pretty good rider, but I could tell you beat me quite easily."

He just smiled. As long as she knew it, he wouldn't rub it in. He quickly dismounted.

She released her left foot from the stirrup and swung her right leg over the pommel ready to jump down.

"Wait, miss!" He strode to the side of her horse and lifted his hands to help. On this, he wouldn't take no for an answer. Mrs. Walker had instructed him how to help a lady dismount. He grasped her waist and lifted her down. Boy, that felt good.

He tried to remember the last time he'd helped a lady get off a horse. He couldn't. Sally didn't ride much.

"Why don't we stretch our legs some before we head back to the ranch?" he suggested.

"I think that's a good idea. But could we first stand here a minute?"

He looked down at her; she probably needed to catch her breath but didn't want to say so. He couldn't help feel superior—and protective.

They were silent some moments, looking at the wide-open spaces. He liked the quietness, standing here beside her.

"What a wide sky," Miss Arnell said with wonder.

"Wide, wide, the open sky," he responded.

"That has a poetic ring."

"It did? It just popped out." He stuffed his hands in his pockets. "My mother used to read us poetry. Maybe some of it rubbed off."

"That's not typical for a cowboy, is it?"

"Guess not." He grinned. "Sometimes I get bored with my own breed."

"Do you read, Mr. Logan?"

"Not much. I was never around many books."

"Would you like to read more? I have a book or two you might enjoy." She looked at him like she was sizing him up. "I couldn't go long without reading. Before I left home, my parents promised to send me more books after I've read the ones I brought."

If this meant more time with her, he was all for it. "Sure thing. Just choose one you think I'd like."

"I'll do that." She tilted her head to the terrain beyond the clump of trees. "Now, would you like to walk a little before we head back?"

"Yes." He chose a course that looked easiest.

They'd gone a ways in silence when she continued the conversation. "I'd like to know about the poetry your mother liked...if you can remember."

"Well...I was about nine when she died, but I remember *Hiawatha*,

On the shores of Gitche Gumee,
Of the shining Big-Sea-Water,
Stood Nokomis, the old woman,
Pointing with her finger westward,
O'er the water pointing westward,
To the purple clouds of sunset...."

"You have a good memory. That's an excerpt from a very long poem."

"I liked it, that's why. I pictured Hiawatha doin' what his grandmother, Nokomis, wanted. She told him to kill Megissogwon, the fierce magician who had breathed fever on the people and murdered her father. When I was a boy, *I* was Hiawatha, shoutin' his war-cry, a death-cry!"

He looked down at Miss Arnell and smiled. "I was blood-thirsty like most boys. I've calmed down some, but I won't hesitate to fight. Mr. Walker knows that.

"And there's somethin' else about that poem. I liked that word *westward*. Maybe that's one reason I came west." He paused. "My mother shared mostly poems with a story to them. 'Good for your age,' she said. But there were others, too—she liked some English poet who loved nature. I caught his love of nature. I especially like wide-open spaces and mountains."

"Even this wind?" she grabbed her hat at a particularly strong gust.

"You get used to it. Here, hold onto my arm, and I'll slow down a bit." He'd seen his stride was a bit long for her.

"Thank you."

Again he experienced a rush of pleasure in assisting her.

"Go on," she said. "Did your mother have any other favorites?"

"Two poets who were married." He tried to remember. "Their name had a color in it. Brown, I think. She said they wrote about human nature and...love." He felt himself blush.

"Yes! The Brownings! Who doesn't love Elizabeth Barrett Browning's poem, *How do I love thee, let me count the ways...*" She stopped for a second, her hand holding him back. She gazed up at him. "You are a surprise, Mr. Logan. A true surprise!"

This ride was turning out better than he'd hoped.

She smiled, then started walking again. They talked on for some minutes, she wanting to know more about his boyhood. He told her about having to scramble for himself and his brother. Finding odd jobs a boy could do. Being hungry. He decided against telling her about drifting into crime. She probably wouldn't understand how hard it'd been, might not trust him anymore.

She suggested turning back.

When they reached their horses, he took her boot in his hand and helped hoist her up, once again glad to help.

They turned their horses back to the ranch and rode companionably side by side. He couldn't have asked for anything better. Well—he *could* think of something better—holding her close after being rescued. But he'd already told himself to forget that.

"Mr. Logan, you're smiling again. One of these times you must let me in on the joke." Her words came gaily across the space between them.

"Oh, I don't know—"

"Uh, oh," she said, laughing. "As questionable as that? Then, I'd better importune you no further."

"I don't know what importune means, but I get where you're goin'. You're right, you don't want to hear what I'm thinkin'."

After a minute he noticed someone in the distance, cantering toward them. He'd been so intent on her and his own thoughts, he hadn't been paying much attention to surroundings. Anyway, their horses knew the way back to the ranch.

He tried to recognize the horseman, but he was too far away.

After a few minutes, he knew. That banker from Buffalo. What in tarnation was he doing here? Nat felt so irritated he couldn't even remember the man's name. He'd never had much to do with banks anyway. Other than help rob them.

Finally he volunteered, "Someone sure is comin' to meet us."

"I wonder who."

He didn't say.

The two parties came closer. "Oh, I do believe it's the banker from Buffalo," she exclaimed. "Mr. Norland, the man I met on the stagecoach, and then saw again when we lunched at the Myers place. How nice!"

A sudden dark emotion shot through Nat. He wondered what would happen next.

Another minute and the banker hailed them. Their horses

stopped, stood head-to-head. "I'm glad I found you." Mr. Norland looked at Miss Arnell. "You know, I came all the way from Buffalo. I was hoping we could ride together."

"How very nice of you."

Nat glanced over to see a wide, pleased smile on Miss Arnell's face.

"Mr. Logan." Miss Arnell turned to him. "This has been a delightful ride. Would you mind if I continued with Mr. Norland? He's come so far."

Nat gazed at the banker and set a smile on his face, "Of course, Mr. Norland can take over." He was determined to make out that this meant nothing to him, but his back had stiffened.

Miss Arnell looked at him more closely. "You're sure you don't mind?"

"No, glad to offer the hospitality of our ranch. As you said, Mr. Norland's come so far."

He nodded to the banker. "I'll be getting' on now and leave it to you to get Miss Arnell back safely."

Norland tipped his hat. It was a dismissal.

Nat directed his horse to circle around the banker. It wasn't until he was a mile away that he remembered he hadn't even said goodbye to the teacher.

8

As they approached the ranch, Margaret felt she was returning from a far country. Riding in new surroundings, and
then being with two such different men, had been stimulating,
but she was ready to come home, to be in the familiar. She hoped
Mrs. Walker would do some of the honors in entertaining their
guest.

Mr. Norland and she had talked on a variety of subjects. The
most entertaining had been his sketch of various people who
lived in or visited Buffalo. Charismatic personalities, like Buffalo
Bill Cody, the great buffalo hunter who was said to be forming
a Wild West Show, and General George Crook, who had fought
the Sioux after they massacred General George Custer and his
troops at the battle of the Little Big Horn.

The banker added, "Englishmen are also coming into the
area, mostly in the form of large enterprises. Lesser sons of lords
who want to make their money in cattle. Lord Frewen south of
you is just such an individual."

When Margaret mentioned Mr. and Mrs. Walker had been
invited to one of Lord Frewen's parties, his eyebrows rose. She
could see his opinion of the Walkers considerably elevated.

"But, of course," he said, "I've discovered there are quite a variety of people in these parts. Even rustlers. That's why you want to be careful with whom you associate."

He had gone on to explain. "It is all right to be friendly with everyone, but it's also a good idea to keep one's distance, socially and personally, from others. Take these cowboys. Most of them have little education. It wouldn't be wise for someone like yourself, who is educated, to associate with them too much."

Their horses had drifted apart, and he kneed his horse closer. "For instance, what is the Walkers' idea of you going out with that cowboy today?"

"I'm to have an escort, for my protection on the range."

"I'm surprised Mr. or Mrs. Walker doesn't accompany you. It would certainly be better society."

"They're far too busy. But I also understand that cowboys are invariably respectful to ladies. Certainly on this ranch, Mrs. Walker wouldn't tolerate anything else."

"That's good to hear. However, I hope she spreads around the favors, and doesn't let you go out exclusively with just one cowboy. He could get the wrong impression. This one today, I thought him rather rough looking. He's not in your class at all."

Margaret was silent a moment, not quite sure how to respond. "It's true Mr. Logan is largely uneducated, but he certainly treats a lady properly."

"I'm glad to hear he's respectful. I still say, however, that it pays to be careful and not pay any one of these cowboys too much attention. It would give the wrong idea."

They walked their horses into the ranch yard.

Mr. Norland helped Margaret down from her horse. His assistance was quite different from Mr. Logan's. Yes, it had been quite unlike Mr. Logan's. It surprised her.

And as far as cowboys went—and her experience was limited—Mr. Logan certainly didn't seem to fit the mold. His feel for poetry, for instance. As far as she could tell, it was not only instilled into him by his mother, it seemed part of his nature.

Colorful observations just bolted out of his mouth. Like a horse out of a chute.

She laughed.

"Miss Arnell, did I do something funny?"

"Oh, no! I was just remembering something from this afternoon. Nothing to do with you." She looked around. "I'm not sure where to leave our horses. Maybe we should walk them to the barn. You are staying for supper, aren't you? Mrs. Walker would certainly invite you."

"That I will. If for no other reason than Mrs. Walker has an excellent cook. But, of course, the Walker ranch has other attractions." He smiled at her.

That sort of admiration almost put her out of countenance. Yet…it was rather flattering.

They approached the barn. "Someone will surely be around to care for our mounts." Margaret said the words quite loudly, hoping someone was around to hear.

As soon as she spoke, Mr. Logan stepped out of the building. "I'll take your horses."

Seeing the two men closely together, Margaret couldn't help notice the difference in their dress. Mr. Logan was in typical cowboy attire, rough jeans and a dark shirt with dusty boots, whereas Mr. Norland had on a well-cut broadcloth suit. The banker certainly looked more refined.

Mr. Logan stepped near her horse and stroked its neck affectionately then looked over at Mr. Norland's. "You've got yourself a fine mare, there. Looks like she's got stayin' power."

"I like to take long rides and purchased her with that in mind. She literally eats up the miles, so it made coming here this afternoon doable." His eyes went to Margaret. "Of course, I had another inducement—"

"I'll take your horses." Nat grabbed the horses' reins.

Margaret glanced at Mr. Logan. He'd cut off the banker's pretty speech.

"Take my arm, Miss Arnell, and I'll escort you to the house."

"Thank you." She couldn't help note the proprietary air with which Mr. Norland had offered. She started walking, then looked back. Nat had not moved, was staring at them.

"Thank you, Mr. Logan."

He held up the reins as if to say, *You're welcome*.

"And I appreciated your escort today," she added. "I enjoyed it." He suddenly smiled in answer. She felt a nice little something pass between them. When he'd left them on the range, he'd given no parting goodbye. Had he been miffed—or something?

So, he was sensitive. After all, he did have a feeling for poetry—that kind of man would be sensitive. She must remember that. She wouldn't want to unintentionally hurt him.

A cowboy and poetry. Who would have thought?

Margaret and Mr. Norland walked to the porch and Mrs. Walker greeted them, "Hello! Supper will be ready shortly."

Margaret excused herself to freshen up after the ride. She changed into a dark green silk, felt the occasion called for something a little more formal. When she entered the dining room, she was gratified to see it look so elegant. A white cloth covered the long table and a candelabra graced either end. Mrs. Walker's wedding gifts, she supposed. A low bowl of flowers had been placed in the middle. Some of the colorful blooms on the house's south side had been sacrificed. In honor of the banker's visit, no doubt.

The seating arrangement had been changed as well. Mr. Walker still sat at the head of the table, but now his wife was placed on his right with Mr. Norland to his left. Margaret sat next to Mr. Norland with everyone else sitting where they were accustomed with the exception of the foreman at the foot of the table. Nat was one place down from his usual seat, beside Mrs. Walker. Margaret was sure both of them enjoyed the proximity. She'd noticed that Mrs. Walker treated him like a son. Oh, she was careful not to show favoritism in front of the other cowboys. But Margaret had seen the little favors Mrs. Walker extended to him.

Nat—for that is how she now thought of him after their ride—had on a clean shirt and his dark hair looked like it had been dunked in water. His face had that fresh-scrubbed look. She smiled to herself. He looked unusually presentable.

After Mr. Walker said grace, Sally and Cook came in with the food. Big slabs of beef with gravy. Two kinds of vegetables had been raided from the root cellar.

Margaret was passing a dish of beets and looking up, noticed Sally bend down next to Nat and place a basket of freshly baked bread in front of him. "You get first dibs," she said in a whisper. Her shoulder touched his and stayed there a moment. Her contact had an air of intimacy, but was done so adroitly that apparently Margaret was the only one who noticed.

Margaret looked away, but couldn't help thinking, *How very forward*. Her eyes went back to them surreptitiously.

How did Nat feel about Sally touching him in that way? He acted as if he hadn't noticed, but it would be hard for any red-blooded male not to. He hadn't moved his shoulder away from Sally, not even a fraction.

Margaret decided to pay attention to Mr. Norland on her right, but he was intent on eating. In fact, everyone was enjoying the dinner so much, there was complete silence.

Finally, the banker broke the spell. "This food is delicious."

"Thank you," Mrs. Walker said. "I'll be sure to pass on the compliment to our cook." She then asked, "How have your visits to the other ranchers been going?"

"Quite well. Yesterday, in fact…" and he told about encountering one of the newer cattlemen in town.

Margaret smiled. He was quite the story teller. Of course, she already knew that.

Eventually, talk went around to Mrs. Walker's pet project, the new school.

Mr. Walker looked proudly at his wife. "Josephine is successful at whatever she puts her hand to. And Nat, here, with the help of our men and neighbors in the area, is building the schoolhouse."

"That's commendable. I firmly believe in formal education," Mr. Norland said. "Have you thought how to furnish the school? What about desks for the students, and another for the teacher?"

"Good question. The desks—" Mr. Walker looked at Nat. "Would that be something you can build?"

"It seems to me," Mr. Norland said, "that you could order them from Cheyenne. Store bought desks would be better. And, if you're short on cash, the bank can help with a loan."

"Well—" Mr. Walker began.

"Not to interrupt," Nat said, "but I think I could make somethin' you need."

"What do you have in mind?"

"Nothin' too fancy at first. A bench for several students to sit on with a back to it. Then a long table for them to write on. I could make as many as you need."

"That sounds good enough, if you can do it."

"Don't you need him on the ranch?" Mr. Norland asked. "With the cows and such?" He paused, then said forcefully, "I'll get you good terms, very good ones indeed. And you'd have something in short order. I'm sure Miss Arnell would like to get started as soon as possible." He turned to smile at her.

Nat cleared his throat. "I'd like to save you some money, Mr. Walker. I'm sure I could do a good job for you."

Mr. Norland looked at Nat. "I'm sure you could." Margaret heard the condescending tone in the banker's voice. "However, it's a matter of time. I'm sure you see that."

"Mr. Walker, if you'd let me off the cattle, I could get started tomorrow," Nat offered.

"We could go to your office after supper, Mr. Walker, and you would see how I would help you." Mr. Norland's tone was compelling. Margaret could see he thought his idea was better than this cowboy's.

"Dessert is about to be served," Mrs. Walker announced. All eyes turned to the kitchen. Sally walked through the door with a large dish of fruit cobbler. The discussion about desks had been skillfully tabled. Mrs. Walker had gone all out with this meal; usually, dessert wasn't served.

Sally stopped at a spot between Mrs. Walker and Nat. Margaret wondered if there would be a repeat performance of what she'd seen earlier. Then, just as Sally placed the cobbler on the table, a baby wailed. Sally jerked around. The woman could not have turned faster and left the room. Margaret's heart went out to the baby—and then to the mother. The room had become quiet, waiting.

Margaret heard the baby's cry soften to a whimper and then stop. Obviously, Sally had picked up her son and comforted him. Her mother's heart had taken precedence over everything. The cowboys started talking again as Mrs. Walker served the dessert.

Suddenly, Margaret felt her assessment of Sally had been too negative and judgmental. Sally had shown Nat undue attention, yet, hadn't she also shown herself to be a devoted mother? Margaret had seen that in the stagecoach, Sally doing everything she could to keep her baby comfortable and quiet.

Mentally, Margaret drew herself up. From now on she would try to be more charitable.

Margaret and Mr. and Mrs. Walker accompanied Mr. Norland to his horse. It had been sent for earlier, saddled, and tied to the front rail.

"Well, I certainly enjoyed myself, Mrs. Walker." The banker shook Mr. Walker's hand. "You think about that loan for those school desks."

"Thank you. The missus and I will talk it over—and, of course, see what Logan can do."

"All right, then." The banker mounted his horse. "I'd like to come again, if I may, Mrs. Walker. Your cook certainly knows her business. And I'd like to take Miss Arnell riding."

"That would be fine."

Margaret felt Mrs. Walker give her consent less than enthusiastically. She wondered why.

They all waved to the departing guest.

Now, a walk would be in order, Margaret felt. Something was niggling her, and she wanted to get to the bottom of it. She stayed at the rail when the Walkers turned to mount the steps.

"You coming?" Mrs. Walker paused at the top.

"I'd like to walk for a few minutes, if it's all right with you. This has been a busy day, and I need to wind down. Think things through a little."

"That'd be fine, but stay near the ranch buildings." Mrs. Walker held out a hand to keep her husband at her side. "Are you sure you don't want to sit on one of the porch chairs?"

"Actually, I think better walking."

"All right. Mr. Walker and I will be keeping each other company in the sitting room. Just don't be too long."

"I won't. Thank you for a lovely evening. The table setting, everything, was special."

"I'd say it was exceptional." Mr. Walker glanced at his wife. "As our cowboys would say, 'You put on the dog!'"

"Well, I have my womanly pride. After all, we entertained a big city banker."

"Ah!" He laughed. "When I saw those candelabra, I knew there was something going on." He put his arm around his wife.

"Good you're going for a walk, Margaret. I need to discuss with the missus why she doesn't put on the dog more often for me." And he hustled her into the house.

Margaret chuckled. It was good she was leaving them alone, to be together in their own sitting room.

She started down the drive. Walking back, she'd take the fork that led to the barn; that way, she wouldn't stray too far.

Dusk was coming on, but the air was mild. It felt good to stretch her legs. She swung her arms as she strolled along. There was nothing like a good walk.

She loved seeing the Walkers together like that. They joked and showed each other affection. She felt lighter in spirit, more able to sort out her jumbled thoughts.

What was bothering her?

It was the two men. So different from each other. A couple of unexpected things had happened this afternoon, small in themselves, but something she wanted to consider.

She thought back to when Mr. Norland had helped her off the horse. He'd grasped her firmly enough, but then let her slide so that she almost fell against him. If she hadn't had the gumption and strength to stop herself, she was sure she would have fallen onto him. And what would he have done? She wasn't ready to be that close to a man, any man. It suggested intimacy. He'd been such a perfect gentleman riding on the range. Now, she wasn't quite so sure about him.

What would her friends say in Chicago? There, she'd been a little bit of a bluestocking. She was admired, that she could tell, but none of the men ever approached her in a romantic way.

Besides, she'd let her aspirations be known. She wanted to become a teacher. Not to marry—at least not right away. When she told people she was going west, that really set her apart. Any young man who approached her talked of adventure, the wilds, that sort of thing. She was leaving, so they didn't talk of romance.

The two girls she'd become better friends with wondered

about the cowboys, what they'd be like. Would they be rough? Romantic, in a tough kind of way? Well, she'd been on a ride with one today. She could tell he was tough, strong, and experienced. In fact, when she compared the way Nat had assisted her from the horse, compared to the banker, Nat had lifted her *up* from the horse. She'd been suspended momentarily in the air like a doll or a little girl. It had been fun, made descending from a horse rather exciting. She'd felt the energy in him but also felt completely secure. As soon as her feet touched the ground firmly, he let her go. As a gentleman should. Whereas the banker, who should have been the perfect gentleman, had held onto her a little longer than necessary.

And something else. At some point in the afternoon, each man had extended his arm to assist her. But, again, there was a difference. When Nat had offered his, she needed it. The wind had buffeted her and the terrain was uneven. She had really appreciated his help. His arm was strong; she could feel the muscle beneath the shirt—which shouldn't have been a surprise. Nat did a lot of physical labor whereas Mr. Norland sat at a desk. Even now, she could still feel Nat's hard muscle.

Mr. Norland had also offered his arm. In the course of things, it should have been a gentlemanly gesture. Yet, he had made such a thing of it in front of Nat. Like she belonged to him. He and she were on the same social level, and he was going to show that cowboy what was what. His touch felt proprietary. She nearly withdrew her hand. Her lips curved up mischievously. She wondered what Mr. Norland would have said to *that*.

Well, there it was. Even though this cowboy was supposedly beneath her, she had actually felt more comfortable with him—or his treatment of her—which was maybe the same thing. Was he more truly the gentleman than the banker?

Now, that was a funny thought.

She turned on the drive and took the fork to the barn. Light was fading, so she'd soon be going in.

Reaching the barn, she was just about to cross in front of the main door when she heard raised voices. Instinctively, she stepped back.

"What were you doin' in my things?" She recognized Nat's angry voice.

"Logan! The other day I saw you put that ring in your pocket, and Mrs. Walker hasn't got it back." The foreman's voice was contemptuous, angry. "Now, give it up."

"Blast you! I'll bring it to her myself. In my own way."

"Likely story. You've been found out, so of course that's what you'll do *now*."

Margaret heard boot steps start toward the barn door. She moved back into the shadows.

"Hey! Come here!"

"I'll take care of it. Get off my back."

"Mr. Walker will hear of this!"

Nat appeared at the door, then rushed in the direction of the corrals.

The foreman stepped out of the barn. "Thief!"

Margaret's stomach knotted. The foreman hesitated some moments then stomped off to the bunkhouse. When he'd disappeared, she stood still some moments. Nat, a thief? She didn't understand.

9

Minutes later, Margaret sat at the small desk in her room, trying to collect herself. The foreman and Nat's confrontation disturbed her. She had just decided that Nat was a gentleman—if a rough, uneducated one—but now, possibly a thief?

What was this West, anyway? In Chicago she would never, ever associate with a thief. What would her mother and father say if they knew she was grappling with something like this?

Margaret bent over to unlace her shoes, finding relief in doing the small, ordinary task. She couldn't even guess how to work through this problem.

Could she ever look Nat in the face again? Talk with him? Have him escort her on rides? Knowing Nat was a favorite of Mrs. Walker, how could she let her know he was suspected of stealing?

She hung up her dress, tried to neatly fold her underthings, but her hands felt clumsy.

Turning down the covers on her bed, Margaret slid beneath them. This was too much to think through tonight. She would try to sleep. Maybe tomorrow she'd have an idea of what to do.

One thing was sure. She had plenty on her plate without adding this new problem. Besides teaching Jason tomorrow, two other children were arriving to be part of the new school. For now, Mrs. Walker was letting her use the ranch house sitting room as a classroom. After each school session with Jason, they would carefully put their school things away so that the room returned to normal. Now, she would need to set up the room for two additional students. And, of course, the challenge would be to see where these two children stood in their learning. If she remembered correctly, one was about Jason's age. The other was older. Maybe she could teach them all at the same time, doing a "review" of certain aspects to see how much these other children knew.

Her mind focused on this new challenge. Relief coursed through her. This was what she loved. Teaching. Opening young minds to the new worlds of reading, writing and arithmetic. Margaret loved the scope and the orderliness of it. Maybe quite different from the measure of orderliness the West presented. She could now guess at the gap—maybe canyon would be more apt—between the two worlds.

Well, she would do what could be done to bring knowledge and order into the minds of the students entrusted to her. That was her mission in this part of the Wyoming Territory.

Margaret thought back to Nat. Well, what of him? Did she need to have dealings with him? Then she remembered the book she'd promised to lend him. Bother! She didn't even want to talk with him. Margaret could see she'd let down her guard on that ride. How could she have been so foolish? Mr. Norland was right. She'd have to keep her distance, draw a line in the sand, so to speak.

However, she would need to give Nat that book. Unless she could send it by carrier pigeon. That brought a smile. She turned on her side, her face nestling into the pillow. Maybe sleep would come after all.

From the barn opening, Nat looked up as Jason stepped out the back door of the ranch house. It was late afternoon. Nat supposed school was done for the day. Returning from riding the range that morning, he'd seen two new children playing outside with Jason. In fact, he'd made a point to steer his horse closer to the house, and when he thought Miss Arnell spotted him, tipped his hat. She had turned away, but he was sure she'd seen him. He shrugged, probably he was wrong. Wouldn't be the first time.

So, the school was growing. He was glad for Miss Arnell. She could do a lot of good.

Which reminded him, tomorrow he and the men would head off to the western range to cut those lodgepole pines for the school. Mr. Walker had said they'd go as soon as chores were over. Cook had been told to send along plenty of food. Both for lunch and late afternoon. They wouldn't be coming back till dusk. Mr. Walker was determined to make a good start on the work, so supper would be late. Nat smiled. Knowing the boss, they might get all the trees felled in one day. Then the next few days, after cutting off the limbs, they'd cart the logs down by ox and sled. Nat liked the way this ranch got things done. No wonder it was one of the best in these parts.

Mrs. Walker's grandson walked up, and he welcomed the lad. "Jason! What you doin' here? You got somethin'?"

"Yes, Mr. Logan. This is for you." He held out a book.

"For me? You read this in school today?"

"No. Miss Arnell said to give it to you. Said you'd talked about it the other day—her giving you a book, that is."

"Ah, yes, I remember."

Surprise and disappointment hit him. Miss Arnell hadn't waited to give it to him herself. It would have been another reason for them to talk...or something. He turned over the book and looked at the title. *Ivanhoe* by Sir Walter Scott. When he opened it a little, he saw a note inserted between the pages. Addressed to him from Miss Arnell. He'd read it after the boy left.

77

"So, Jason, when are we goin' to start your ridin' lessons?"

"Grandma said after I review the ABC's and learn my numbers to 100."

"Well, let's git goin' then. How long d' you think it'll take?"

"Depends on Miss Arnell, I guess. Those two new kids are slowing me down. I was doing real good before they came."

"You just keep at it." Nat reached out to ruffle the boy's hair. "I expect it'll be a few days before I'd start you anyhow. Tomorrow the other cowboys and me are off to fell those trees for the new school."

"I wish I could see that!"

"It'd be interestin', that's for sure. An education of sorts. Yet, it'd be a little dangerous. Being around those fallin' trees—you got to watch it."

"I'd watch myself!"

"Sure you would. But your ma and grandma would have somethin' to say about that." Nat laughed. "A lot!"

"Oh, I know. Mother says I'm her 'precious.'" Jason scrunched up his nose in disgust.

Nat laughed again. "See what you mean. But I was 'bout your age when I lost my ma. I'll never forget that. So just appreciate yours. Treat her nice, like a lady. You're lucky to have someone who loves you so. After my ma died, I didn't have anybody like that."

Jason stared at Nat. "Your ma died? That must have been bad. But you still had your dad."

"Nope. He died from influenza when I was real young. Ma had us two boys to raise, all by herself. That's why I say, appreciate yours. Obey her. Honor her, like the Good Book says."

Nat tousled Jason's hair again. "Enough of sermon. Now git back to the house and behave yourself."

"Okay, Mr. Logan!" Jason turned and started to run.

"Thanks for the book!" Nat called after him.

Soon as the boy disappeared, Nat took out the note from

Miss Arnell. It had been folded over with a sharp crease. So sharp it was difficult to open. He found his fingers fumbling, even shaking a little. Fool, to be so nervous over a simple note. It was probably nothing. Yet, he read it eagerly.

This is a good tale from a master English storyteller. It contains colorful descriptions of outlaws, a tournament, and the divisions between Jews and Christians. Have you heard of Robin Hood, King John, and Richard the Lionhearted? I believe this author was a good judge of human behavior. Some people find the work poetic. It takes place in 12th Century England. I hope you like it.

Huh. He was hoping for something a little warmer than, "I hope you like it." Almost sounded downright impersonal. She'd said she enjoyed that ride with him. Why didn't she say something about them getting together again to talk over the book?

She could have said reading this will make you a more educated cowboy, someone the other cowboys—*and I*—will look up to. Someday—*at my side*—I'll have you help me with my students.

He laughed. Now that last was a dumb thought, his imagination was getting carried away again.

He held up the book. It looked a long one, and he hoped it didn't have too many big words. He didn't want to look dumb in front of the teacher, although she knew he didn't have much education. Anyhow, he'd do his best.

In fact, he'd get right at it tonight. Then, maybe after he came back from the trees, they could talk about the story. Maybe she could help him with words he didn't understand…that sort of thing.

Josephine looked up as Margaret entered the room. Every time she saw the young woman, a satisfied glow came over her. What an inspiration to have her come and teach. Josephine could already see Jason had taken to her and improved in his studies.

"Come, sit, Margaret." She put down her pencil and shoved aside the ledger she was working on. "I need a break from this. Numbers were never my strong suit. Now, what's on your mind?"

Margaret sat in the indicated chair, was about to say something, then seemed to change her mind. Finally, she began.

"First of all, I want to tell you how well your grandson is doing. I'm amazed how quickly he learns something new. I rarely need to repeat myself." She placed her hands neatly in her lap. "The two new children are sweet, but either they are shy or are quite behind in the basics. Maybe I'll delegate Jason to work with the boy while I spend time with his sister. I've found that a student—in this case Jason—will learn a lesson more thoroughly when teaching it himself. So, we might kill two birds with one stone."

"You have my permission to do whatever you think best. *That* you know, Margaret." There was a long, silent pause.

Margaret looked down at her hands in her lap. Josephine noticed they weren't relaxed; they were restive, fidgety, and she was twisting her ring around her finger. "That's a lovely ring, Margaret. I've been meaning to tell you. The amber stone suits you."

Margaret looked up, concern marking her features. *There's something bothering her, but, unless, she tells me, I have no idea what it might be.* Mrs. Walker set herself to wait patiently.

"There's one other thing," Margaret began. "I've been thinking about my rides out from the ranch. Would it be possible for me to ride by myself? I would be careful not to stray too far from the house."

A long moment passed before Mrs. Walker answered. "I don't think so. I know Mr. Walker wouldn't hear of it. Both of us feel responsible for your safety. What would we tell your parents if something happened to you?" She paused, her woman's intuition suspecting some little bump in the road of human relations. "Did anything untoward happen on your ride with Mr. Logan? I hope he was a gentleman."

"Oh, he was. It's something completely different. But now that you mention it, I would prefer not to ride out with him again. If Mr. Walker insists on an escort, I could try the other cowboys you have in mind." Margaret's eyes were troubled. "I do appreciate all you're doing for me, and I don't want to appear ungrateful—or fussy. But, if you could arrange it—"

"Well, yes, of course." Josephine looked at Margaret closely. "You're sure nothing went wrong on the ride? I know Mr. Norland appeared unexpectedly. I hope Nat took it well."

"Oh, yes, yes! He took it just fine. It's something else." She glanced down then looked up again. "If you don't mind, I'd rather not explain."

Now it was Mrs. Walker's turn to search for words. "Of course, Margaret. I'll tell Mr. Logan. Probably after they fell those trees, though. I think he rather liked escorting you, and this would come as an unwelcome surprise. I don't want his mind wandering off this particular job. Felling trees can be dangerous. The men need to keep their wits about them."

"Thank you. Thank you, Mrs. Walker." Margaret started to rise. "That's all I had on my mind."

Mrs. Walker had the feeling that this escorting business was what Margaret had really come to talk about. She watched as the graceful young woman left the room. Now, what brought that on? She knew Nat still had his wild moments, yet she'd instructed him so carefully in what a gentleman should do. It was a puzzle.

She reluctantly placed the ledger solidly in front of her and firmed her resolve. She was determined to would finish the accounts this morning.

Nat directed the boys to the grove of lodgepole pines. "Let's start where the trees are spaced out a little. It'll make things easier till we get the hang of it."

Mr. Walker came up to him. "Why don't you and a couple of the boys show how it's done. Some of them are new at this."

"All right. Over there I've marked a tree off by itself."

The cowboys gathered around and Nat took up the axe. "You all stand at the side. That's the best place to be when a tree comes down."

"That's right," Mr. Walker agreed. "Never get in back of the tree. You can be seriously hurt if the tree butt kicks back during the fall."

Nat patiently showed how to notch the tree, then started a level cut opposite it. "Now don't go all the way. Leave a little 'bout in the middle to act like a hinge."

Mr. Walker added, "Now boys, when a tree starts to fall, if you can, get behind a standing tree to protect yourself from projectiles and debris. We don't want anyone hurt."

Nat finished the cut then quickly stepped off to the side as a loud crack split the air.

"Timber-r-r!" the men shouted as the tree began to fall. Snapping, ripping, and crackling followed, then a huge *booming* sounded as the tree hit the ground. A cheer went up.

"There we go!" Mr. Walker shouted. "Now, Nat, scatter these men so they don't get in each other's hair. Teams of two. Boys, you can see the trees marked for cutting."

A few hours later, the men had felled a good portion. Mr. Walker called a lunch break and each man went over to the chuck wagon. "Take some extra time to rest," Mr. Walker added.

"Then we'll go at it again."

Nat decided to get off by himself. After eating, he planned on taking a little *siesta*, as his Mexican friend would say.

He walked some distance and found a large rock to sit against. He was hot, but the wind cooled his face. He dug into the plate of beef and beans, then gazed off to the south, remembering the last time he was here locating these lodgepole pines—when he discovered rustlers driving off some of their cattle.

Disgust rose up in him. He hated it when men stole what others had worked hard for; he'd finally woke up to how wrong it was. When he was younger, he'd been a fool. True, necessity had driven him to it, the stealing and all. But it'd been bad, all the same.

From time to time as Nat got older, he did get a paying job. But it never seemed enough. He'd blow money in town. Then steal some more to make it to the next meager pay. After all, he'd reasoned, he and his brother had to eat.

However, there came a time when they got into bigger stealing. Regular like. And wouldn't talk about getting a job.

That last time, because they were brothers and used to sticking together, Nat had agreed to hold the horses while Lem and a couple of his friends hit that bank. Nat hadn't wanted to. For some reason, robbing that bank had woken him up. He'd decided this was the last time he'd do anything like that. Afterward, he and Lem had words. Lem just didn't understand.

So they'd parted ways. Nat had traveled north and found this job, determined to stick with it, no matter what. At first it was hard, because he didn't know all that much about cattle. He'd taken to the horses, like a sponge to water. Horses had personality. They were sensitive, loyal. More like a person.

He looked off in the distance across the plains with the Big Horn Mountains at his right. Where was his brother now? Seeing that horse with the half-moon on its rump…he thought back to when he'd been in the Occidental Saloon, trying to pick up news. Looking over the room, he'd finally made his way over to a lone drinker. Rough type with a missing front tooth. Obviously a loner. Yet the man allowed Nat to sit down at his table.

Nat had let the silence lengthen. After a while, the man said he was from down south a ways, didn't talk about working on a ranch. He wouldn't say he was from the Hole-in-the-Wall; anyhow, nobody would openly admit that. But after an hour of the man drinking and a good bit of quiet, Nat got around to reminiscing about his brother and that half-moon horse. What had that old man said?

"A half-moon horse? Yah, I seen it. What d'ya say your name was?"

"Logan."

"Yep. I remember him, haven't seen him for a spell. Sure did set store by that horse." Then he added, "Yah...I was in prison once. Just visitin', you understand." He slammed down his glass. "But sometimes cellmates get shut of each other." He wouldn't say anything more. Even when Nat bought him another drink.

But that last expression had a worrying, bad sound...like his brother and that horse had gotten separated—maybe forcibly—and it was a final thing.

10

After supper, Nat caught up with Mrs. Walker's daughter in the hallway. He had heard she and her mother were riding into Buffalo the next day, and was glad he caught her alone. "Ma'am! Could I ask you somethin'?"

Allison turned around and smiled. "Certainly."

"I hear you're goin' into town tomorrow and wonder if you'd do me a favor. I'd take care of it myself, but I'm workin' hard on those trees for the new school."

He drew a lump of cloth from his pocket. "This is a secret." He gingerly undid it and held out a ring.

"Is that a ruby? It's lovely." She handled it carefully. "I seem to remember Mother lost a ring such as this."

"Well, this is it." Nat beamed with pleasure.

Allison broke out into the widest smile. "Where did you find it?"

"I found it in the barn, hidden in the dirt and muck. It needs better cleanin' than I can do—and polishin'. Stuff is stuck in the swirly parts. I wondered if you'd try to find someone in town could do the job."

"Nat, that's the sweetest thing. I could hug you. Mother will be so excited. This ring was one of her most prized possessions.

I know how she treasured it—one of the few things Father gave her when they could ill afford it."

"The only thing is, don't tell your ma. I want to surprise her with it before the school raisin'. So she can wear it then."

Allison hesitated. "I'll see what I can do. But Buffalo is such a small town. What should I do if I can't find someone to help me?"

"Well, try real hard. Sure, I could give her the ring like this. But I want it all shined up pretty like. She's quality, you see, and I don't want to give her anythin' less." He thought for a moment. "You could try Doc Watkin's place. He might have somethin'." He smiled. "He's got a cure for everythin' human. Ought to have a cure for a ring."

She laughed. "Nat, you have such a unique way of saying things. I'll miss it when I leave for New York. My husband's there, temporarily, on business. I'm going next week, leaving Jason here." She held out her hand. "I'll see what I can do. And, I'll be sure to keep it from my mother. I can always tell her I'm going to the doctor—something for Jason before I leave."

She had just walked to her room when Mrs. Walker entered from the sitting room. "Nat, could I see you in the office for a minute? My husband told me you felled all the trees for the school, and I've been waiting to talk with you about something."

* * *

Nat strode down the steps from the office in a hurry, but not so as to let anyone guess how upset he was. Just now he wanted to get shut of all women. Especially Margaret Arnell.

Deep embarrassment had shot through him when Mrs. Walker told him Miss Arnell no longer wanted his escort. Mrs. Walker said she didn't know why. But those were the teacher's wishes.

He could see it was hard on her, telling him. Something in

him wanted to spare her saying anything more, but he had to ask. "What about the other cowboys?"

"It seems she'll try them."

"So, I wasn't good enough for her."

"Nat, she didn't say that. In fact, I was sure to ask if something had happened that made her uncomfortable. Like your not being a gentleman. But she said, no, it was something else."

"Somethin' else?"

"That's what she said. She didn't confide in me." Mrs. Walker hesitated a long moment. "Do you think you could ask her?"

"No!" Just the thought of bringing up the subject with the teacher had him breaking out in a sweat. No, if she didn't want him, she didn't want him. Simple as that.

He stepped into the bunkroom; most of the boys were out and about yet. But they'd be here soon. He walked to his bed. Beside it was a little pile of his stuff with the book tucked underneath. He hadn't broadcast his possession to the boys. Just read it quietly here and there. No sense in making them jealous.

But now he bent over and took the book from the stack of things. He'd a mind to give it back to Miss Arnell. With Jason as messenger. He gripped it hard. Emotion came over him all of a sudden. There were so few books in the West, and the thought of giving up this one was painful. It was his opportunity to read one, and from one of the best storytellers, Miss Arnell said.

If he sent it back, she'd probably think it was too hard for him. And think even less of him. Darn that woman. Well, he wouldn't give her the satisfaction. He'd read it all right. If he didn't know a word that was important, he'd ask Mrs. Walker.

Did Miss Arnell think he was dumb? Well, he'd show her. He was smarter than she realized. In fact, he probably knew more about life than she had in her little finger.

In his mind he saw one of her little fingers. They *were* little. And slender. Once again he felt her hand on his arm. It made him feel more like a man.

Well, that was over.

He put the book away and hunkered down on his bunk.

But his mind wouldn't leave alone what she'd said about not wanting his escort. He wondered if it had anything to do with that banker. After she'd rode with him, by comparison, Nat looked like a hick. That was probably it. He *wasn't* good enough for her.

It was just as well he'd be gone most of the day, getting those logs ready for the school. And making the furniture. He'd show her he could do quality stuff. Life wasn't all book learning.

He turned on his side, looking around the bunkhouse. The boys didn't have much. A lot of it was worn and pretty beat up. Sometimes he just had a longing for finer things. Gentle things. Was that what a woman brought to a man's life? He remembered his mother—and missed her. Well, he was glad he had Mrs. Walker from time to time.

He chuckled wryly. There was Sally. She was friendly, maybe a mite too much. He could always spend some time with her.

"So, all the trees have been transported down to the school site?" Mr. Walker leaned back in his chair, looking across his desk at Nat.

"Yes, sir, about a mile from here, north toward Buffalo. The limbs are off just the way you asked. Now we need to square 'em. Takes extra time, of course, but they'll last longer that way."

"Good. So, do you think we'll be ready for the raising by next week? I have to give the missus the go-ahead. She wants to inform all the neighbors, even those without kids. Everybody'll want to be there."

"Then tell her to start invitin'." Nat took up his work gloves. "Is that all, sir?" On the boss's nod, he started to rise from his chair when a loud knock sounded.

"Thought I heard a horse outside. Nat, go ahead and answer the door."

Nat swung it open, and Major Wolcott strode inside.

"Glad to find you're in, Walker."

"Hello, Major. What's on your mind?" The boss rose and motioned to the cattleman. "Have a seat."

Nat wondered if Mr. Walker wanted him to stay. He had a feeling this was about the homesteaders and cattle. He threw his boss a questioning look, and was motioned to wait.

"What's this about, Major?"

Major Wolcott swore. The rancher looked every bit as belligerent and upset as his big frame conveyed. "It's those homesteaders near my spread. I'm tired of them coming onto my property and watering their cows off my stream. I've a notion to put a bullet somewhere it'll hurt."

"Well, those homesteaders have been watering their cows there a good while. They probably feel they have right of access because of usage. Have you filed a claim on that part of the river?"

"You bet I have. A little over a week ago."

"Just a week ago? What have you done about informing the homesteaders?"

"Told them it was mine, to get off my property."

"That would come as an unwelcome surprise. Where are they going to go for water?" Mr. Walker let the question sink in. "I'd say there was plenty of water for you both. Could you give them a right-of-way, particularly since they were using it before you filed a claim? That would be the right neighborly thing to do."

"I know what you're getting at, but I don't want to encourage them to stay." Major Wolcott shifted in his chair. "More will come, you know that, and then there won't be enough water. I've got to take my stand now. Maybe you haven't had trouble like this."

"Well, I wouldn't call it trouble. I have two families on my eastern border, but we've gotten along." Mr. Walker stood. "You know, my wife has the idea of bringing the big ranchers and the homesteaders together with a school. All would be free to send their children."

"The school is a good idea. But I don't know about letting those homesteaders send their children, especially the new ones. We can't encourage these people to keep coming. First, they take our water. Next, it'll be our cattle. You know I've been missing some."

"Last time we talked I told you it was more than likely rustlers. They're around these parts and the homesteaders are getting blamed for the stealing."

"What are you going to do about that?"

"One thing at a time, Major. We got to get this school built first. Nat here thinks it'll be ready to raise by next week. You're invited. My Josey is one hospitable little lady, and you'd be more than welcome. You can meet the neighbors and have a great feed."

"I'll see." The big man rose. "In the meantime, I want you to think about how we're going to deal with the problem of missing cattle. I still think the homesteaders have a hand in it."

Mr. Walker held out his hand. "I'll see what I can do."

Major Wolcott shook it hard and turned to go. He glanced at Nat. "You're a witness to what we just said. If he forgets, remind your boss he and I got a deal." He marched out and closed the door firmly.

Nat looked at his boss to see his reaction.

Mr. Walker ran his hand through his hair. "I hate to see Major Wolcott up in arms. He can be a firebrand. But we have other neighbors to consider as well." He looked Nat straight in the eye. "Keep your ears to the ground. I still think our missing cows can be placed right at the doorstep of rustlers. Like one of those gangs from Hole-in-the-Wall. They've got a reputation and I've gotten over the thinking we're too far north of them." He paused. "I might send you out for a few nights, camp out secret-like, and see if you come up with something. Most of this rustling is done at night. What you saw during the day was unusual.

"But let's get this school up first. I want to keep my wife happy, and maybe she has the right idea about bringing these big cattlemen and homesteaders together. At least, it's worth a try."

"So, after this school business, I camp out. Is that all, sir?"

"Yes. Glad you stayed for this last bit. I want someone else's brain working on this problem."

Nat nodded his support, then walked out onto the porch. Colburn was just coming up the steps. His favorite person. He noted a steely look in the foreman's eye. Now, what was needling him?

Ten minutes later in the bunkhouse, Nat received the message Mr. Walker wanted him back in his office. Nat put down the lariat he was mending. A bad feeling welled up in him. If it had something to do with the foreman, he was in hot water. Dang it!

He was about to exit the bunkhouse when some distance away he saw Miss Arnell getting ready for her daily ride. She stood by her horse, waiting for Shorty to help her up. Shorty for escort? Nat couldn't help smirking. A more lame-brained cowboy didn't exist in these parts. And she deserved him.

He watched Shorty stoop to take her foot to assist her up into the saddle. Unintentionally, he let her foot slip and she fell against the horse. Nat almost had it in him to feel sorry for her. But not quite. Actually, he was sort of amused to think what was in store for her with Shorty.

He settled back to watch the show. Shorty tried again. This time Miss Arnell clung to the pommel and pretty much got herself up into the saddle. It was an awkward business. Shorty grabbed the dragging skirt of her riding outfit, lifting it for her as she swung her right leg over the side-saddle pommel. "Please! Don't!" Her voice had an edge. "I can handle it from here."

Shorty had the grace to look embarrassed. He took one last glance at the teacher, maybe to see if she was okay, then made for his horse. Nat smiled grimly. She'd think twice about saying she didn't want the likes of Nat Logan escorting her. Why, he was an expertly trained escort compared to Shorty. Yes, the teacher's ride would sure be different with Shorty—either upsetting or extremely dull.

She might even beg to have Nat back. He straightened. Then, again, maybe he wouldn't have *her* back. This thing could work two ways.

The two riders approached, and he slid out of sight. As they passed, he heard Miss Arnell say a kind word to Shorty. And just as suddenly, a streak of kindheartedness ran through Nat. What had Mrs. Walker said to him again and again? "Nat, you've got to forgive people." He knew *that* was right. It'd always been a problem with him.

After the two horses passed, Nat stepped out of the bunkhouse to look at the riders. The way Miss Arnell sat a horse, the way she rode, was a pleasure to watch.

He strode off toward the ranch office.

When Nat entered, his suspicions were confirmed. Colburn sat across from the boss, and neither man smiled at him. *Here it comes.*

"Nat," Mr. Walker began. "We've got a problem. Why don't you explain, Colburn." He added as an afterthought. "Nat, take a seat."

"If you don't mind, sir, I'll stand." Somehow he felt better able to deal with this situation, standing.

Colburn turned in his seat to look at him. "I came to Mr. Walker with the fact that I caught you with Mrs. Walker's ring, and even after I said somethin', you didn't return it. That's stealin'."

"What do you say, Nat?" Mr. Walker's voice was hard, not affable like he'd been a short time ago.

"Yes, I found the ring. While I was cleanin' barn stalls."

"Cleaning stalls?" Mr. Walker said sternly. "You've got better things to do." He looked at Colburn. "Whose job is that?"

"Shorty's."

"Then why in tarnation wasn't Shorty cleaning those stalls? Wasn't he doing his job properly? We don't waste Nat's time cleaning the barn. He's needed for building the school. Then I want him breaking those new horses we brought in from the wild."

"I hear what you're sayin', boss." Colburn paused. "But about this ring business—"

"Yes." Mr. Walker brought himself back to the business at hand. "So, what do you have to say for yourself, Nat?"

"I mean to give it to Mrs. Walker, but I'm waitin' for a special occasion to surprise her."

"Likely story!" Colburn's voice had an edge. "Now that you're caught."

"It's true. Mr. Walker, I sent the ring with your daughter, when she went into Buffalo today. She's goin' to get it cleaned and polished. But it's a secret. Mrs. Walker's not to know!"

Silence followed. Nat watched for Mr. Walker's reaction.

The boss sat quietly, apparently weighing Nat's story against what Colburn had said.

Nat didn't like the quiet. He'd been a fool to wait so long. He should've given the ring to Mrs. Walker and been done with it. She could have got it polished herself. Still, he hadn't wanted to give it to her so messed up.

Mr. Walker's gaze went to the foreman. "You may go,

93

Colburn."

"But Mr. Walker—" The foreman started forward in his chair.

"I don't want to hear any more about it." His tone tolerated no argument. "Nat, you can stay for a minute."

Colburn gave a hard glance at Nat and left. The door just missed being slammed.

Mr. Walker's chin had dropped, he looked up at Nat from under shaggy brows. "I'm sorry all this happened. You're a good person, an excellent cowhand. Thanks for your honesty." His head lifted. "Mrs. Walker will be excited. I'll let you handle the surprise." His face brightened. "Maybe, just maybe, Shorty might have a replacement cleaning that barn."

They both laughed.

"But, really, Nat. I wish you and Colburn got along better. He's a good foreman, has been with me from the beginning. He's just set in his ways."

He rose. "Okay, you can go, the ladies should be back from Buffalo. Hopefully, my daughter will have that ring all ready to go."

───────◦◉◦───────

Margaret fastened a clean collar on her dress. This afternoon's ride was something she hoped not to repeat. It had been silent, Shorty hardly saying a word. And, to save her life, she wouldn't have gotten off her horse for a walk—as she'd done with Nat. Getting on or off a horse with Shorty's help was something to avoid. She could still feel her body slam against the horse as she fell on his first assist.

She smoothed her hair. Well, she was ready for supper. Seldom had she felt so hungry. Opening the bedroom door and stepping into the hall, she spied a man and woman in close contact. Nat and Allison. Nat's back was to her so she couldn't see clearly, but she thought she saw their hands meet. Had something passed between them? She quickly stepped back into her bedroom, embarrassed. She didn't know what to think.

After a moment, she peeked out the door. Both were gone. Relieved, she walked to the dining room. Thankfully, she wouldn't have to look at either of them; they sat at the opposite end of the table, on Mr. Walker's right and left. Her place was next to Mrs. Walker with the foreman sitting across.

For the most part, the meal was quiet, the men as hungry as herself. As they were finishing up, however, good-natured joshing bandied back and forth from one cowboy to another. Talk escalated until a noisy buzz filled the room.

Then someone stood at Mr. Walker's end of the table and hit a fork against a glass again and again. The sharp tinkling sound caught the attention of the men, and conversations dropped off. Margaret looked down the long table. Nat stopped tapping the glass with his fork.

"Ladies and gentlemen!" He looked over the length of the table. "We have a happy occasion to celebrate." He held up something wrapped in a piece of cloth and inclined his head to the boss. "With Mr. Walker's permission."

Putting his chair back out of the way, he sauntered down the length of the table, and stopped beside Mrs. Walker. "Ma'am, I have somethin' for you. A surprise. Somethin' I hope you'll really like."

She gazed up at him, smiling.

Margaret also looked up, rapt. He had the complete attention of everyone at the table. He swept up his hand in a large arc and, with a flourish, deposited the little bundle on the table in front of Mrs. Walker.

"What is this, Nat?" Her voice was hushed.

Everyone at table craned to see.

Mrs. Walker took up the small cloth and unwrapped it. "Oh, Nat!"

Her eyes filled with tears. She put her hand over her face.

Margaret stared at Mrs. Walker, then at the ring. She felt herself get still all over. Then she glanced up at Nat. He was watching her.

She lowered her gaze. If he only knew what she'd been thinking of him. Heat crept up her face.

Margaret looked across the table at the foreman. He was staring at something over her shoulder, as if ignoring the whole situation. She wondered if he was feeling ashamed—as she was.

Mrs. Walker held up the ruby ring. "The lost has been found!" The cowboys clapped and cheered.

She put the ring on her finger and rose. "Thank you, thank you, Nat," and she stepped over to wrap her arms around him in a big, motherly hug. When she let him go, she looked down the table at her husband, and held up her hand triumphantly. A huge smile lit up his face.

Margaret was the first of the company to rise and hug Mrs. Walker. How happy she was for her. But she avoided Nat's gaze. Others came over to see the ring and offer their congratulations. A busy, noisy gladness filled the room. Margaret kept a smile on her face, but as soon as it was socially acceptable, she left the room.

11

Margaret opened her eyes to a dark bedroom and wondered what time it was. Dawn had not yet come. No noise broke the night stillness.

She turned over to go back to sleep. But even in her half-awakened state, her mind stole back to the previous evening. Once again, she sat at the supper table. Nat surprised everyone by presenting the ruby ring to Mrs. Walker. For Margaret, surprise was too tame a word. It had shocked her. And such was her shame, she couldn't keep her eyes on Nat's when he looked directly at her.

She stared at the wall, knowing her request that Nat no longer accompany her needed to be addressed. But how? The trouble was she hadn't told either Mrs. Walker or Nat the reason. She wasn't sure which of them to talk with. Or how to clear up the problem. She had left it all so nebulous—never mentioned the ring and her suspicions of Nat's theft.

Finally, she sat up in bed and adjusted the pillow behind her. She could tell she wasn't going back to sleep anytime soon.

Part of the reason she felt muddled was that she was confused about Nat. Originally, she had pegged him as just another cowboy, but a resourceful one. Then in that Buffalo restaurant he had actually carried on an intelligent conversation.

A few days later, on their first ride out from the ranch, the subject of poetry had come up. Of all things. She'd been surprised at his poetic sensibility. In fact, he'd challenged her thinking. More than that, there'd been a sweetness mixed in with the challenge.

They had something, it seemed, in common. She then offered to lend him Sir Walter Scott's novel. And truthfully, he'd treated her more like a gentleman than the banker.

But then overhearing the foreman's accusation and jumping so readily to a damaging conclusion, she'd cut off further dealings with Nat. And further friendship. She had stirred up a hornet's nest—a swarm of her own making. The sad thing was—the problem had never existed.

Would it be possible to get back that ease she'd had with him? It was more than just asking him to be reinstated as her riding escort. There was that "finer something" that also needed to be restored. If he was as sensitive as she believed him to be, he would have been hurt, offended. She had slapped him, figuratively speaking, and slapped him rather hard.

At the table last night, she'd felt so ashamed. When he looked at her after presenting the ring, honestly, she couldn't look him in the eye.

What should she now do?

She sat quietly, slumped against the pillow. Painfully, her mind wandered over the various possibilities. Finally, her eyes searched the darkness overhead. *Lord*, she prayed, *what should I do?*

The answer came clearly, like an arrow into her soul.

First thing in the morning, before your teaching day starts, go to Mrs. Walker and ask for Nat's reinstatement. Then apologize for any distress you've caused.

Two new girls, a little older than her first pupils, had been added to Margaret's class, and she'd asked them to write a short essay describing their house, ranch buildings and animals. She wanted to ascertain their writing ability as well as to learn about their homes. The three younger students were to trace their ABCs.

The quiet seat work enabled her to hear voices next door in the office. No words could be distinguished, but one voice belonged to Mr. Walker, the other, to Nat.

Margaret thought back to her conversation earlier in the day with Mrs. Walker. How relieved she was when Mrs. Walker merely said she was glad Margaret had changed her mind about Nat. He wouldn't be able to resume his escort until after the schoolhouse raising, because he was, in fact, supervising it. And even then he would still share the duty with the other cowboys.

That was fine with Margaret, just so this barrier she'd erected between Nat and herself was removed. Of course, he and she would never be close. He and Sally obviously had some kind of long-standing friendship. Margaret wondered what it had been. She doubted if Sally would act so familiarly with Nat if there hadn't been a history of…intimacy.

Was the West this free in its morals? Never, never would she have seen that kind of deportment in her Chicago society. Of course, she didn't deny there were rough places in the city, a seamier life. Even though they'd had that terrible fire just twelve years ago, with so much of the city destroyed and people reassessing what was really important in life, part of society had now returned to "normal."

Just then, Jason approached her and held up his work. She checked it over. "Jason," she said quietly. "Will you please write your numbers—far as you can." He needed to stay busy as long as the others were working.

He returned to his place and sat down, then looked up at her shyly. Margaret smiled her encouragement, and he settled right down to work. What a nice boy. If only her thoughts would settle down as nicely.

She found herself straining to hear the voices next door. Nat's voice, his sentences had their own rhythm, a certain gait— like a horse. And with its ups and downs, his voice's inflection had a lilt all its own. She smiled inwardly. His use of the English language was far from perfect, yet somehow it suited him. The pitch of his voice had a lower octave with a certain edge. It "cut the mustard" as the expression went. A voice that could command.

Then suddenly, conversation in the office stopped.

She heard footsteps. Had the outside door to the office opened? Margaret strained to hear.

Boots strode the length of the porch. Nat's. Even his step had a lilt. He walked quickly, with energy. Something quickened inside her hearing that gait.

She knew he'd been out at the school site earlier in the day. Would he remain at the ranch longer this afternoon?

<hr />

Nat closed the office door and stepped onto the porch. He and Mr. Walker both agreed that squared off logs lasted longer than ones rounded with the bark still on. Water would get into those cracks between logs and eventually rot them. They wanted this schoolhouse to last.

He decided to make his way to the kitchen, starting around the porch, instead of from inside the house. Didn't want to disturb Miss Arnell teaching in the sitting room. He figured he was in enough disgrace. For what, he didn't know. First, she'd requested he no longer accompany her on rides. Then last night, when he'd given Mrs. Walker her ring and looked right at her— she looked down and afterward paid him no heed. She was the first to leave the dining room.

Anyway, now he'd get something from the kitchen to eat. Maybe Cook would give him some treats for the boys working back at the school site. Opening the door, he smelled something good. Something sweet.

"Hello, Nat!" Sally looked up from the colorful cloths she'd spread out on the kitchen table.

She looked real perky, like she was glad to see him. More than he could say for Miss Arnell. Seeing Sally's welcome made him feel good. A man liked to be greeted nice-like by a woman.

"Whatcha doin' Sally?" He crossed the room.

She held up a long, triangular piece. "I'm makin' pennants—for the school shindig next week. Pretty nice, huh?"

"Yup." He leaned over the table. Mrs. Walker must have raided the dry goods section of the store in Buffalo. Especially the bright colors. "This will be downright cheerful lookin'. Where ya goin' to hang 'em?"

"For starters, we thought the front edge of the food table. Then when you're done with the school, we'll tack up a couple strings of 'em inside the school. Just before the dance. That'll make it right festive, don't you think?"

"Good idea.

"And while you men are workin' at the school site, the women are plannin' on comin' here. Put up the food, temporary like, in the kitchen. Then when you men are 'bout done, we'll head on over to the school and set up the food. Outside if the weather's nice, or inside the school if the weather's bad." She lifted her hands and snapped her fingers. "Either way, we're goin' to have ourselves a celebration."

She stood and started humming a catchy tune, sashaying her hips and shoulders as she made her way round the table to Nat. "Come on, Nat. Let's warm up for that dance." She put herself right in front of him, close.

Nothing much he could do but oblige, so he put his hand around her waist and took her outstretched hand in his. He was ready to step out when she beat him to it and led him around the room. At first, he balked a little, but then got into the spirit of things. Sure felt good to be light-hearted again.

"I wouldn't miss that dance for nothin'," she said after finishing the tune. "I'll be sure to save you a dance or two, seein' you're the best dancer in these parts. Besides," she swung her hips again, "we're such *friends*, aren't we?"

The way she said *friends* got Nat's imagination going, remembering her kisses before she ran off with that ne'er-do-well and had a baby. He bet she was suggesting some time together at the shindig. Away from everyone. An uneasy feeling welled up in him. "Friends, yes. But now you're a married lady." He smiled, wanting to soften what he'd just said. "But we had fun while it lasted."

"We sure did. But, you know, I'm afraid that husband of mine is long-gone. I don't think I can wait much longer to have a real father for my son." She looked up at him, her eyes shining all appealing-like. "In the meantime, 'til I find somebody, I'm wonderin' if you could show Davy a little fatherly attention?"

"Well...." What was she suggesting now?

"Oh, nothin' much. Just hold him and let him hear your manly voice. It won't matter—he doesn't know if you're his father or not. But I do want him to grow up to be a real man— like you."

"I don't know much about babies."

"I'll show you what to do. Like I said, nothin' much. Just let my little man know there's a man around."

That moment they heard a cry from an adjoining room.

"That's my son. Stay here, while I get him."

"Hey! Where's Cook? Can't she help? I just came in here to get somethin' to eat and maybe take some food back to the boys."

"Cook's out in the garden." She held up her hand to stop him from leaving. "Wait just a minute." Then she darted into the adjoining room.

A minute later Sally entered the kitchen holding a sleepy-head. "Ah…look at him, Nat. Isn't he a darlin'? He's just up from his nap." She held her son out toward him. "Here, you hold him while I get a dry diaper and some playthings." Nat struggled to get a better hold of the child while Sally popped out of the kitchen once again. As whimpering started, he thought to pat the boy lightly on the back.

"Now, remain quiet while I go to the kitchen. I'm going to borrow some measuring cups from Cook for our arithmetic lesson." Margaret gave her students a last look before she hurried down the hall. This lesson needed to be practical as her youngest girl wasn't catching on. Opening the kitchen door, she saw the room was empty—except for a man and baby.

Nat, his back to her, was holding and soothing Sally's little boy.

"Okay-y-y. You be quiet now." He rocked the child in his arms. "Good little man."

Margaret watched him a long moment. When the child started to wiggle in Nat's arms, he said, "There-e-re, little bronco. Don't you get restless." He made gentle cooing noises.

Now, where did he learn that? It was as if he was born to the task and caring for his own child.

Margaret's breath suddenly stopped and held. The thought was a strange one. Even if Nat wasn't the actual father, he *could* be a father to this child, the way he was acting. It surprised her. She hadn't visualized him settling down. He acted so footloose and fancy free. She had the impression, despite Sally's occasional "ownership" of the cowboy, that he was too much the bachelor.

Standing still, looking at the affectionate scene, Margaret suddenly couldn't look any longer. Clearing her throat with a "huh-hum," she opened the door farther and walked in.

Nat turned.

"I've come to borrow something from Cook," she said. He hadn't smiled. It was apparent Mrs. Walker hadn't talked with him yet. "Do you know where she is?"

"Sally said she's out back in the garden."

At that moment, Sally entered the room, smiling at Nat. Belatedly, she noticed Margaret. "Oh, Miss Arnell, can we help you?"

Margaret heard the word "we," as well as the possessive note in Sally's voice.

"I need to see Cook about something."

"She's out back."

"Then I'll go outside and find her." Quickly she stepped to the back door. She felt very much *de trop*.

She was also confused. The way Sally had just acted, Margaret could almost hear the wheels turning in Sally's mind. *A father for my baby, a father for my baby.* Nat did look quite the father, cuddling the little boy.

Had Sally forgotten she was married? Margaret wondered… if the husband didn't show up, was Sally already thinking of someone to fill that role? Nat, maybe?

Margaret could see the way the wind was blowing.

12

"L ord Frewen, how good of you to come to our school raising." Josephine extended her hand.

He bent over and brushed it with his lips, then looked up and smiled. "The building looks about completed. I'm sorry I wasn't here earlier."

This man's charm was palpable. Josephine returned the smile. "Ah! No one would expect you to help put up the walls. They're now putting in the plank flooring. We're just pleased you're here, and honored."

"Well, this is a pleasure. I like people, and it gets a little lonely at my ranch with Lady Frewen gone."

"How is your wife? Will we see her in Wyoming Territory again?"

"She's doing fine. Of course, she's back in New York with her father—in the lap of luxury. I'm afraid life out here was rather more isolated than she expected. She was game at first. And I tried to give her every convenience she'd had in the East. But that last hunt was too much for her. So—I doubt if she'll return here."

How well Josephine remembered. One couldn't expect everyone to weather a miscarriage the way pioneer women did. Clara Frewen was accustomed to the very best doctor within easy call. Here, it could take a day or more for Doctor Watkins to be contacted, then longer before he arrived to help, depending where he was in the Territory.

"I can see you're going to have plenty of food. I came at just the right time," Lord Frewen teased.

"Well, of course. And aren't you accustomed to being waited on hand and foot?"

He laughed graciously. "It's true, the other ranchers around here, particularly the women, wonder at the number of servants I brought with me. For my wife's sake, you understand. I couldn't expect her to rough it like I've done on occasion."

"Yes, I heard about that forty-mile trek you made on foot to Rock Creek after your horse went lame."

"Well, necessity is the mother of invention, as they say. I couldn't let snow drifts and mountains get the better of me. And, I might add, a few blisters."

"Of course not," Josephine quipped. "Just kill yourself in the process. Then you wouldn't have to worry about rustlers, grasshoppers, or prairie fires taking over your ranch."

"True!" He chuckled. "However, you must know, we Englishmen are hardier than you might think. And I've never been accused of lack of invention. Some even call me foolhardy."

Now Josephine laughed. "I admit, you have quite a reputation. In fact, few here would vie with or challenge you on that. Speaking of your ranch, how goes business?"

"Josey, will you round up everyone? It's about time for those few minutes of calm you wanted." Her husband looked around as if in a daze. "Where's my Bible?"

Josephine could see the cowboys weren't the only ones who needed some respite before the dance began. It would do them all good to have a bit of quiet.

As everyone settled on the grass, George stood at the head of the gathering. Pride rose in her. She had married a *man*. How proud she was to be his wife. They made a good team. He always said he couldn't have made it without her. Not only in the practical doings of ranch life, but in the personal support which he'd wanted and needed. She thought of those times they would talk in the sitting room, in the walks they'd take around the ranch, and when they comforted and nourished each other at night. Sometimes they both went right to sleep. But other times...she smiled.

George looked at her as the crowd was quieting. He saw the smile and returned it. He hadn't known what she was thinking, of course, but she could assume his thoughts were pleasant as well.

Jason came up to her. "Can I sit by you?"

She put her arm around him and looked down at his soft, dark hair. Nothing warmed her heart like this grandchild.

"Ladies and gentlemen!" her husband called out and within moments, silence followed. "We want to welcome you today. And to thank you for your hard work, both the men who helped put up the school and the ladies who prepared all this good food. In addition, I'd like to introduce some of our honored guests." He began with Lord Frewen, Major Wolcott and then Mr. Norland.

Josephine had noticed like Lord Frewen, Mr. Norland arrived just in time to congratulate the men on their hard work. He went around quietly, not making too much of his late arrival, but still trying to ingratiate himself with all the men. Then, the same with the ladies, thanking them for the food. He'd pretty much claimed Margaret, always circling back to her.

"And now," her husband continued, "in dedicating this school, we want to take a few moments to read words from the book of Proverbs. This first is from Chapter 4 Verse 7. 'Wisdom is the principal thing; therefore get wisdom: and with all thy getting get understanding.'

"You know, the key word in Proverbs is wisdom. Do you

know what that means?" He paused and looked over the crowd. "I don't expect you to answer out loud, but I want you to think about it." He paused a bit longer. "It means the ability to live life skillfully. Now, we ranchers all want that. And, it's something we want to pass on to our children."

He turned a couple pages of his Bible.

"I've got another verse in Chapter 8 Verse 11. 'For wisdom is better than rubies; and all the things that may be desired are not to be compared to it.'" He looked at Josephine. "My wife understands that. She lost the ruby ring I gave her, and Nat over there," he nodded to the back of the crowd, "found it. Was she elated!

"But I know my wife well enough that if that ring had never been found, what she really values is wisdom and understanding. The kind that's mentioned here in Chapter 1, Verse 7." He turned back a few pages. "'The fear of the Lord is the beginning of knowledge....' That's the kind of knowledge my wife really values. And it's the kind of knowledge she wants passed on to our children and grandchildren. It's why she started this school, why she sent off to Chicago for our fine teacher who I'll introduce in a minute."

He looked over at Josey and nodded his appreciation. "Thank you, dear. I'm proud of you.

"But now I want to read the rest of that Verse 7. It says, 'but fools despise wisdom and instruction.' Ladies and gentlemen, we want no fools in Wyoming Territory." His voice was stern. "I'm saying that for both the ranchers, such as myself and Major Wolcott here, and also the homesteaders at our gathering. We want to get along, and we hope to pass this on throughout the Territory. We'll need to do it with intention. But we can start here—with our own example."

He paused a long moment. "Now, I want to introduce someone who will help us impart good learning and wisdom to our children and grandchildren." He held out his hand toward the teacher. "Miss Margaret Arnell! Will you stand, please? And do you have a few things to say to these good people here?"

The banker, sitting beside Margaret, helped her rise. She smiled her thanks and raised her voice to address the gathering. She began explaining that the McGuffey Readers she'd brought from Chicago would help the students obtain a first-rate education.

"First and foremost, these Readers uphold the tenets that Mr. Walker has just put forth, the importance of wisdom and understanding, and how knowledge begins with the fear, or reverence, of the Lord. It is something I believe wholeheartedly.

"We already have five students in the school and are looking forward to adding more." She looked around the group, smiling. "If you have any questions, please feel free to ask me any time during the evening."

The crowd clapped, and she curtseyed, at which everyone chuckled. When she sat down, the banker helped her once again. He said something quietly in her ear.

Josephine looked around. Where was Nat in all this? Of course, he had been right in the middle of the school raising, directing the operation, pitching in and working as much as any man. No wonder he hadn't had time for the social "niceties" that Lord Frewen and the banker had attended to.

She located him standing behind the food table with a couple of the other cowboys. They'd all donned the clean shirts she'd insisted on. She'd seen to it, too, that several buckets of water were placed behind the school so the men were able to wash up before putting on their shirts to be ready for the dance.

The fiddler she'd engaged sat by the table. She made sure he had a seat. He'd be working his tail off the rest of the evening.

Gracious! Where had her thoughts been straying? Her husband was about to pray, and she was off in Timbuktu. She bowed her head, determined to join him in spirit.

Margaret looked around the schoolhouse at everyone having a good time, talking and laughing, and lining up at the refreshment table. The fiddler had announced a pause in the dancing. The room was hot, so she was glad she'd worn her lightest cotton dress; its lime green flowers cooled the eye. And the room was fresh with the smell of new wood, the floor with its pristine boards swept clean after being laid. Tonight those boards were feeling the weight of many feet.

She'd had no time to sit out a dance before another cowboy came up and asked for her hand. She never realized she would be so popular. Of course, with the greater number of men compared to women, she shouldn't have been surprised. Women, especially unmarried ones, were scarce, so naturally she'd be in demand.

Lord Frewen and Mr. Norland had claimed a dance each. Mr. Norland said he would like more, but realized the ratio of men to women. Margaret saw that as much as he would like to dance again with her, he wouldn't take the chance of angering the cowboys. They might not have much money at present, but one could never tell about the future. The banker made plain his interest in her, but she could tell he had his eye on business as well.

Mr. Walker hadn't asked her yet. His wife had said he was a good dancer, but he would make sure his cowboys had "first dibs."

She'd just danced with Shorty. Gracious! Somehow, they'd gotten through the first half of the song. Thankfully, another cowboy had cut in.

One of the few she hadn't danced with was Nat. Well, it served her right the way she'd treated him. Mrs. Walker let her know she had talked with him, so at least his escort would resume. But after Nat passed up another dance with her in favor of an older matron, Margaret knew something was wrong.

Pride had kept her from saying anything to him. Now, if

there was any opportunity, she would broach the subject. He glanced her way, and she promptly smiled, thinking he might need encouragement to approach her.

She walked over to the refreshment table, took a proffered drink and seemed to consider the different items to eat. Someone tapped her on the shoulder, and she turned, expecting to see Nat.

Shorty beamed. "Miss Arnell, be honored if ya'd dance with me again."

Margaret's stomach dropped. *Where was Nat?* She looked down on Shorty from her greater height. "Thank you, but..." Just then, Nat stepped to her side. "...I promised Mr. Logan the next one. And you and I have already danced." She said it teasingly to soften her refusal. She looked up at Nat, hoping he'd now ask her.

His eyes crinkled at the corners. He'd probably seen her earlier suffering through that dance with Shorty. "May I?" He held out his hand.

"Yes," she said, and put down her drink. The fiddler was about to start another tune. Nat led her out, placing his hand on her waist, the other grasping her hand in a firm grip. Then at the music's start, he swung her out. After their first energetic circle around the floor, he shortened his steps, slowing their pace. This was her opportunity.

"Thank you for this dance."

He nodded.

"This gives me the chance to apologize. When I asked that you no longer accompany me on my rides, it was a mistake on my part. Will you forgive me?"

"Of course." One side of his mouth quirked up. "Glad I finally meet with our little schoolmarm's approval. It's enough to boost an ignorant cowboy's confidence."

She laughed up at him, and his hold tightened, and he swung her out again.

They circled the floor, and Margaret could sense something had changed. At the beginning of their dance, Nat's natural energy had propelled them. Now, a lighter exuberance drove him. His mood had lightened.

Was she reading this aright? Oh, what did she know about cowboys anyway? They all had their own style dancing with her. She wondered where Nat had learned such skill. Mrs. Walker? Yes, she was sure that good lady had taken him under her wing. Well then, she would stop analyzing and just enjoy the time with a man who knew how to dance.

Nat guided her decisively, yet gently.

She wished the fiddler would play longer. Or that Nat would ask her for the next one. She smiled up at him, knew her eyes were shining. She couldn't help it. She was so glad she'd apologized. It had broken the uneasiness, that little barrier she felt when they first started to dance. Now they were in harmony with each other. This was something that satisfied her soul. She wondered if he noticed as well.

This augured well for their friendship. She didn't know how long she'd stay in Wyoming, but this would be good to have—friendship with a man who was more than the average cowboy.

As the music ended, he swung her in close. Her breath caught.

He laughed down at her then eased her away. "Didn't mean to get carried away there, Miss Arnell. Just gave into the urge, I guess. You sure can dance."

"I will say the same of you." Her heart was beating fast. Of course, they'd been going like the wind. The pace she'd noticed in his walk extended to his dancing. "I really enjoyed that. Thank you."

"Now, if you'll excuse me," he said and lowered his head in a quick little nod, respectfully, like a gentleman in Chicago would have done. She looked after him as he wove his way across the room. There was a long pause in the music. The fiddler had stopped to take a drink and stretch his arms.

She glanced once more in Nat's direction. He was approaching Sally at the refreshment table. She was all smiles and animation. He held out his hand and she grasped it, and he led her out to where other couples were waiting for the next dance to begin.

Several of the cowboys from their ranch noticed and motioned to let the two have the floor. The rest of the dancers hastened to the sides of the room.

The fiddler called out, "What song do you want?"

"Skip to my Lou!" Nat shouted back and positioned Sally in the center of the floor. The fiddler lifted his instrument, and with a robust thrust of his bow the song took off and so did Nat and Sally.

Margaret wondered if the West had heard of exhibition dancing, but that's exactly what this was. Nat dipped and swung Sally around to the lively fiddling. The crowd started clapping in time. The two dancers whooped it up, thumping the floor with their feet, emphasizing the beat of the music. Margaret knew Nat had enough energy, but Sally?

She looked to be in her element, enjoying every moment of this dance with a man who could really partner her. Partner? At the word, Margaret's mind checked.

But Sally was married. She'd also heard rumors about Sally and Colburn the foreman—something about their past. Margaret looked around the room to locate him. He was to her left, his face grim. Was it true then, that he'd carried a flame for Sally before she'd left the ranch a year ago? He obviously wasn't pleased to see Sally dancing with Nat. Her pleasure showed all too clearly in her face.

Not only was she beaming, but once in a while she'd shout out a whoop. That would have never happened in Chicago. But with this crowd clapping, and a few of the men joining in and stomping, it fit right in. The whole place was happy and excited. No wonder the floor had cleared when Nat and Sally had stepped up. They had obviously been partners before.

Margaret's dance with Nat had been nothing like this.

But, Margaret told herself, theirs had been sweeter. And, of course, she wanted more decorum in dancing. It's what she was accustomed to.

As the song was finishing, Nat grabbed Sally at the waist and swung her up in the air with the crowd shouting and clapping. Sally dropped down into his arms, remaining there a long moment. The fiddler's bow came off the strings with a flourish. Nat swung Sally out to stand beside him. She curtsied, and he saluted with a bow.

Margaret was glad their dance was finished. While it had been a real exhibition of skill and high spirits, she had been all but holding her breath the entire performance. But why? Ordinarily, she would have enjoyed it immensely. Now, she just couldn't say.

But it had been good. Very good, she admitted.

The crowd came together after that, some gathering around Nat and Sally, congratulating them.

The fiddler began another song. Margaret saw Nat lead Sally to the refreshment table for something to drink. When another cowboy offered to lead her out to dance, Sally gestured "later." She and Nat took up their drinks and headed toward the door, exiting the building.

Mrs. Walker gazed after them.

13

Josephine's heart sank. She hoped Nat and Sally wouldn't be gone long...for the longer they were gone...it just wasn't wise.

She'd had second thoughts about letting Sally stay on at the ranch. In fact, she'd almost said no. But when she saw that baby, she couldn't imagine a mother taking care of that child anywhere but in a home with a degree of stability. And where was home for Sally—with her husband absent? Home was apparently here, with Cook, her aunt.

At least, that's the way she'd worked it out in her mind. But Josephine had warned Sally that if there was anything untoward—like what might be going on with Nat—she could no longer remain at the ranch.

What should she do, follow them outside? That seemed a bit much. They were both adults.

Colburn stood near the door. He looked nervous, on edge. It was plain to see he was nettled about Sally leaving with Nat.

So, she wasn't the only one worried. He'd had it in for Nat for some time. It would only need Nat and Sally doing something foolish to set off Colburn. And Josephine wanted no trouble, no violence at this school raising.

Colburn's arm twitched, his shoulder hitched up in a jerk. He made for the door.

Oh no! Josephine looked around for her husband's help. He was busy in conversation with Lord Frewen. Neither man would appreciate her interruption. On second thought, maybe this situation needed a woman's touch.

She walked past a couple of people, reached for the door and closed it behind her.

Which way should she go? Off to the right she saw Colburn approach the wagons and buggies. To her left, the horses had been staked. And Nat loved horses. She set off in that direction. Hopefully, she would find Nat and Sally before Colburn did.

Out a ways stood a tree which the tethered horses obscured. She wondered if the two she sought were there. A couple of the mares moved, and she saw Nat and Sally. He was leaning against the tree with Sally close. At that moment Nat put his hand on Sally's shoulder. Patted it. Was he comforting her? Then Sally stepped nearer. So close. If Mr. Walker and she had been that familiar before marriage, it would have indicated they were engaged. She saw Sally put one arm around Nat's neck.

Josephine's heart dropped. If Colburn saw them now—

She wouldn't allow any trouble here. This event was supposed to bring the big ranchers and homesteaders together. She didn't want any conflict on these grounds.

She'd have to make her presence known before Colburn discovered them, but she'd try to avoid embarrassing the couple.

She walked up to one of her own horses and, catching its bridle, began to pat and talk to it. She raised her voice just enough to make sure Nat and Sally realized her presence.

Stepping around the horses, she once again observed Nat and Sally near the tree, but now standing a decorous distance from each other.

Josephine approached them with a smile.

"Oh, I'm so glad to see you, Sally. Your baby is getting fussy.

and Mrs. Roberts, I'm sure, would like you to tend to him."

Disappointment flashed across Sally's face, but she offered, "Thank you, Mrs. Walker. I'll go right in."

As Sally started toward the school, Josephine kindly added, "By the way, that was quite some dance the two of you put on for us. Made me wish I was young again."

Sally smiled, nodded her head in acknowledgement and went ahead to the school.

"I haven't danced with you yet, Mrs. Walker," Nat offered. "How about takin' a turn with me 'around the floor? Here," he held out his arm, "let me escort you back."

"I'd like that very much. Maybe we can get in on one of the last dances. Our fiddler is winding down." She took his arm.

At that moment, she noticed Colburn standing near the horses. He didn't look any too happy. How much had he seen? Well, if he wanted it out with Nat, he could do so at the ranch, and she'd turn a deaf ear and a blind eye. Sometimes it paid to have the sitting room and bedrooms of her home on the far end—away from the bunkhouse.

Margaret watched Mrs. Walker walk toward her. "My dear," Mrs. Walker said, taking hold of her arm, "Let's join Lord Frewen and Nat. It's seems they're having quite a conversation."

Margaret wouldn't have approached the men on her own, but with Mrs. Walker taking the initiative, it would be all right.

"What are you men laughing about?" Mrs. Walker asked. "Or isn't it fit for genteel ladies to hear?"

"Nat and I are reminiscing about that big hunt last year." Lord Frewen beckoned the ladies join them. "I know you remember that, Mrs. Walker."

"How could I forget? I'd never been on anything so well-organized and luxurious in these wild parts."

117

"That's the reason I engaged Buffalo Bill as guide and scout. I'd heard about his prowess from my father-in-law." Lord Frewen looked at Margaret. "Miss Arnell, maybe you don't know this, but my father-in-law is the famous New York financier, Leonard Jerome. Back in '71 he and his brother Lawrence had a memorable hunt. The Jerome brothers, along with other dignitaries gathered with Buffalo Bill near Fort McPherson—in Nebraska.

"That hunt was one of my father-in-law's favorite stories. He told me great preparations had been made for it, including the food, which was the finest. The general at the fort sent a troop of cavalry to meet their party at the train. When they rode back to the post, they saw the regiment drawn up on dress parade. The band struck up a martial air and General Sheridan himself reviewed the cavalry."

Lord Frewen told the tale with all the vivid detail of his colorful personality. Margaret could see he was a born raconteur.

"At the end of the hunt, Bill was voted a Mighty Hunter. They called him *Nimrod*, no less. I'm a pretty good shot, but Buffalo Bill is unbelievable.

"We didn't have quite that fanfare for our hunt, but we tried our best to make it memorable."

Lord Frewen flashed his engaging smile.

"That's why I wanted Buffalo Bill in charge. Nat, here, was second in command."

He turned to Nat. "When you rode beside Buffalo Bill, he told you a story about him and the army, back in '69. About his bringing fresh meat into the soldiers' camp." He clapped Nat on the shoulder. "Tell that one."

Mr. Norland walked up to their group and stepping near Margaret, took her elbow and held it a long moment. She looked at Nat just then, and saw that he noticed.

"Mr. Norland!" Lord Frewen greeted. "I was just about to have Nat tell what a tremendous shot Buffalo Bill was. Bill was

118

famous for riding his horse at full tilt and taking down a buffalo with a single bullet. Go ahead, Nat."

Nat grinned. "Wal, as you said, this took place in the spring of '69. Buffalo Bill was scoutin' for the Fifth Cavalry, and was told to relocate with them from Fort Lyon, Colorado to Fort McPherson, Nebraska.

"It was a large command. Would you believe, 76 wagons for food and supplies for the soldiers? Now, the average distance they covered was only ten miles a day, so by the time the troops reached the Solomon River they'd run out of fresh meat. Colonel Royal, the commandin' officer, asked Bill to look up some game. So Bill said, 'All right, sir. Will you send a couple of wagons along to fetch in the meat?'

"The colonel was real curt in his reply. 'We'll send for the game, Cody, when there's some game to send for.'" Nat smirked. "Apparently, he'd had little experience with Bill—

"That settled the matter, of course. But Bill rode away, a little ruffed up in temper.

"Only he wasn't long in roundin' up a herd of seven buffalo and headin' them straight for camp. As he drew near, he rode alongside his game, bringin' them down, one after another. Now, until only an old bull remained. And that one he killed, almost dead center of camp.

"The ruckus in camp was bad, and those chargin' buffaloes nearly stampeded the picketed horses. Colonel Royal had watched the hunt with the other officers, and after all was said and done, he was pretty angry. He demanded, 'What does this mean, Cody?'

"'Why,' said Bill. 'I thought, sir, I'd save you the trouble of sending after the game.'

"The colonel had to smile, though I'm thinkin' the other officers enjoyed the joke more than he did."

Margaret and the rest of the group laughed, enjoying the joke quite as much.

The banker leaned toward her and said softly. "When it's time to go, may I escort you back to the ranch, Miss Arnell?" His words, however, carried to everyone in the circle.

"Oh! I was just about to offer myself," Lord Frewen said light-heartedly. "Surely, a lord's request will trump a banker's."

"I didn't realize I was so popular," Margaret said. She was pleased, but for the life of her, she didn't know what to say next. She glanced at Mrs. Walker.

"Well, I will break the tie," Mrs. Walker said, laughing. "I need her myself, and since I'm the Grand Dame of this occasion, I take precedence over both of you."

She turned to Margaret. "You and Cook will bring the decorations and other items back to the ranch. Nat, I'm commandeering you to drive the wagon. In the meantime, I'll gather up things here, making sure the extra food goes home with these families. Afterward, Nat, you can return for the farm table and such. By that time, everyone will have departed. Before we leave with that second wagon, I want to make sure all the loose ends are tied up." She looked around brightly at their circle.

Relief flooded through Margaret. Mrs. Walker had adroitly taken care of a socially sticky situation. Leave it to the *Grand Dame*.

Nat helped Mr. Walker load the wagon.

"That does it," Mr. Walker said. "Let's get Miss Arnell onto the seat first." The big man took the teacher's hand in his and helped lift her up. "Nat, you go next, then I'll help Cook."

As soon as Cook settled herself, and Nat lifted the reins to slap the horses, Sally hurried up with her baby.

"Mr. Walker! Can I go along? Davy is gettin' so fussy and needs his bed-y-bye."

"His what?"

"His bed! He's overly tired."

"All right, but there's no more room on the wagon bench. Can you ride in back with the stores?"

"Oh, let me sit behind," Cook offered. "I can climb back easy as pie."

Nat wasn't overly pleased Sally was coming, but he could see everything was being arranged, so he might as well go along. He turned toward Cook and gripped her hand to assist her over the bench.

She chose to sit with her back to the seat. "This will work just fine. I'll hold onto the side of the wagon. Now, Sally, you get on up."

Sally handed her son to Mr. Walker. He held the baby with one arm while helping her up with the other. "Thank you," she said, and held out her arms for her son.

Nat waited until she settled Davy in the crook of one arm and grabbed the edge of the bench to steady herself. But then she said, "Wait!" and shifted her son to the other side and Nat felt her hand wrap around his arm.

"Thanks, Nat," she said quietly.

Nat looked ahead at the horses, but out of the corner of his eye saw Miss Arnell glance their way. She couldn't help but see Sally nestle against him. An uncomfortable feeling welled up inside.

Earlier, the thought surfaced that Mrs. Walker had orchestrated him taking Miss Arnell home, relieving her of having to choose between Lord Frewen and Mr. Norland's offers. And Nat was all too glad to comply. But Mrs. Walker also knew the teacher and he had been at outs with each other, and he welcomed the opportunity to make further amends. He thought they might talk on this ride home.

But now, here was Sally. He suddenly upbraided himself for thinking unchristian thoughts toward her. She couldn't help it, poor thing, with the baby and all. He'd just have to make the best of the situation.

Yet, he'd seen Miss Arnell stiffen. Dang it! Just when things had started to get friendlier between them.

Nat slapped the reins to get moving. But gently. A baby was onboard.

He hadn't driven a hundred yards when he heard a horse come up from behind. He glanced back. Colburn. What in tarnation was he here for?

Nat kept his eyes looking ahead. He'd just ignore the man. They rode another hundred yards, but Colburn stayed off a way, to the left of Sally.

Nat put two and two together. In his own way, Colburn was staking his claim. Irritation rose up in him. And a competitive streak. Just because Colburn wanted Sally didn't mean he'd get her. After all, Sally had chosen to come home with Nat. He'd had a feeling all along the baby was just an excuse. She could have chosen a spot somewhere on the school grounds to sit quietly with her son, lulling him to sleep. But she hadn't.

Nat felt her move a little closer. This was getting complicated. He wanted to keep Sally as a friend, didn't want Colburn butting in on that. Yet, he glanced at Miss Arnell. If she could sit any stiffer, he didn't know how. She was like an iceberg.

But he admired Miss Arnell. Had seen right off what a lady she was. And liked it that she recognized his leaning toward poetry. But he was afraid she was out of his league. He remembered the way the banker had sidled up to her again and again during the evening. Why, even Lord Frewen had offered to escort her back to the ranch.

Yes, she was one fine woman. Looked fine, too. Today, he'd noticed right off how good she looked in that light green dress. It showed her figure in all the right places. Probably one of those fancy dresses from Chicago.

He just had to face it, though; she was out of his reach. In fact, both these women were. Sally was married.

But there was something here he didn't understand. To-night, when Sally and he were standing by that tree, she'd wondered out loud about her husband. Felt badly, wondering when she'd ever see him again. Nat wanted to comfort her, so patted her shoulder. She'd stepped closer and put her arm around his neck—just like old times—but suddenly he could feel things getting out of hand. Sally was just making herself too...willing, and he was having trouble not letting her cuddle up to him the way she used to.

She was about to tell him something, something in the nature of a secret, he thought, when they'd heard Mrs. Walker by the horses. And he started feeling even more uncomfortable with Sally so close.

Actually, it was good Mrs. Walker had shown up when she did, because he'd known it wasn't right the way they were standing so chummy-like. Even now riding home, Sally was snuggling up to him. Why did she make up to him so? Yet, at the same time he felt competitive with Colburn over her attentions, her friendliness. He didn't want to lose that.

He glanced at Miss Arnell. He wanted to say something, anything, to warm things up between them, but she was looking like that was the last thing she wanted. She had apologized during their nice dance together, but an apology was a long way from genuine friendship. And, anyway, he didn't see much hope of a friendship there.

He thought of Mrs. Walker. Now, *they* were friends. But he had to be careful not to take up too much of her time. She had a lot to do on the ranch. And there was always Mr. Walker who had priority.

The mile back to the ranch, no one was saying anything. Not even Cook. Too much was going on underneath the surface.

Nat directed the wagon into the ranch yard. He glanced left. When the wagon slowed, Colburn said hello to Sally, then followed them around to the back of the house. Nat parked the wagon near the kitchen door.

Colburn dismounted. It didn't take much of a brain to guess what he meant to do.

Nat started to rise.

Just then Shorty galloped around the corner of the house. *What was he up to?*

Colburn lifted his arms to take Sally's baby and offered to help her down.

Sally glanced at Nat, a question in her eyes.

"Go ahead," he said, his eyes moving to Shorty who had sidled up his horse near Miss Arnell.

"I can help you, Miss Arnell," Shorty said, jumping off his horse.

Dang that Shorty. Some of Nat's confusion regarding these women suddenly disappeared.

"Put up your horse, Shorty, then come back and help unload."

He'd be jiggered if he'd let Shorty put a hand on Miss Arnell. He jumped off the wagon. Besides, this was his—he was about to say—job. No, this was his *pleasure.*

He looked up and caught the teacher's eye, and held out his arms.

"Now, Miss Arnell!"

14

Josephine took down a piece of decorative pottery to dust. She was giving the sitting room a thorough cleaning, now that Margaret was installed in the new school.

She would admit to no one but herself that she had intervened in Lord Frewen and Mr. Norland's offers to escort Margaret home, having her instead go with Nat.

The way Nat and Margaret had danced together—there'd been *something* there. As the dance went on, Josephine noticed a particular harmony between them. Nat swept Margaret along and she followed his lead gracefully, fitting herself to him. They were beautiful to watch. Was it more than just a good-fellow feeling? Attraction, maybe?

At any rate, she was glad the misunderstanding had been cleared up between them. Having them take the supplies back to the ranch, Josephine wanted to give them an opportunity to be together longer, to possibly talk.

She put the piece of pottery back on the shelf. Dusting didn't take much thought, and it gave her an opportunity to think, really think through things, separate the wheat from the chaff.

That Sally! Josephine had been so upset seeing Sally outside with Nat that she'd been on the verge of telling her to find another home. Yet, the baby held her back. Little Davy had won her heart.

However, the picture of Nat and Sally standing so close together at that tree still troubled her. Again the thought came: such closeness suggested more than just friendship.

Josephine confessed she was confused. By Sally, particularly. Sally was a married woman, and she didn't like to think Sally was lost to all propriety.

And Nat. Why had he allowed Sally to be so close? Moreover, he had shown chivalry, maybe interest, in the teacher. What were his intentions?

As much as possible, Josephine wanted relationships on the ranch to be good and above board.

Should she say something to Sally or Nat?

She reached for her only figurine, that of a mother and child. A sweet feeling welled up in her. She remembered holding her daughter like this.

Nat was like a son to her, and she wanted the best for him. Besides that, Nat was her "spiritual child." He had come to her on more than one occasion for advice.

But Josephine realized much of what constituted the Christian walk, Nat would need to discover for himself. She couldn't spoon-feed him all the answers.

Josephine put the figurine back in its place.

On the other hand, there was also a place for talk, for "figuring out" life with another believer.

What should she do?

Then she remembered her husband had said something about sending Nat to scout the western range. He'd be gone a few days, camping.

Now would be a good time for that, give Nat thinking time away from the ranch. Away from the distractions of these women, especially Sally. If her husband didn't send Nat out in the next day or two, she'd remind him.

This would also give her an opportunity to let this whole question rest for a bit. Surely, during that time the Lord would guide her.

———————◦◦◦◦———————

Nat struck a match to the small pile of kindling in the depression he'd chosen. If rustlers roamed this area, he didn't want his fire seen. He looked up at the looming Big Horns. No one except Mr. Walker knew his reason for being here.

When he'd talked with Lord Frewen at the school raising, Nat discovered he was missing cattle as well. Of course, Lord Frewen's ranch was to the south of the Walkers'. He suspected, and Nat agreed with him, that Indians off the reservation were helping themselves to his cattle, especially when the government didn't come through on the promised rations. The Sioux were never ones to stand on ceremony with the white man.

Nat remembered how they had outnumbered Custer at the Little Big Horn, just miles north of here. Thousands of warriors surprising a little over 200 U.S. soldiers. Nat had always wondered what Custer was thinking, what he must have felt seeing that horde of Indians charge up the hill. He'd probably no time to feel the fool, just set about being the general he claimed to be, fighting with everything in him.

Nat had followed the investigations with avid interest. Even now, seven years after the fight, the details were unclear, since none of Custer's men survived the battle.

Nat remembered the difference in weapons between the Indians and Custer's soldiers. True, the Indians had bows and arrows, but they also had repeating rifles, whereas the soldiers had only single shot rifles.

Those soldiers never had a chance.

He made sure his own firearms were good, particularly his rifle. His Winchester 73 was accurate and could shoot the distance. His horse was the best he could find. Outlaws never had inferior horses, needed fast ones with endurance. They never knew when they had to outrun a posse. Nat had learned quality firearms and horses were important during his days on the wrong side of the law.

Of course, that was all in his past. Yet, in a situation like he was in now, dealing with possible rustlers, Nat knew they'd have the best in both firearms and horses. And he should have nothing less if he'd have any chance of apprehending them without getting himself killed.

After making coffee over his fire, Nat sat against a large rock and looked at the area around him. A bunch of Walker cattle roamed in the distance. He studied the landscape in front, then to his right and left. That hunt he'd been on with Buffalo Bill, the scout had talked about the importance of being aware of the layout of the land—rocks, hills and trees where enemies might be hidden.

"You want to spot them before they see you. Any irregularity in the landscape, where a hump appears that wasn't ordinarily there, is suspect. Someone might be trying to hide who wants to surprise you." Buffalo Bill said that his ability to memorize the topography of the land while scouting for the army, had saved his hide more than once.

Well, Nat hadn't seen too many Indians in these parts, not to say they weren't here. But he had no intention of being surprised by them or any rustlers in the area. To that end, he kept himself and his fire hidden.

Despite the uncertainties that marked his time on this western range, he was glad to be here, alone. It gave him time to think. Life at the ranch had gotten a little tricky with Sally. And he didn't know what to think about Mar—Miss Arnell.

Day before yesterday he'd escorted the teacher on her ride, and it had gone well. She had warmed up a bit. They'd talked about the opening chapters of *Ivanhoe*. Nothing big, mainly going over what happened so far. He could tell she was trying to interest him in the story. Who was against who and all. "Conflict" she called it. He grimaced. Conflict was a whole lot easier reading about than living it.

He didn't mind what went on between cowboys—angry words, and a fist fight now and then. What bothered him was this thing with women. One woman was hard enough. But he figured he had two to deal with. Two impossible ones.

Sally was married but was going after him like she wasn't. And Miss Arnell? She stirred something in him. He knew she was out of his range, and she acted like it, but that only seemed to egg him on. He thought back to their recent ride. He had put himself out to entertain her, make her laugh, came up with thoughts about the book that surprised even himself. Then, he put all that gentlemen stuff he knew into the ride. Thought he'd handled it pretty well. He sure didn't want her snubbing him again.

It was a tricky thing, what he was doing. Wasn't sure just *what* he was doing. All he knew was that he didn't want to appear dumb. For some reason, even though he knew he wasn't Miss Arnell's equal, he wanted her to think he could have been, if he'd had her education. He didn't want her bored with him. And then, if he was honest, he wanted her to feel a mite excited going out with him. What did they call it—a little flirtation?

That's probably all it was. No hope of it going further. It was fun, though, and it sharpened him up. He liked a challenge. He'd been getting bored before she came. But reading *Ivanhoe*, talking it over with her—just being with her—had taken the boringness out of life.

And Sally? Well, he had to admit she'd done the same for him, in a different way. He wasn't quite sure the difference, but with Sally, now, it was like going back to the comfortable, yet exciting times they'd had before she'd left. He'd always looked forward to—

Well, back then they'd got carried away. He had even considered asking her to marry him. Then he'd been blind-sided by that traveling salesman. Been a long time since he felt that surprised. And angry. But then time had taken care of that, too, and he'd forgiven her. After all, they'd had good times, dancing and carrying on. She was fun.

He'd been young enough, fool enough, not to pay much attention to Colburn. Couldn't blame himself much, though. The man had played his cards so close to his chest Nat hadn't known he liked Sally until she ran away. Then Colburn swore something fierce.

Out here on the range, Nat was glad to be out of all that confusion. Life was simple, at least for now. The night air was cool and he smelled the sharp scent of nearby pines.

What he should do is scout around. He doused his fire.

The hill at his rear provided a good lookout. He started the climb, choosing to step on grass clumps to avoid the crunch of loose rocks.

The dark sky had just enough light. He stopped before the crest of the hill, not wanting to disrupt its outline. No one was supposedly around, but you never knew. He looked around from his new vantage point.

There. Off in the distance to the right, a spot of fire.

Cowboys from another ranch? This was the Walker spread, though it was open range where other cattle wandered. But cowboys rarely camped in a group like that, especially at this time of year. He saw no reason for it.

Rustlers?

In the direction where those men sat, a good bit of scrub and grass would give him cover.

His stealthy approach took so much time his muscles were tight with effort—as well as with worry.

Finally, he reached thick brush some distance from their fire. If he strained, he could catch a bit of what they said.

"Cattle...canyon...won't be missed."

Nat's heart pumped faster. He took off his hat and peered around the brush.

Five men.

He gripped his rifle. Surprising them, he knew he could take down two, maybe three. His finger hovered close to the trigger. He'd like to show those rustlers—dang, if he would let them steal Walker cattle.

He slowed his breathing.

But that would be a fool move. The odds were against him. The others would come at him with a vengeance, and he'd be dead. No good to Walker cattle or his boss.

"Later...get others on the plain."

He was so busy with his own thoughts, he'd just about missed that last. They'd come back?

Where were they driving those steers from the canyon? To the Hole? Rebrand them and return later for those on the plain? That'd work.

He suspected—and he wasn't the only one—that outlaws from Hole-in-the-Wall rustled what cattle they could, then spirited them away.

"Okay. Let's saddle up!"

Nat's thoughts snapped back to the thieves. He'd wait to watch where they headed. One man rose and the others followed, the last one kicking dirt on the fire.

Horses had been staked at the side of the camp. The rustlers mounted and started west to the Big Horns.

Yeah, some of those Walker cattle had probably moseyed into that canyon where a stream ran and the grass was green.

On his haunches, Nat peered out from his hiding place, trying to see their mounts better. He wondered....

There it was. A half-moon on the rear of one horse.

The following week while Josephine was dusting her pottery, Nat sauntered into the room.

"Need help, Mrs. Walker? I have a free hour."

She turned from her dusting. Suddenly, she *knew*. It was time for that heart-to-heart. "How's your work going on the ranch?" She smiled. "And relations with the other cowboys?"

"Work's pretty good, ma'am. Dealin' with the boys? All right, except 'you know who.'" He grinned. "But some of that's my own fault. I realized that out on the western range. Awhile back I was pretty young and acted it. Colburn's so serious, I never paid him much attention. He's got a pretty thin skin, and I should have caught onto that."

"Nat, I can see you becoming foreman of a ranch someday or even working a spread of your own. You've got it in you."

She turned away from him to pick up another piece of pottery—it gave her the opportunity to ask her next question without seeming so direct. "Considering the future, have you thought of yours?"

"Well…I mentioned it some to Mr. Walker…maybe he told you. I'd like a spread of my own someday. Somethin' with horses. And just enough cattle to keep us in beef."

"What about a wife? Practically speaking, there aren't many women around, certainly not enough for all the men in the West. We've got one single girl on our ranch, and another who acts like it."

Josephine hesitated, put the piece of pottery back on the shelf, then decided to plow ahead. "I don't know what to think of Sally. She seems to keep after you."

Nat was silent.

She continued dusting the shelf with her back to him. "And I'm sure she's missing that father for her son."

There! She'd said it, put something in Nat's hopper to think about…and she might as well keep going, now that she'd gone this far. "But I also wondered if you might be interested in the teacher."

"Yes…well…."

More silence followed. Mrs. Walker decided she better turn around and see what was going on in Nat's mind. She was on rather sensitive ground.

Nat looked a little confused. "You have any more to say?" he asked.

"I don't know if I should."

"From anyone else, I wouldn't ask. Consider it interferin'. With you, it's different, you've got my interests at heart." The corners of his eyes crinkled. "You're like my mother. A mother a man appreciates after years of rough and tumble livin', after bein' away from home a while. So shoot."

"All right." She lowered her voice to soften what she said. "Sally is a very pretty young woman, and it's my observation she uses it for her advantage. Now, if she truly values you as a friend, and treats you as such, that's all right. But is that the way she treats you? She is a married woman, and in my estimation, hardly acts like it. Usually, I can't tell what she's thinking; in this case, though, it's fairly obvious. I'm mostly concerned about you."

She put her dusting cloth aside. "What kind of things do you talk about with Sally? You have a good mind, Nat, and I can see it developing. I could ask the same thing concerning the teacher. What do you talk about with her?"

He didn't answer right away, and to give him time she sat down in one of the large leather armchairs. She then asked, "What kind of acquaintance or friendship do you have with either of them?"

Maybe she didn't need to say more. She could see Nat was thinking.

But then she suddenly decided to press on. "You know, a woman is meant, by God, to be a source of beauty to a man. There are different ways of measuring beauty. But if the beauty is only physical, or skin deep as they say, that kind of beauty—

after marriage—can lose much of its appeal if it's not buttressed by beauty of soul. By that I mean a woman who has worthy thoughts, a woman who is kind, and a woman who is, above all, faithful to her man. The union with such a wife can ripen and sweeten—and deepen—as the years go on. My husband and I are proof of that.

"The thing to have is discernment. And, along with that, determination to live a pure life. This is sometimes difficult. We all experience temptation, but we have the Holy Spirit to give us strength in difficulties.

"I think of a favorite hymn by Issac Watts:

Holy Spirit, Light divine,
Shine upon this heart of mine;
Chase the shades of night away,
Turn my darkness into day.

"What I'm getting at," Josephine asked carefully, "is what kind of woman do you want for a wife? Is it someone to play around with, to have fun with? That can surely be part of the relationship. Or will it also be someone with whom you can build a life? Continue to grow...together?

"You know, life can get hard, and the playing won't last unless there's something deeper between you and your wife."

Nat was gazing into the distance. She saw a shadow of something cross his features. Was it sheepishness? Guilt? Either way, he was obviously thinking. Good.

15

Nat stepped out of the bunkhouse and saw Miss Arnell lean on a rail of the corral, looking over the horses. Today was Saturday, Miss Arnell's day off from teaching, and it was his turn to take her on her ride. He wondered...and finally sauntered over and stopped by her side.

She turned to him. "Hello. It's a beautiful day, isn't it?"

"Sure is." He rubbed his chin to gain a little time. And build up his courage. "Some time back...I mentioned a canyon I thought you might like to see, for a little adventure. On our ride later, would you like to go a bit farther? Say, to that canyon?"

"Oh!" She stood up straighter. "Would you take me there? I'm ready to take on something new."

"Sure. The weather looks fine for a longer ride, though you never can tell about afternoons. But we can't let that stop us."

One of the horses came up just then and nudged him. Nat reached up and stroked the mare. "If you'll tell Mrs. Walker what we have in mind, I'll make sure Cook packs us sandwiches and somethin' to drink. The ride's some miles and we'll get hungry. There's a place in the canyon for a picnic—that is, if you've a mind to."

"I'd like that very much."

"Good. I was thinkin', too, of a place we might climb. Leave the horses and go up the rocks a bit. It's a pretty easy ascent, but you want to have your sturdiest shoes or boots." He glanced down at the foot peaking from underneath her skirt. "Not them dainty things you're wearin'."

Margaret gave him a look. "I never wear these riding."

His eyes caught her expression and he smiled. "Okay. I was thinkin' of something real sturdy, thick in the sole." His glance went again to her elegant shoe. *Those do make a foot awful pretty.* He glanced up and found her looking at him. Feeling himself redden, he wondered if she'd read his thoughts. To cover the awkwardness, he said, "Well, all right then. How about startin' out right after noontime?"

"That would be fine."

His mind went over the terrain. It was rougher than she was used to and the ride longer, but they had the whole afternoon. This had been just what he'd been hoping for, a change from his usual work. After Mrs. Walker's talk with him, he was looking forward to spending more time with Miss Arnell.

The distance to the canyon was farther than Margaret had expected. Their ride stretched over miles of prairie grassland. She loved looking at the mountains, but their distance from the ranch had deceived her.

But for all that, she was enjoying the ride. Above and around her, the sky was a deep glorious blue. Wyoming sky!

She glanced at Nat. A finer looking horseman would be hard to find, even among the young men who rode the parks in Chicago. It didn't matter that Nat wore a rugged shirt and jeans compared to their tailored riding outfits. He looked every inch a man, a rider who knew his business. It appealed to something deep within her. Competence, that's what it was.

She was trying to bring about something similar in her students. Training their minds to read and write. Do arithmetic. Give them something to take with them into life to feel more competent. They might not realize it now, but times were changing and it behooved a person to be able to read and write. To know mathematics. It was worth the work.

But she hadn't come out here to worry about school. This was her opportunity for a real adventure, and she appreciated Nat giving it to her. He had work around the ranch that needed doing, of that she was sure. She'd learned what a valuable ranch hand he was.

Margaret glanced over at him again. He rode easy in the saddle and was good to look at. Any woman would think the same. Sally surely did. Her mind went back to the schoolhouse dance. Margaret never remembered dancing with such vigor. But it had been nothing compared to the dance Nat and Sally had exhibited. Now, that was spirited.

She couldn't figure out what was really going on between them.

But she hadn't seen them together much lately. In fact, it'd been rumored Nat had been out on the range, on some special assignment for Mr. Walker. She wondered if he hadn't been sent out to get him away from Sally. After all, Sally was a married lady. She knew Mrs. Walker wouldn't countenance anything unseemly in that relationship.

Well, she didn't either. While she respected Sally as a mother, it rankled that she was so free and easy with Nat. If anyone should be free with Nat, it should be an unattached woman. Like herself. But that, of course, was out of the question. Their differences in education were too pronounced.

Glancing at him, he seemed perfectly content. Maybe he was as glad to get out of his normal routine as she was. And, maybe, a little glad to be with her? Even though she didn't consider him husband material—

Was it her vanity that wanted to be appreciated as a woman?

Well. Enough of that. She wished she'd known about this trip some days in advance. It would have given her something to look forward to. But she'd put that out of her mind. She was here and would pay attention to her surroundings. It wasn't every day she was treated to an outing like this.

They crossed several depressions and skirted around low hills, but as they continued, the approach to the canyon leveled out.

At the canyon opening, she felt excitement rise up in her. What lay ahead? Walking the horses into its mouth, they stopped at a rocky stream which barred their way.

"The horses can pick their way over the rocks," Nat assured her. "Just give 'em their head.

Margaret held onto the pommel as her horse navigated the rocks. This wasn't riding in a Chicago park. Nat led the way; he turned and looked back to see how she was doing. She was determined to appear competent, not as unsettled as she felt. She gave him a confident smile.

The canyon opening seemed to be fifty or sixty feet across. Trees and brush followed the stream bed. She liked seeing the greenery. In the East she had been accustomed to lots of it.

There'd been a breeze on the plain, but as they progressed farther into the canyon, the wind died down. Margaret took off her jacket and draped it across the pommel.

"Good idea, ma'am. You want to keep from gettin' hot and sweatin' too much. That way you won't get so thirsty. 'Course we've got plenty of water along." He offered a companionable grin.

Margaret smiled to herself. No gentleman in Chicago would warn her about sweating, much less say the word.

She went back to studying the canyon. Walls loomed up on either side. At places it would widen some, but the general impression was one of narrowness, the sides now only forty or so feet apart. The air was very still. She couldn't hear birds—or any kind of sound except the rushing stream.

"When we round that next bend, I've got somethin' to show you," Nat said. "It's gettin' a bit close here, so you better follow behind me."

Margaret held her mare back and let Nat precede her.

The canyon narrowed even more, and rounding the bend, she saw huge slabs of vertical rock on either side. "The colors!" she exclaimed. "They're so dramatic." Enormous buff-colored stone streaked with black rose up around them. "I've never seen anything like it."

"Me either, and I've ridden a few canyons."

"You mentioned we would climb. Surely you didn't mean here."

"No!" He laughed. "Even I wouldn't attempt this. But it's so beautiful, I wanted you to see it. In a few minutes, we'll go back to where the horses can graze. Nearby we can have our picnic after the climb."

Margaret marveled at the place. At times, they skirted the very edge of the stream, the canyon walls came so close.

"Let's go back now," Nat said.

When they reached the place Nat had in mind, he offered, "We can take a drink, splash our faces to cool off and then let the horses drink." He pointed. "Right up there is where we'll climb. You feel up to it?"

"Yes, but only after I've stretched my legs a little. I don't see how you cowboys endure so much time on a horse."

He laughed. "That's why half of us are bowlegged. Once you dismount, if you walk back and forth some, you'll be okay. I'll hobble the horses near the grass. Then we'll climb."

After he assisted her off the horse, Margaret particularly noticed Nat wasn't bowlegged. He stood straight and tall. If he weren't just a cowboy, she'd be proud to have him escort her anywhere. Even in Chicago.

———————◄○►———————

The ascent proved harder than Nat remembered; he hadn't thought in terms of a female climbing it. But Miss Arnell seemed game enough. He led the way, showing her where to place her feet. Looking down at her, he noticed she was breathing a little hard. Her normally ivory skin was flushed, the light brought out the red glints in her brown hair. He stared at her a moment…making sure she was all right, then made himself turn and concentrate on the climb ahead.

They were about two-thirds of the way up, could start to really see up and down the canyon. "Don't look down. Not just here," he warned.

He stepped up onto a large boulder and reached down to help her. At that moment one of her feet slipped and her hands shot up in alarm. He reacted instantly and caught her arms. He held them tightly for a few seconds, then drew her up by brute strength. Once he got her up on the rock, he held her against him, leaned away from the edge. Their breaths came in gasps.

She was trembling. He knew the thought of that near fall was working on her. He held her tighter. "I've got you now. You're all right." He made his voice as sure and strong as he could. Truth be told, he felt a little shaky himself—which was unlike him. He was known for his fearlessness.

He continued to hold her close. She fit against him so fine.

As his calm returned, he began to feel the humor of the situation. Heck! He wasn't going to be first to break this hold.

Then he felt her stiffen and start to draw away.

"Thank you," she said, a wary look in her eyes.

He decided to reassure her and make the whole thing a joke. "Hey, anytime you need a leanin' post, just call on good ol' Nat. Even horses like to hang 'round me."

She laughed.

It was all right then. But her closeness had sparked something in him—he hadn't wanted to let her go. He'd better watch his step. He doubted Mrs. Walker would approve of him making up to the teacher, and he sure didn't want to disappoint "Ma."

He glanced away, over the mountains. Probably he should think of Miss Arnell like a sister. Especially her being a school-marm and all. Why, he could barely write. She would certainly have none of him—in the particular way that had crossed his mind.

Suddenly, he felt embarrassed, what was he thinking anyway? He hastily offered, "Just a little more way to climb—don't worry, I'll help you—then we'll rest at the spot I have in mind."

She took a deep breath. "You weren't joking when you talked about an adventure."

He handed her up to a ledge where he helped her sit, careful to keep his touch impersonal.

They rested for a minute, admiring the view. Then he took out the field glass he used on the range and pointing it north-west, found what he was looking for. He held out the glass to her and pointed in that direction. "Do you see that cliff way out there? Look for somethin' unusual, somethin' that's not rock and scrub."

She took the glass and peered through it, moving it slowly up and down, then to the right and left. "I don't see anything out of the ordinary."

"Here, let me get it aimed right, then you grab hold and see if you can spot somethin'."

He got close, his cheek near hers. As soon as she moved to look through the glass, he leaned away. Her nearness had once again triggered something in him. He'd wanted to turn and brush her cheek with his lips, press them there.

Stop cowboy. That would end whatever trust she had in him. But he knew if he'd done that to Sally, she would've turned her face to his so their lips met.

"Ah! Is that a nest?"

"You found it." A sharp pleasure shot through him.

"Why, I think I see a couple of little eagles in there. Eaglets!"

"Ya sure enough do." He made himself focus on the delight of her discovery. "Just think of two little bird-lives in that aerie."

She looked at him. "Aerie! You know that word?"

"Aw…I read it in a book of poems Mrs. Walker lent me."

Admiration glowed from her eyes.

He felt good. Almost as good as if his lips were on her cheek. Almost.

She turned back and looked through the glass again.

"Actually," he began, "this is the first time I've seen two little eagles. Up 'til now, there's only been one. So this is special."

"They're perched so nicely on the edge of that nest. Gracious, it looks like it's made of sticks. Rather rough, isn't it?"

"The parents keep addin' to it year after year. They'll use that same nest a number of times. It looks as if one of them is off huntin' food."

"Yes, I see just one adult, perched off a way from the young."

"Eagles can sit like that for hours. If she turns her head, you'll see a golden color on the back of her head, runnin' down her neck. That's why they're called golden eagles."

"She just moved her head! I see it—a golden brown color." Miss Arnell watched a bit longer, then lowered the glass.

"Now, if you keep your eyes open on our rides," he said, "you might see one huntin'. Golden eagles like the open, semi-dry places we have on our plains. It's somethin' to see, the way they dive out of the sky. You won't believe how fast. And they're so high up, it's a wonder they can see anythin' on the ground. But they do. They go right to their prey, grab it with their talons without touchin' the ground, and make off with it."

"That sounds fascinating. If you see one hunting on our ride back to the ranch, be sure to tell me."

Nat smiled. "I'll do that. And while we're up here, why don't you look around some with that glass. There should be some mountain flowers...on that ridge to the left."

After a few moments of quiet, he suggested, "We can stay here as long as you like, then we'll go on back down and have our lunch."

She laughed. "That sounds good. I'm getting hungry. Is it easier going down than coming up?"

"That depends." He tried to think from her point of view. "Come to think of it, sometimes it's harder." At her quick glance, he added, "But don't you worry, I'll be sure to keep hold of you. I don't want you fallin'."

Yes, he'd make sure she got down okay. He'd keep close, go down before her by just a little. He'd take her hand in the tricky spots or steady her arm. He smiled to himself. This outing was turning out better than he'd imagined.

———————◁▷———————

He helped settle Miss Arnell near the stream.

"With the canyon walls so near, it feels a protected place," she said.

"Yes. You can relax after that climb. And this late in the summer, the stream is a gentle rush between the rocks. In the spring it can be quite a torrent, that water comin' off the mountains from melting snow. We'd hardly be able to hear each other speak."

They ate their sandwiches and talked of many things. He didn't know when he enjoyed a time more.

Drinking the last of his coffee, head tipped up, he noticed clouds moving overhead. He hadn't seen them before now. The canyon walls blocked out much of the sky. And, of course, the horizon. His jaw tightened. They'd stayed longer than they should've.

"Here!" he said, rising. "Let's get our horses and get on back to the ranch. Those clouds might bring rain."

After steadying her horse, he hefted her up into the saddle. "I'll lead the way. I want to pick up the pace."

As soon as they exited the canyon, they felt the wind had picked up. Clouds had bunched, turning dark.

Man, he wished he'd kept better track of the weather. He'd been so engrossed in what they were saying—

He pushed the horses to make better time and kept thinking of the terrain ahead, knew they would be exposed to the brewing storm. The country was open, pretty much flat, except for a few small rises and several depressions.

Lighting streaked across the sky. Thunder rumbled.

They passed down into one depression and up the other side. How much farther could they go before the downpour hit?

He looked back, the storm with its threatening clouds was moving close to the earth, rolling along the horizon.

Thunder followed lightning closer and closer together. Two miles from the ranch the wind suddenly swept down and brought a spatter of rain.

A second depression was just ahead. They'd better take advantage of it. He helped Miss Arnell slip off her horse, then quickly untied a couple items off his saddle. He thrust them at her.

"Quick! Spread this ground cover in the depression. Then take the slicker and cover yourself. I'll be with you in a minute."

He led their horses some yards away, keeping them to the low ground of the depression. He anchored their halters in a stalwart bush. Giving them each a reassuring rub on the neck, he said, "There. You'll be all right."

It began sprinkling harder and then the sky abruptly darkened overhead, blotting out the light.

He ran the few yards to where Miss Arnell had taken cover underneath his slicker. He got down on the ground and lifted it slightly. "I'm afraid I'll have to join you under there."

"Please don't stand on ceremony. It's beginning to rain!"

He lowered himself beside her. "Lie down. We don't want to stick up and attract any lightning." Suddenly, rain pelted the slicker. "It's comin' now!"

There wasn't much cover for the two of them. "We'll have to bunch up some," he said. "Get on your side and bend your knees, and I'll bend mine behind yours. Then scoot near me. Don't worry, I won't bite." With one hand he held the slicker firmly over their heads against the wind. With the other he reached over her and held it around them. She was enclosed—against him. The rain beat down on them.

If they came through this storm all right, he wasn't going to feel so badly about it, because as the wind and rain raged over them, she pressed herself against him. He had determined to protect her, like a guide or brother. But those brotherly feelings were deserting him. With her pressing so close, he felt less and less like one. Well, he'd just have to bear it.

His face rested on top of her head. He let his lips press against her soft hair. Yes, he'd just have to bear it. He smiled to himself.

The storm was moving fast, but he didn't think it would pay to get from under their cover too quickly. Not long and it would lessen, but he wanted to make sure the storm was well past. He wondered if he shouldn't wait until the rain stopped completely so she wouldn't be all wet riding into the ranch.

"Mr. Logan," she asked when the rain had slacked. "Do you think the storm has passed enough for us to start back?"

"Good question. But I think another minute." And he determined to enjoy that minute to the full.

16

Margaret bent over and unlaced her riding boots. Nat had insisted she wear her heaviest footwear. He had been right, on more than one account.

Today had been an adventure. That canyon! They'd ridden into it a couple miles to see those fantastic, buff-colored boulders streaked with black. There was something exotic about the place she'd never forget. Who would have thought such a spot existed? She was glad Nat had taken her there.

For a few minutes she let her mind wander over the events of the day, paused at the instances when Nat and she had shared something unusual.

A couple of times she'd been more scared than she admitted, like the climb up the side of the canyon. She'd done fine the first third of the way, but as it became more difficult, she...well, she refused to give up. After all, she'd told him she was out for a little adventure. But when she slipped—

Even now, the thought brought a shudder. That little bit of weightlessness when she dropped clung to her memory—in the most horrible way.

If Nat hadn't reacted with lightning reflexes, she'd have tumbled down, over and over. It was a dreadful thought. She'd not share that experience with her parents.

But then the moment Nat caught her and pulled her up, holding her tightly, she felt so secure. She finally calmed down. He hadn't held her a moment longer than a gentleman would who had rescued a maiden. Well, not much longer. She had to admit his firmness felt so wonderful she had clung to him a bit. And when she began to feel uncomfortable, looking up at him with that question, he released her, joking as if there was nothing in it. His sensitivity surprised her.

Margaret climbed into bed and pulled up the sheet and blanket.

So they had continued their climb up the side of the canyon. She thought back to Mrs. Walker's words on that first drive into Buffalo, how her husband had insisted Nat accompany them— for safety. Yes, Nat could certainly be trusted for that.

In the storm, too, he had been protective, in the best sense of the word, caring for both the horses and herself. She turned in bed, the bedclothes wrapping tightly around her, bringing back those minutes under Nat's slicker when she'd been tight against him. The slicker had acted as a close protection over them like they were in a cocoon. Warmth spread through her.

It had seemed perfectly natural. Maybe it was because of what had happened earlier before that afternoon. She had come to feel comfortable and safe with him. He'd been a gentleman, so she had no fears of his taking advantage of her. Yes, he had been physically close, nearer to her than any other man of her acquaintance. But it'd been protective in nature.

She trusted him. He would not go farther than society dictated—though that same society would have questioned them, seeing them like that under the slicker. But this is one time society would have been wrong.

Josephine sat at her sitting room desk, once again doing the accounts. She was not particularly good at arithmetic, but she was the designated bookkeeper. Her husband certainly had enough work on their spread. Getting this out of the way, they could discuss the numbers after supper, then have some special time together. She smiled. Thankfully, the week had been quiet, her husband and the boys working the range.

"Mrs. Walker! Mrs. Walker! Come right away!"

Josephine turned.

Sally ran through the front door like a whirlwind, carrying her baby. "Out front there's a man half dead on his horse!"

Josephine quickly rose.

"He needs help bad, but I can't do anythin' till I get Davy settled."

"Take the child to your aunt, then run back to help me." Without another look at the girl, Josephine rushed through the door and down the steps. Hanging over his horse's neck was one of their neighbors, a homesteader. One arm was feebly wrapped around the pommel. He wore no hat, his face was bloodied. He'd been beaten—badly.

"Mr. Reid, can you sit up a bit? What happened?"

He winced as raised himself. "I just come from town for supplies…some men came at me a couple miles back…dragged me off my horse."

He swayed in the saddle, she reached up to steady him.

"Much obliged, ma'am…if you could help me some…don't want my wife to see me like this…it'd worry her."

"I'll find someone to get Mr. Walker off the range. He should know about this. We'll get you fixed up and settled in bed for a while. Then I'll send one of our boys to your wife so she won't worry too much."

Sally descended the stairs.

"Good! Here's help."

"What can I do?" Sally asked breathlessly.

"You hold Mr. Reid on one side while he slides off his horse. I'll take the other. Mr. Reid, you go ahead and gentle yourself off the horse…slowly now."

He slid off the horse, trying not to lean on the women too heavily.

"Sally, gently now. We'll take him to the sitting room, on over to the couch."

With infinite care, they helped him up the steps—Josephine blessed her husband for making them shallow—and walked slowly across the porch.

Gaining the couch, Josephine said, "Help him sit first, then ease his upper body down. Yes, that's it. And Sally, help him lift his legs up on the couch."

"My dirty boots, ma'am!"

"We won't worry about that. This leather can stand up to a lot. It's seen worse." Josephine looked up at Sally, "Please get him some of our medicinal drink."

Sally gave her a questioning look.

"The brandy. In the cupboard to the right of the stove. Way back."

Sally left, and Josephine turned back to her neighbor.

"I don't drink, ma'am."

"Well, we don't either. This is purely for medicinal purposes. After you've had a few swallows and relaxed a bit, I'll examine your arm. Don't worry, I've seen twisted arms, broken arms— the lot—on this ranch. With a doctor so far away, I've had to learn a few things."

Josephine wondered who could have done this. Could it have been outlaws? They were around, she knew. Or was it trouble brewing between the big ranchers and the homesteaders? "Anything else you can tell me about what happened?"

"Ma'am…they kicked at me. Told me…I had no business settlin' where I did. Said to pack up and leave…me with a wife and two children.

Wincing again, he lay motionless a moment before continuing.

"I got mad…tried to give 'em tarnation…was that angry. But they gave me tarnation instead…and then some."

"Oh, Mr. Reid! I'm so sorry."

Sally approached with the bottle and a glass.

Josephine reached out to take them. "Now, if you'll pull up that straight-backed chair for me to sit on."

Josephine poured a little brandy into the glass. Sitting near him, she lifted his head slightly and held it to his lips. "Just a few swallows."

He coughed.

"That's all right. It's strange tasting and you can feel it going down. But it'll do the trick. Trust me."

She took her time helping him. He didn't like it, but he did as he was told.

Josephine looked up suddenly. "Oh, I almost forgot. Sally, go to the bunkhouse. There's got to be someone around. Have him ride out to the range and get Mr. Walker to come in—along with one other cowboy. I want to send someone to Mr. Reid's wife with a message."

For once, Josephine thought, *I'm glad Sally's here.*

Josephine entered the sitting room right behind her husband. Supper had been finished for some time, and everyone taken care of. She was relieved to finally be alone with him.

"Here, sit on the couch with me," he said. "I think you ought to know something."

She'd made sure the couch had been cleaned as soon as Mr. Reid was settled in the buckboard. He had insisted on getting home as soon as possible, afraid to leave his wife alone that night.

"I wish Hiram had stayed," Josephine said. "He was so badly hurt. One of our boys could have remained with his family and done the chores."

"I told Rolly to take care of Hiram's animals, and see what kind of help he needs beyond that."

"I'm so glad you arranged that."

Her husband took her hand and patted it. "There's more to the story. I didn't want it spread about. This afternoon, on the way to tell Hiram's wife, Nat saw a bunch of cowboys at Hiram's boundary. Two of them had just finished pulling down his fence. The wires had been cut into short lengths and piled here and there. That wire's now useless."

"Oh, George!"

"I know." He put his arm around her and pulled her in close. Josephine felt they both needed this. Her husband was tough, but he had a soft place in his heart. Especially for someone starting out like Hiram. Like they'd begun years ago—and struggled.

Josephine let the silence envelop them, bringing a degree of comfort. She prayed silently. Then she asked, "Do you know whose cowboys they were?"

"Nat recognized two of the boys. Moreton Frewen's men."

"Oh, no! Why?"

"He followed through on his threat to make an example of any homesteader who settled on his property. His foreman Fred Hesse must have given the go-ahead."

"That makes me feel sick."

"Yes, and Frewen doesn't even own that land. He uses thousands and thousands of acres of open range that don't belong to anyone, whereas Hiram legally owns that parcel. Ironic, isn't it?"

Righteous anger started to boil up in Josephine. She pulled away from her husband so she could look him in the eye. "What are we going to do?"

"We'll inform Sheriff Canton in Buffalo. The trouble is, Frank Canton is sympathetic to the big ranchers. And the rub is that the big ranchers have so much power. I've seen the way they operate in Cheyenne. The Wyoming Stock Growers Association is dominated by the cattle barons, and the WSGA is hand-in-hand with the whole political system up there, which affects what happens in our neck of the woods. It's a hard nut to crack."

"God forgive them. But I can hardly believe this of Lord Frewen. He seems so charming."

"Well, he is, Josephine. Yet he's also got a self-righteous 'I'm right, no matter what' streak in him that can't see any other way than his own."

"That's so sad."

"It is. Part of it comes from the way landed gentry in England think. On their land, they run the show. The common people who work for them don't have much say. That's what Frewen is used to, and only the good Lord could change his mind. It's deeply ingrained in him."

He paused then added, "Frewen actually has more problems than that. He owes money right and left. His charisma helps him get loans from people, but he's such a poor manager, I doubt he'll ever be able to pay them back."

Josephine searched her husband's face. How disappointing to discover all this. It made her appreciate her husband's honesty and integrity even more. She slipped her arm around his neck, and held him hard against her.

17

Nat tried not to let feelings of disgust well up in him. He'd walked outside by the kitchen window on an errand for the foreman, and now Cook motioned him inside to do something for her. If he knew her, she'd have him running all over the place.

Someway, he had to get himself promoted. This business of being at everyone's beck and call...he didn't cotton to it. He jerked open the back door and let it slam shut.

"Here!" The cook pointed to the stove. "I've done lost track of time. Take this pail of hot water to the teacher's room and throw it into the tub. She'll be back in a few minutes, so hurry. I can't leave the stove without burning this sauce."

The teacher's room? His interest picked up.

Cook gave another stir to her sauce. "Nat! And don't clunk so with those boots. Be quiet so you don't disturb Mrs. Walker. You cowboys make enough ruckus on this ranch to last her days on end."

Grabbing the bucket of hot water, Nat stepped out the door and treaded silently across the hall.

He'd been in the teacher's room only once, and that just briefly to deliver a heavy box from Chicago. He hadn't let himself linger. Now, with her not there, maybe he could glance around some. He'd been curious about her room. Noiselessly, he opened the door.

Nat froze. The teacher, her head turned away, was lowering a white garment down her arm. Her creamy neck and shoulder were exposed. Another curve showed down her front. Bowled over, he stood looking. He had to close this door, but as he did so, he found himself staring until the door finally shut.

He glanced up and down the hall. No one had seen him. What was he thinking, continuing to look at Miss Arnell like that?

Luckily, she hadn't seen him—he thought—or else she'd have let out a scream or something.

He stood still a few moments, gathering his wits.

What should he do? He was expected to deliver this water for her bath. Darn it!

Maybe he'd just knock on the door and wait for her answer. When he entered, act like nothing had happened.

He knocked and heard a startled, "Yes?"

"Miss Arnell, I'm here to deliver some hot water."

"Oh! Give me a minute, please."

Yeah, he bet it'd be a minute. A long minute before she made herself presentable. Knowing that, he put the bucket down and stood patiently waiting.

"You may come in now."

He stepped in and saw her fully dressed, sitting demurely at the desk, writing. Except her shoes were lined up to the right of where she sat. She hadn't taken the time to put them back on. And she seemed intent on her task.

"Cook asked me to deliver this hot water," he began. "Where would you like it?" It'd be better to feign complete innocence. Not even suggest it might be for a bath.

"In that tub behind the screen, please."

He shouldered his way gingerly around the opening. There

was none too much room. Carefully, he poured the hot water into the hip bath.

"I haven't seen one of these in a while." He hoped what he said sounded normal, conversational like. "My mother used to have one." Mothers were always a safe topic. "She smelled like rosewater after a bath. We young'uns loved to nestle up to her afterward."

All of a sudden, his words seemed wrong. A picture of him nestling into the teacher's arms after a bath came unbidden.

"Yes, well that's that," he said heartily as he stepped from behind the screen. "Anythin' else we can do for you?" Saying "we" instead of "I" made it sound more impersonal. He had no idea how she was feeling about him being in the room...standing right by her bath....

"No, that will be all."

He was half embarrassed, yet he wanted to guess if she'd known he'd opened the door earlier. He paused a moment and looked at her more closely. She continued to write. The cheek turned toward him looked a bit rosier than usual. But not much else was different.

"Thank you, Mr. Logan," she said simply, turning from her writing, looking suggestively at the door.

He took the delicate hint and started toward the exit. But then, before he stepped out, he glanced over his shoulder. His eyes caught hers and, for a moment, something leapt between them. Something almost physical. He stood mesmerized, like he'd heard about with those snakes in India. Her look kept him there, as if her eyes were saying the opposite of what she'd just said with her mouth.

She was the first to break the spell. "Thank you, again." She nodded a dismissal.

"Yes, ma'am." This time he seized the door knob and bounded through the opening. He needed to get out—pronto. In those few moments, he'd become a mite too desirous of

155

staying put.

It wasn't proper for him to be there in the first place, alone with her like that. Usually, the cook would have done the honors with the water—except for her sauce about to burn.

Crossing the hall, he stopped at the kitchen door and grinned. Reckoned tonight at supper, he'd never enjoy a sauce so much, it reminding him of what had just happened. He'd be sure to compliment Cook.

But no way would he say anything about the teacher being in the room. And that look in her eyes...he didn't quite know what to make of it. But it was something he would think about...that, and some other things that hadn't escaped his notice.

His grin widened.

———————◦◦◦———————

Margaret put down the pen she'd been holding and thought about what had just happened. While undressing, she'd sensed something and turned, just in time to see the door close. Had Nat opened the door, seen her, and then quietly closed it? If so, how much had he seen? Her already warm cheeks grew warmer still. She sat some moments longer at her desk.

That door should have been bolted. She thought she'd done so. Well, it was her own fault then.

Poor man, subjected to such an embarrassing scene. She was sorry for that. Really sorry, for Mrs. Walker had told her Nat had become a believer just a short time ago. Margaret didn't want to be a stumbling stone, him thinking about her in an improper way. Besides their rides, when they did talk about the book she'd lent him, she had no intention of becoming more than a casual friend. Although he was handsome enough, there was no way they could become more than cowhand to teacher. Why, she had years of education beyond him.

She'd thought through this all before, so why was she going over the same ground again? For a husband, she wanted someone she could respect, look up to as her equal or superior. That was her ideal.

How should she handle this incident? It would be impossible to ask him about it. That would only draw too much attention to it and make the time they spent together embarrassing for them both. Her finger traced a circle on the paper on her desk top. It would probably be better if she acted as if nothing had happened. Just greet him as she had before.

But there was that *look* they'd shared before he left the room. Would she ever forget that? It was the kind of penetrating look one shared with someone with whom one was intimate.

Oh, dear! Her hand flew to her face.

What had she started by forgetting to lock her door? She rose suddenly and purposefully walked across the room and snapped the bolt in place. She felt so embarrassed she cringed inside. Back at her desk, she all but yanked off her blouse. Before her water got cold, she'd better get on with that stupid bath.

———— ◦◦◦◦ ————

In his bunk that night, Nat lay awake, unable to sleep. Two of the other cowboys were snoring—which didn't usually bother him.

…And he had complained about doing Cook a favor. If Cook knew what a favor she'd done him— He'd be thinking about Miss Arnell's white skin for many a day.

Lord help him. What had got started here? Maybe nothing good, at least for him. He wanted to be a godly man, the kind of man Mrs. Walker had told him about. He really did. And he suspected this daydreaming of his would fit into the "forbidden" category.

But then again, he wasn't exactly sure of that either. It was beautiful, that shoulder and arm. And that other part, that slope down her front that bulged up some. Mrs. Walker had told him the Lord said, "whatsoever things are lovely…think on these things." But he had a feeling that was stretching things in this situation.

It would be best to keep things a bit impersonal with Miss Arnell. Friendly, of course, but impersonal.

But he'd really liked it when Miss Arnell gave him that book and they talked about it. He wanted more than one book though. Wanted to get an education. He didn't want to be a dum-dum, a dummkopf. He'd been called that once as a boy. He felt his face redden just remembering.

Could he ask Mrs. Walker about getting more book learning? Would she think that was out of line? He didn't want Mrs. Walker suspecting there was anything improper between the teacher and himself. But more schooling was something he wanted.

Why?

Well…maybe that was better left unanswered for the time being. He just knew he was bound and determined to get more education.

Nat woke from his dream. It was a wonderful dream. He'd seen Miss Arnell again, turned away from him, her beautiful skin exposed.

Now, he was a cowboy who studied terrain. And he thought about that particular bit of terrain. It was a private part of her he was sure no other man had laid eyes on.

A deep urge took hold of him. He didn't want another man seeing that.

Then out of the blue, he wanted Miss Arnell…wanted her for himself.

He could see her on that ranch he'd get someday. Them sitting on the porch together, talking…and doing some of those things husbands and wives did.

He whispered her Christian name: *Margaret*….

Just as suddenly, he turned over and hit his pillow.

This was pure foolishness, him thinking this way. How would that ever happen, the ranch, and her sitting there with him?

He'd learned that banker was supposed to stop by the school tomorrow and escort her home to supper. Was that why she had that bath in the middle of the week?

That tom-fool banker.

He made Nat mad. Plum mad.

18

Margaret rode sedately beside Mr. Norland. *Sedate* would be the right word to describe this ride. She glanced at the man in the saddle. He rode well, if a little stiff. Not as effortless as Nat.

She'd certainly had an opportunity to see Nat's handling of his mount in that canyon. It required deft management of a horse and, at times, he'd gone ahead of her to make sure the way was passable. Also, the manner in which he dismounted a horse was a pleasure to observe, a fluid movement. And often, how he handled the reins, one hand holding them while the other rested on his leg.

But this quiet ride with Mr. Norland was probably good. Her thoughts went to those three new boys in school...they came two afternoons a week until the fall roundup, after which they'd come full time.

They'd overcome their shyness, their quietness, or whatever one wanted to call it. They liked to tease two younger girls, throw bits of outside debris at them in class when her back was turned. She'd hear one girl squeal and quickly turn around, only to see all three boys working studiously.

Once, she'd caught one of the boys glancing up, a knowing

smirk on his face. At times, she felt they not only wanted to bother the girls, but were out to get under her skin as well. She'd need to think of better ways of handling them. She was determined to keep control of her classroom.

As she and Mr. Norland neared the ranch yard, the cowboys could be heard whooping and hollering.

"I wonder what's going on." Mr. Norland lifted up in his stirrups, craning his neck. "Sounds like the boys have themselves some entertainment. Shall we investigate?"

Margaret hoped it wasn't too wild. Mr. Norland might not be accustomed to such, being city bred. But she said, "Yes, of course."

They rode to the cottonwoods by the stream in back of the house. A crowd of cowboys had gathered.

"Let me help you dismount," Mr. Norland said, alighting. She lifted her leg over the pommel, ready for his assist. His hands grasped her waist. After she descended, she felt his hands linger. Deftly, she drew away.

How differently Nat helped her. He would lift her up and swing her around like he would a child to "give a little ride." In that movement, Margaret felt his love of play, how he liked to have fun. His sense of humor showed itself even there.

In contrast, Mr. Norland's assist felt serious, earnest, and maybe a bit possessive. She still felt the imprint of his hands on her waist. Almost she said something, then decided against it. Maybe that was just his way. And after all, she might be reading too much into it.

———————◦◦◦———————

Josephine stood watching from the kitchen window. Her "boys" were at it again, egged on by Sally. That Sally. Well, she supposed cowboys had to have their fun. Except when the two cowhands were Nat and Colburn. With them, a spirit of fun wasn't always evident.

She hoped it all stayed in good spirits, particularly when she noticed her grandson Jason and his best friend nearby. They'd run home as soon as school was out, had their cookies and milk, then raced outside to join the cowboys.

Maybe she better see what was happening.

Nat and Colburn stood at the base of a cottonwood tree in the row along the stream. Cottonwoods did best by a river or some other water source. That's why she and her husband had taken pains to water the grove of cottonwoods they'd planted in front of their house. They wanted a good windbreak for their home.

Josephine could see that even her husband had joined in the cowboys' fun, standing near the two competitors—Nat and Colburn—watch in hand. Apparently, he was the timer.

At that moment Josephine saw Margaret and Mr. Norland walk up, leading their horses.

"Hey, wait a sec," one cowboy shouted. "Let the school teacher and her beau see the action." Everyone turned to the newcomers.

Josephine thought the cowhand's choice of words unfortunate. As far as she knew, Margaret hadn't set her cap for the banker, and this would just embarrass her. Mr. Norland was sure to take it the wrong way, too. She doubted he knew cowboys loved to joke. They had so little fun, working long hours on the range. When life was dull, something like this added a little spice.

Her husband walked over to Mr. Norland and held out his hand in greeting, invited him and Margaret to see the competition.

He motioned the circle of cowboys to spread out, making room for the new arrivals. At the end of a day, the boys would be hot and sweaty, unless they'd dunked or washed up in the tough by the barn. Apparently with this in mind, her husband guided Margaret and Mr. Norland to one side, a little apart from the cowhands. Relief swept through Josephine.

"Okay boys!" Mr. Walker shouted. "I'll toss a coin to see who climbs first. Colburn, you call it."

"Heads!"

Josephine saw her husband flip the coin in the air, catch it and slap it on the back of his hand.

"Heads! Colburn, you called it. You want first or second?"

"First."

"All right. Position yourself at the base of this tree. When I shout 'Go,' climb as fast as you can, untie that red neckerchief up there and come on down. When you hand it to me, I'll call time. Get set!"

Josephine saw they'd chosen a tree with a couple of good limbs positioned near the base. It made a good climbing tree.

"Go!"

Colburn jumped to grab a high branch within reach, thrust his foot on a lower branch and hoisted himself up. He climbed grabbing branches and catching footholds. Quickly he untied the red neckerchief, clamped it between his teeth and hurried down. He jumped from the lowest branch and shoved the cloth into her husband's hand. George glanced at his watch and shouted out the time.

Sally came up to Colburn, congratulated him on his good time and hugged him.

"Hey, if I knew I'd get a hug from Sally, I would've signed up," one cowboy shouted.

"Yeah, and broke your leg comin' down that tree," Shorty yelled. Laughter broke out.

Josephine's eyes went to Nat. She saw him glance at Margaret and swing his arms from the shoulder, warming up.

"Come on, Nat!" Sally encouraged. "You get a hug for tryin'. The winner gets a kiss."

The cowboys guffawed. Sally had just upped the stakes.

163

Josephine knew anyone of them would have liked that kiss.

Nat positioned himself at the base of the tree.

"Go!" shouted her husband.

Nat jumped and grabbed a branch to hoist himself up like Colburn, slamming his foot on the same lower branch, then upped the tree like a lumberjack. He swiftly untied the other neckerchief and jumped down to a lower branch, missed it, dropped a couple of feet but quickly caught himself on another branch.

"Jiminy!" Josephine's grandson cried out. The crowd held its breath.

The missed step had cost Nat, but without hesitating, some distance from the ground, he slung himself feet first, landing at her husband's feet and stuffed the cloth into his hand.

"Winner by two seconds!" her husband cried out.

A smile broke over Nat, and he stretched up his arms in victory. Josephine saw his quick glance at Margaret.

Sally sashayed up to Nat and gave him a long hug and his victory kiss. Josephine hardly dared look at Colburn.

⁕

Margaret stepped into the hall from her bedroom deep in thought.

She was still trying to understand all that had happened yesterday when Mr. Norland escorted her home from school—and its aftermath.

She'd been spellbound by Nat and Colburn climbing that tree, so strong and agile. Particularly Nat.

Mr. Norland had snickered quietly near her ear, "Boys will be boys, won't they?" as if such carryings-on were beneath him. She'd treated his question as rhetorical, because she hardly knew how to respond. She herself had had nothing but admiration for the cowboys.

Later, after supper, just before she saw the banker off to Buffalo, he'd said how enjoyable the time had been with her, that he'd like to do it again. On second thought, maybe she could stay over in Buffalo, and he'd show her a proper time.

She'd remained quiet, determined to see him off, promising nothing.

Giving a last wave, and turning away, she noticed a cowboy duck around the corner of the barn. She saw too little for recognition; however, there'd been a decisiveness in the movement. No, more than that, it had seemed angry. Had he been somehow upset by her goodbye to the banker? Maybe. Did it matter?

Now, just a few steps from the sitting room, she noticed voices, their tone confidential. Instinctively, she knew she should turn back, but recognizing Nat talking with Mrs. Walker, she paused.

A special relationship existed between these two. She wondered why, they were so different. The cowboy was, for the most part, rough and uncultured. Mrs. Walker was not only educated, but wise. She had that fine sense of dealing with people and judging situations which few possessed. For herself, Margaret found Mrs. Walker someone in whom she had complete confidence, a woman who could be her mentor.

"…I just can't seem to do the right thing," Nat was saying. "Every time I get around that man, I want to challenge him to a fight or tell him to lay off her. Sooner or later I'm goin' to lose my temper."

He exhaled a long sigh. "What do I do? This last time I was around him, I came so close—to makin' a complete fool of myself—not because he'd get the better of me in a fight, but in words, if we got into an argument. If I told him to lay-off, he'd ask me why, and start talkin' circles 'round me."

"Yes, I can see that. But," Mrs. Walker said, laughing, "he gets under my skin, too."

"He does?" Margaret heard the surprise in Nat's voice.

"Yes. He's quite sure of himself. A little too much swagger for my taste."

"Anyone else see that?"

"I'm not sure. Of course, I'm an old lady and have been around some. I can usually recognize the difference between someone who's true-blue and someone who's out for his own interests. The way I've sized him up, I think he's someone who'd change his viewpoint if something worked to his disadvantage. He thinks of himself, first and foremost."

"Dang! Thought I was the only one who was thinkin' that."

"Sometimes we women can spot these things." Margaret could hear the smile in Mrs. Walker's voice.

"Really? I don't think..." Disbelief colored his words.

"Maybe not immediately. Sometimes a woman, a young woman, particularly, can be rather foolish if she's paid enough attention. If she's complimented and fussed over...."

In the silence that followed, Margaret thought Mrs. Walker was letting Nat think that through.

"Let me put that better. When a woman is shown she's *valued*, that changes her perception of the relationship. You know, that's what it really comes down to—a woman wants to feel valued. Maybe even more than that...cherished."

A pregnant silence followed. Then, a sudden, masculine, "Hm-m-m."

"Yes, Nat. A man starts by being thoughtful to a woman. Instead of thinking of what he wants, he considers what might please her. Now, when a man is in love, his mind naturally runs on these lines. After marriage, when he *has* her, he can often forget this and take her for granted. That is never good. One's spouse should be first in consideration. He or she should be made to feel special and important, just like during courtship. However, it's easy to get lazy. To start thinking of oneself first, of one's own comfort and desires."

Margaret heard Mrs. Walker shift in her seat, then she

continued. "That's not the way Christ would have it. Think for a moment how much He gave of Himself—how He sacrificed for us, loved us. Nat! He gave His all.

"As followers of Christ, we should seek to do the same. We all tend to be a bit selfish, thinking primarily of ourselves. But when we start to see the light on this, we can choose to put the other person first. To show him or her loving consideration, even when we don't feel like it."

Margaret felt the force of the words. She wondered how Nat was reacting.

In the ensuing silence, it dawned on Margaret she'd been eavesdropping—in the most shameless way. There'd been that first twinge of conscience, but she became so interested in what was said, she forgot herself and stood listening to this very personal conversation.

Softly as she could, she turned back to enter her room.

Closing the door, she wondered, who were they talking about? Who was getting under Nat's skin? One of the other cowboys? Someone in town? And the woman he wanted to protect, who was she? Someone he obviously put a lot of store by. Sally?

An uncomfortable warmth sprang up in her.

Was that jealousy? No, she was sure that would feel like a hot flame. Besides, why would she be jealous of Sally? She did have to admit, though, that if Sally wasn't already married, she and Nat would be a good match.

Nat and herself? She laughed quietly. They'd be a perfect mismatch.

She certainly didn't want people thinking of them as a couple. For safety reasons, he accompanied her on rides. The country was rather wild, and she wanted to explore—satisfying that curiosity that was part of her nature. Mrs. Walker said she was not to ride alone any distance from the ranch, and Mr. Walker backed that up. Both knew her parents and felt responsible for her safety.

So, it was right and proper that Nat accompany her on the range—along with some of the other cowboys. But she shouldn't show him partiality, although she had to admit, he was rather a favorite.

Something about him interested her. He had a curiosity about life she'd seen in few others. He liked learning. She'd seen it in his reaction to Scott's novel.

She considered the situation. What she'd like—would be to see him educated. He looked fine enough on the outside. Strong. Broad-shouldered. Those light gray eyes, standing out against his tanned skin, were almost piercing. They could glint, flash right into a person.

Actually, he was rather a man to be reckoned with.

If only he could be educated. Her eyes looked unseeing at the objects in her room, visualizing a possible future for Nat. He could be a prized student. She could see the potential. Wouldn't it be something if he'd develop into an educated man?

She thought back to Mrs. Walker's words: "…how Christ gave Himself for us." Maybe she should consider giving a little more of herself. To Nat. After all, she was a teacher.

She would be careful to keep it purely professional. Only to help him. After all, she could never be romantically involved with a cowboy—much less marry one.

19

Margaret stared up at the ceiling. She wasn't sleeping. Finally, she gave up and rose from her bed, wrapped herself in a robe and quietly made her way out the door onto the porch.

A light shone in the office at the other end of the house. It was late, near midnight. What was Mr. Walker doing up so late? That afternoon he'd twisted his ankle and was supposed to stay off it. In bed.

Silently, she made for the easy chairs at the end of the porch, opposite his office. She snuggled down into one.

Muffled voices came from the office, but no distinct words. She could discern a number of men talk, ask questions, make comments....

Then Nat's voice.

She sat up a little straighter, now wished she could hear what was being said. Of course, this was none of her business. Still...something was going on.

The air was colder than she'd expected. Sitting there, she wished she'd brought something for extra warmth, a blanket or afghan.

The voices stopped. Chairs scraped against the wood floor.

Were the men finished? Maybe she should go back inside. She didn't want to be seen.

Just then a couple of the Walker cowboys burst out the office door. She shrank back into her seat, making herself as inconspicuous as possible. However, they were in such a hurry, they never glanced her way. Were they off to do something which required haste? Something important?

She looked for Nat. Surely he would be coming out soon. Several others exited, and again, no one noticed her.

When Nat did step outside, Mr. Walker followed him to the door, leaning on his makeshift crutch. Margaret felt momentary sympathy for the ranch owner. But he wasn't letting his ankle keep him down.

The dim light silhouetted Nat's broad shoulders. Mr. Walker quietly gave him a last instruction, shook hands with him, then stumped back inside. For a few moments, Nat looked over the ranch yard, apparently deep in thought. Scanning the area, his head inevitably turned in her direction.

Without acknowledging he'd seen her, he started down the steps to the yard, but then paused, retraced his steps back onto the porch and walked quickly in her direction.

She sat very still, only moving her head slightly so as to seem to be looking at the stars and not at him.

He stopped in front of her.

She felt terribly awkward in her sleepwear, sitting outside at this time of night. Should she rise to her feet?

Finally, she stood. Nat seemed even taller in boots—and her in slippers.

"Did you hear?" he asked, just above a whisper.

"No... I came out only moments ago because I couldn't sleep." Her curiosity got the best of her. "It's unusual to have a meeting this late...." She let the rest of her sentence drift off, hoping he'd pick up on her implied question.

"We're goin' out tonight," he answered quietly, "a group of

us cowboys to take care of some ranch business." He paused, then added, "It's secret, so don't say a word to anyone."

A warm glow crept over her. He trusted her.

In the silence which followed, she sensed his alertness, as if he was considering whether to say more.

He placed his hands on her shoulders. His eyes held hers. They were shadowed in the dim moonlight. Still, intensity was there, giving them life. "A couple weeks ago, one night I heard you prayin'. You were lookin' up into heaven...so confidently." He cleared his throat quietly. "After I leave, would you pray for me and the boys?"

He'd seen her praying?

Then she realized the *mission* tonight—for that's how she now saw it—was potentially dangerous. Why else this meeting at night when everyone was asleep? Her mouth opened—to say—she didn't know what. All she knew was that a dread had taken hold of her.

He waited for her answer.

Finally, she breathed, "I will pray. Certainly."

"Thank you!" he whispered. Then, unexpectedly, he bent down and placed his lips on hers.

Instinctively, her hands reached up and clutched his coat.

His lips, warm and reassuring, held hers. Then he lifted his head.

Her hands dropped as, suddenly embarrassed, she realized she'd been holding onto him tightly.

His own hands left her shoulders, and he turned and stole across the porch, running down the steps to catch up with the others.

She stood, staring. This had all been so sudden, she tried to think what had actually happened.

One thing loomed large. She had never been kissed like that. Actually, she'd been kissed only once before in her life, a peck on her lips, something she had not wanted or welcomed. This was so different.

But this kiss, had she actually prolonged it by holding onto him? She didn't know. It had taken her unawares.

What did he mean by kissing her? There was no romantic "understanding" between them. Not even a suggestion of one. They were certainly not engaged to be married. So, why had he done it?

How cold she felt. Holding her arms around herself to keep from shaking, she scurried back to her room, flung back the bed covers and snuggled underneath. As she curled up, trying to get warm, she thought about the cowboys riding out to do some secret ranch business. But Nat had come back on the porch and asked her to pray. She *would* pray.

She clasped her hands and prayed for everyone's safety. Especially Nat's.

Then as she lay in bed, she relived those moments between Nat and herself. Something had passed between them, something real and precious. What was it? She didn't quite know— but it was more than physical.

Something sweet... something *tender* had passed between them.

Yet, it *was* also physical.

Had her lips clung to his ever so little? Suddenly her cheeks felt hot. She was sure, now that she was being honest, that she *had*, just as her hands had clung to his coat. Had he felt it? Had it communicated more than she meant?

What *was* her relationship with this cowboy?

She could now see it was unusual. Was it a special *friendship*? Surely, it could be no more than that.

But...had this kiss potentially opened the way for something closer? If it had been just a friendly one on the cheek or forehead, or even a quick peck on the lips, she could have judged it to be a token of sweet friendship. That's what it should have been.

However, she was afraid this kiss had gone beyond that. She

didn't know how far…inexperienced as she was in this kind of thing.

Could she ask anyone? Mrs. Walker?

Hardly. That good lady would be shocked, and maybe talk to her husband about it. Things as they stood between Nat and herself would certainly change. Probably, he would no longer be allowed to escort her on outings from the ranch. Nor do any of the little offices he performed for her, such as getting the stove started in the school to ward off the morning cold, or making sure one of the boys did, if he couldn't be there.

Oh, God. Where is wisdom here? The surprise, the shock of it, registered in force. Her hands clenched under the covers, her mind reliving that kiss. How could she keep Nat as a friend? Only a friend?

———————◦⋈◦———————

Nat ran down the steps of the porch, elated. What a kiss. He'd done it impulsively. She'd looked so beautiful with her hair down and all. He'd felt in need of something, emotionally and spiritually, before riding out on this mission.

And she'd given it to him. In giving herself, he'd felt a benediction, a blessing. The spiritual side, as Mrs. Walker would say.

For a moment, he paused in stride. From around the barn's corner, he heard the nervous bantering back and forth of the cowboys before riding out.

He had to settle down before joining them. Because that kiss—the physical part—he didn't remember one affecting him quite this way. It had been pure pleasure, and then to feel her hands grab his coat and hold on for dear life. He wanted to help her, protect her. Had her lips clung to his just a bit?

After that he wanted to let his hands slip down from her shoulders onto her waist and draw her tight against him. Give her a kiss to overturn her apple cart.

But that would have frightened her. And spoiled, maybe, the sweetness of what they'd just shared. Because it *was* sweet.

No, he'd done right to leave it at that.

With that decided, he turned the corner of the barn.

From the knot of cowboys and horses waiting, Gus hailed him. "What you lookin' so smiley about? You's like a cat just lapped up the cream."

"Couldn't make you understand if I tried, Gus."

"Ah! That Sally see you off—or somethin'?"

"No. Now let's attend to business." Nat stepped into the saddle, took up the reins and signaled the boys to follow.

Despite the darkness, their horses moved out at a canter. The trail was one they'd ridden many a time, out to the western herd they now aimed to save from rustlers. Hank had sent in word. He'd been positioned along the flank of the Big Horns, south of the herd when he saw a group of riders. Ever since Nat had witnessed rustlers steal part of their cattle and learned of a return, Mr. Walker had positioned lookouts to relay the message along with Hank.

It was fortunate Colburn happened to be in Buffalo. The foreman would have run this mission differently. Now Nat was in charge and glad of it.

He knew only too well what kind of men these rustlers were, and he knew how to lead the others to deal with them. Besides, he was bent on discovering that half-moon bronc and the man who rode him. Mr. Walker maybe wouldn't see it this way—how this needed to be done—but as far as Nat was concerned, this mission would keep that bronc and its rider in mind.

Approaching the Big Horns, Nat led the boys around the cattle and turned south. They rode without talking, and he signaled one cowboy after another to drop out of the bunch to hide back in the trees and brush along the edge of the mountains. This was to be a surprise party.

One of their lookouts reported the rustlers had made camp

a mile or so south of the herd. Apparently, they'd come a piece and decided to eat and rest before striking.

Nat was the last to settle into place. All was quiet. He judged it to be about four in the morning, had a feeling that when dawn broke, they'd see their friends coming from the south. But first that crowd would send a scout to make sure no one from the Walker ranch was about. Or, if a cowboy or two was around, he could be easily taken out of action.

After the rustlers began their roundup, he and the men would make their move. He'd ride out first with the rest of the cowboys quickly following his lead. They'd rush out of the mountains quietly, surprising the thieves.

The element of surprise was important. They wanted to disrupt whatever plan the rustlers had made, end the stealing once and for all—at least with this gang—make it so rough they'd leave Walker cattle alone. It was going to be tough, but everyone here rode for the brand and was up for it.

Nat had also told the men if they saw the half-moon horse, to signal him. He'd tackle that one himself. By hook or crook, he wanted to find out what had happened to his brother.

A slight breeze blew off the mountains. Nat turned up his collar and opened his saddle bag for some beef jerky. This'd be breakfast. He'd sure need it for what was coming. Chewing on a strip, his mind wandered back to Margaret...for that's what he now called her, at least in his mind.

No more *Miss Arnell*.

What they'd shared back there on the porch had been sweet.

But it was more. With his experience, *he knew*. There'd been something real personal in it. Something one shared only with someone special.

Was she too special for him? She was from an educated family, and Mrs. Walker had implied her family was well off with a beautiful home and all. Certainly, a sight better off than him.

He was just a cowboy. But had a nest egg set aside. As soon

as God had become real to him, he'd a change of heart and stopped blowing his money on wild times in town. Started saving for the future. A future with someone special.

He shifted in the saddle.

Now, that kiss. He didn't know exactly what it meant, how far it took them—friendship, that's what she'd want to call it, he was sure. Though he felt it pointed to something more.

Well, if he got back from this mission in one piece, he'd see how things stood with her. For now, he would have to let what happened between them settle down.

He looped his arms around the pommel and relaxed in the saddle, waiting.

An hour passed, or was it two? He stood up in his stirrups to survey the scene better, slowly, so as not to attract notice from anyone with a field glass. Every move of his—and of his cowboys—should be slow and measured.

From his slightly higher vantage point, he thought he saw movement from the south. He waited another minute.

Sure enough, a lone rider appeared. He kept on coming, scanning the resting herd. He would also be looking for Walker cowboys.

Nat heard the first bird song of early morning. Couldn't but feel the strangeness of it, beauty in a day that would begin with an attack. A fight where someone was sure to get hurt or maybe killed.

The rustler reined in his horse, surveyed the scene a minute longer, then raised his arm, motioning the others in.

They came in on a trot, sure of themselves.

Nat smiled. *Don't be too sure, partners. My boys and I have a little surprise.*

He waited until the gang had circled part of the herd to start them south. Then he nudged his horse out of hiding.

Here we go boys!

20

Nat aimed his rifle at a rustler riding in from the far right. The bullet he squeezed off hit the thief and he slumped in the saddle. Nat's shot was the signal for the others to let loose. He'd told them, "We don't want these rustlers comin' after Walker cattle again. If one gets away scot-free, fine. He'll warn others to stay away."

Confusion broke out among the rustlers. Some charged the cowboys, others broke away, trying for cover. With guns going off, the cattle stampeded, bellowing. Turmoil had hit the once quiet prairie.

Nat spotted the half-moon horse in the distance. He slapped the spurs to his mustang. A few bullets whipped the air near him, and he lowered himself against his horse.

Galloping, Nat focused on the half-moon horse and its rider. The man spied him coming and shouldered his rifle, aiming for him. But Nat hugged so close to the horse's neck, running directly at him, that the thief hesitated pulling the trigger, unable to get off a good shot. Drawing his six-shooter and sliding his arm beside his horse's neck, Nat aimed. The first bullet missed. The next one hit the man's rifle, jarring it aside, spoiling its aim. *Pure luck*, but he'd take it.

His horse ran beyond the rustler's. The thief threw his rifle up once again, and turned in the saddle. A bullet *whapped* the air close to Nat's ear. He twisted around and let loose a couple of shots. One bullet hit the thief's shooting arm and his rifle slithered into the dust.

Nat whipped his horse back to the rustler's, crowding it and hammered the butt of his rifle at the thief, whacking his neck and head. The thief lurched over in pain.

Jamming his rifle back down into the scabbard, Nat pushed himself off his mount and onto his opponent. Both leaned over the side of the horse, then broke free of the animal and hit the dirt. The fall jarred Nat, but he felt a momentary, grim satisfaction the robber landed underneath. His fist aimed for the man's head, but his knuckles slid off his face. Nat grabbed the rustler by the shirt collar, leveling as many hard punches as he could. Blood spurted from his nose.

"Where'd you git that horse?" Nat yelled. No answer. "I asked you—" Nat twisted the collar of the shirt, choking the thief. "What happened to the man who owned that horse?"

The rustler coughed to get his breath. "Sold it t' me."

"Liar! My brother wouldn't have done that." Anger kept surging through Nat, he drew back his fist to smash another blow. "What happened? Where is he?"

At that instant a gun roared near Nat, deafening him. Sharp pain shot through his shoulder. The arm he'd just raised, dropped. Unrelenting, Nat gripped the man's collar with his other hand and lifted him to bash his head on the ground.

But something struck Nat's head brutally, and he blacked out.

An unsettled edginess had plagued Margaret all night. She had prayed and prayed. Finally, just before dawn, she'd fallen asleep. Upon wakening, in full daylight, she wondered what was afoot.

It being Saturday, there was no school. She was relieved for she couldn't be away from the house, not knowing what had happened to the cowboys. She made her mind veer away from one particular man.

At breakfast, she asked Mrs. Walker when the cowboys might return. And then quietly added, "What had they planned on doing?" As she was asking the question, Sally entered the dining room, much to Margaret's chagrin. Had she heard? Mrs. Walker gave her a warning glance, signaling she'd answer later.

Margaret knew this was supposed to be hush, hush. Had she gotten so little sleep last night, her anxiety such, that she'd lost her discretion about when or when not to speak?

Sally approached the table and asked if they wanted more coffee and continued fiddling around the room. Margaret pretended nothing was amiss and talked with Mrs. Walker about Friday's school.

After breakfast, Margaret made straight for the sitting room. Mrs. Walker had left for the kitchen, but Margaret was certain she would join her.

Margaret tried not to move about restlessly as she sat in an armchair, waiting. Hearing footsteps, she looked up in relief as Mrs. Walker entered the room and sat at the end of the couch nearest Margaret. Dropping her voice to a low, confidential level, Mrs. Walker asked, "Did you guess, then, something important was happening?"

"Yes," Margaret said quietly, and told what she'd seen at midnight, how Nat had come to her asking for prayer without revealing the nature of the expedition. "Though I did wonder why they rode out in the middle of the night. It occurred to me it might be dangerous. After that, I hardly slept."

"We've had trouble with rustlers." Mrs. Walker then explained that Nat had discovered the thieves would return to steal part of the western herd. "So, last night our cowboys rode out to take care of the problem. I don't know exactly how. My husband wouldn't say."

Margaret stared at her. So it *was* dangerous. She sat quietly, hardly knowing what to think, much less what to say.

Her mind went to Nat. Was he all right? And that kiss, had it been a farewell? Had he needed something to take with him?

But had she given too much, unknowingly encouraged him to think it more than it was? She was still confused as to what had happened. And more than a little foolish.

Yet, she was concerned about the mission. So that's what she and Mrs. Walker discussed.

———————◦◘◦———————

Margaret heard commotion in the ranch yard, horses riding in, men calling to each other.

The cowboys were back.

She rushed out the door. Cowhands and their horses milled about. She stopped at the edge of the porch, uncertain what to do. Where was Nat?

Then she spotted him, slumped over his horse. And tied on. Her hand flew to her mouth.

That moment, Sally stepped out the door, holding Davy. Margaret heard her intake of breath.

"Nat!" Sally sobbed out. "Here, take Davy," and she thrust the child into Margaret's arms.

Stunned by what was going on and with the child unexpectedly shoved on her, Margaret felt unable to move. Instead, she held the child close.

Sally ran to Nat. Her arms went up, encircling as much of him as she could.

Seeing Sally cling to him, Margaret felt a strange tightness in her stomach.

After some moments, Sally called to the nearest cowboy. "Here, help loosen this rope holding him. We'll take him inside."

Just then Mrs. Walker rushed down the steps past Margaret. She immediately located Nat and asked, "What happened?"

"Two hurt, Ma'am," the cowboy answered. "Gus and Nat. Nat's the worse. Shot, then bashed on the head. He's been out most of the ride back."

"The boys can take him to my room, Mrs. Walker," Sally said. "I'll be glad to care for him."

"With the baby and all? No, no."

"Cook can keep Davy."

"Thank you, Sally, but I'll have Nat brought to Jason's room, next to ours. That will be the quietest place. My grandson can sleep either in our room or in the sitting room."

Relief flooded Margaret. Mrs. Walker was right. Nat should be in a room near her. She was like a mother to him. Whereas Sally—

Margaret's thinking suddenly cleared. She'd lost her mind if she'd let Sally nurse Nat. Not that she herself had much more claim to him.

But the picture of Sally sitting near him, cooling his forehead with a wet cloth—doing anything for him—angered Margaret. If Sally could offer help—Margaret could surely offer it as well. She would sit with Nat, watch him, help him eat broth, whatever was needed.

Nat hung over the neck of his horse. What had happened? He had only a blurry, faint recollection. His whole body ached, especially his shoulder.

He tried to look up. Where was he? The ranch? How did that happen—weren't they out on the plains, near the Big Horns?

He tried to think back.

Rustlers. They'd had a job fighting rustlers. Did they get rid of them? Fog rolled in and out of his consciousness.

Someone was at his side. Sally? What was she doing here?

Yes, he was back at the ranch. He could hear noises around him. Horses. Cowboys talking it up.

He felt terrible, couldn't think straight.

"Nat." Sure hands took hold of him. Mrs. Walker. At once he felt comforted.

They helped him slide off the horse. "Watch that right shoulder," someone said.

He remembered now. He'd been shot. For a moment his brain cleared, and he swore silently. Would they have to dig the bullet out? Hopefully, it'd gone clean through.

One of the cowboys got under his left shoulder, holding him up. "Let's walk now, Nat," the voice encouraged.

Then someone got under his other side. Someone short, keeping away from that right shoulder. "Come on, Nat. I've got you now. You'll be all right."

Sally? She wrapped arms around him, helping him along with the cowboy on his other side.

He felt like a sack of potatoes. Could barely manage to put one foot in front of the other. The fog started taking over again. All he wanted was to lie down.

Stairs appeared. He tried to lift a leg. Never felt so slow in his life. Or so foggy headed.

Finally at the top, he stopped for breath. Glanced left at a woman holding a child. Like Mary and baby Jesus. Sweetness touched him.

His eyes tried to focus. It wasn't Mary and Jesus. Margaret... but whose child was she holding? Surely not her own. He couldn't think.

No, she didn't belong to anyone. His mind stuck on that thought. She was free.

Fog came in again, and Margaret seemed far away. He tried to see her face, meet her eyes, but couldn't focus.

Suddenly his feet gave way, and he felt himself slump.

21

"Doctor Watkins, he's right in here." Josephine led the doctor into the back bedroom. "I'm so glad you made it as soon as you did. Nat's like a son to me."

"Have you kept him quiet—and still as possible?"

"Certainly. That is, once he got here. He was out on the range, taking care of ranch business for my husband." Josephine looked at her husband. She didn't know how much to say.

"He was shot," Mr. Walker said. "Lost some blood. But it's the blow to the head we're concerned about."

"We'll see what we can do. I'll examine his head first. Keep him warm, and let's move him slow and gentle. Then I'll take a look at that shoulder. Did the bullet go on through?"

"Still in there. We've disturbed him as little as possible."

"Good. Now, Mrs. Walker, unless you have a strong stomach, why don't you wait outside."

"I have a strong enough stomach, Doctor. My husband with his sprained ankle is limited in movement. Just tell me what you need, I have a girl waiting outside to take orders."

"All right. When I dig for that bullet, I'll use chloroform. We want to keep this boy quiet with that injury to his head." The doctor pursed his lips. "Let's get on with this then."

———————◦⬩◦———————

Cook handed Margaret a bowl of broth on the tray Mrs. Walker had directed her to take. Earlier that day Mrs. Walker had fed Nat herself. They were following the doctor's directions to the letter. All yesterday, he'd ordered Nat have nothing until he came out of his fog.

The door to Jason's bedroom was slightly ajar. Margaret balanced the tray on one arm while she gently pushed open the door.

The room was dim, but as soon as Margaret saw the room's extra occupant, her chest tightened.

Sally sat at Nat's bedside, holding his hand as if it was hers to claim. Nat's eyes were closed.

For a long moment, Margaret stood at the door opening, not knowing quite what approach to take. Finally, she told herself to *act normally. What would you do if Sally wasn't here? Just do that.*

She walked quietly into the room and Sally looked up. "Oh, hello, Margaret."

Sally rose and moved aside items on the bedstand, then turned and grasped the tray. "I'll take it now."

Margaret held onto the tray as Sally tried to draw it away from her. "Mrs. Walker instructed me to take this to Nat. And, aren't you wanted in the kitchen?"

That was a white lie. Margaret felt warmth rise to her face. Of course, Sally would be wanted in a general sense, but….

She had never confronted Sally in this way. Margaret softened her voice. "It's kind of you to offer, but I'll do this."

A hard, intentional look grew in Sally's eyes. "Since I'm already here, I can continue on. Nat and I are old friends, you know. Feeling poorly as he does, I'd think he would want someone familiar and comfortable around."

The woman just wouldn't let go. A wave of anger swept over Margaret.

But she made herself stand quietly—she wouldn't allow herself to show how upset she was. "Like I said, I believe I should follow Mrs. Walker's instructions."

Sally finally let go of the tray, turned and took Nat's hand again and squeezed it. "That's all right, Nat. I'll be back later."

Margaret stepped aside to let Sally pass and waited until she left the room. She turned to Nat. His eyelids fluttered, seemed half asleep. Had he been at all cognizant of the little drama taking place over him?

Margaret set the tray on the bedside table and sat in the chair Sally had recently vacated. It was still warm. That irritated her. She almost stood up.

Why was Sally here in the first place? She'd probably stolen in without anyone knowing. Mrs. Walker had led Margaret to believe no one was with Nat, that he was sleeping and would wake up shortly and need nourishment.

She'd better put Sally out of her mind. Margaret wanted to focus on Nat and what he might need.

She looked at him closely. She could hear his soft breathing. A minute passed. Hearing his breath, here in the bedroom, affected her strangely. Tenderness welled up in her.

Slowly, his eyes opened and his head turned toward her. "Mar...garet," he murmured. Then he just looked at her, like he was in a dream.

She was tempted to reach out and take his hand. Bring flesh and blood reality to him. But she hesitated. Had Nat ever held her hand, the way close friends do? Or in the way a man and woman do who mean a great deal to each other? No, he hadn't. Then she wouldn't. She wanted him to initiate that. Besides, she would not stoop to Sally's level.

She took up the bowl and spoon. "Nat, I have some broth

for you. Good beef broth that Cook has made."

Belatedly, she saw he was too horizontal to be fed properly. He should be raised some. She put the bowl back on the tray.

"I need to put that extra pillow behind you—so that you can take this broth." She leaned over him to retrieve the other pillow on the bed. His nearness stirred a response in her. She backed off a little, held the pillow while he tried to raise himself. He grimaced in pain.

"Your shoulder! Oh Nat, I'm not thinking. Let me help you."

Bending over, she placed her arm around him and, lifting him as best she could, wedged the pillow beneath his head and neck. She felt his body heat. Her responding warmth was more than just tenderness. It brought to mind their closeness on the porch before he left for the rustlers. And his kiss. She kept trying not to think about that. But now with him next to her and them alone with each other....

Here she was, responding to his breathing, his nearness— wanting to remain close to him. It confused her. What was she about?

She brought herself up short. This shouldn't be about her. It was about getting Nat back to health. He had felt very warm when she'd been so near, helping him with the pillow. Was he all right?

"I wonder if you're running a fever." She placed her hand just below his hair line. Touching him brought another unexpected pleasure.

However, she kept her voice matter-of-fact. "You do feel a little warm. Then again, maybe that's to be expected. After I help with your broth, I'll ask Mrs. Walker."

She put a cloth on his chest up to his chin. "This is in case we spill." She smiled. "But we will do our best, Mr. Logan." She used his last name to bring some levity into the situation, as well as a little needed distance. Yes—she needed this last.

She dipped the spoon into the broth, carefully brought it to his mouth. "Now, Mr. Logan...."

◆———————◦═◦———————◆

Nat's shoulder pained him when he switched positions in bed. Doc sure must have done some digging. Was that yesterday or a day or two ago? He'd lost track of time.

Mr. Walker stumped into the room. "How you doing, son?"

"Good 'nough. For a while there thought I was going loco." Nat gave a crooked smile. "My head's clearin'. Good to feel I can think straight."

He changed position again, determined not to let the boss see how stiff and sore he felt. "By the way, what came of our fight with the rustlers? No one's breathed a word."

"Doc wanted you quiet, and my wife enforced it. But I guess it's all right to tell you now. Those rustlers had it pretty rough. Two are pushing up daisies. Several more injured, seriously, I think. A couple got off scot free and high-tailed it out of there. Our boys let the injured go back south."

He leaned on his crutch. "Truthfully, we didn't want to be bothered with 'em. I doubt very much if they'll be back. Next time they'll pick on an easier ranch."

"Good. After all this," Nat nodded at his injured shoulder, "I hoped we had us some good results. When can I get out of bed? We got that fall round up 'round the corner."

"You need to give that hole a chance to heal over before you do any of that. Sure glad I never had to put up with a bullet hole." Mr. Walker grinned. "Before I forget, I want to thank you for the fine job you did leading our men. I was telling Major Wolcott the same, but, you know, he's got this bee in his bonnet about homesteaders stealing his cattle. I told him it was rustlers, but he's sticking to his guns. A lot of the other big ranchers are, too. They're already talking about cutting out nesters from the roundups.

"That's not fair."

"Sure isn't. I don't know where this all is leading. But that's not for you to worry about. I just dropped by to thank you for what you did for the ranch. Colburn was sore he missed out on the action. Of course, he wouldn't want to be where you are now. I'm sorry you got injured."

"All in the line of duty, sir."

"I don't know if you'll be able to do much on the roundup, but afterward, there's a little project Mrs. Walker has in mind."

"Oh?" *Anything that good lady wanted was fine with him.* "What's on Mrs. Walker's mind?"

"She's told me how much you like learning and would like more. So, how 'bout sitting at the back of Miss Arnell's school-room?"

Nat sat up straighter. *Here was an unusual proposal.* "For how long? I've got a powerful lot to learn," he said, laughing.

"Well, a few days at least." Mr. Walker's mouth slid up in a half smile. "I'll have to say, the real reason Mrs. Walker wants you there is to keep a few rowdies in line. This would be after the roundup. They'll be leaving school to help with that. Seems there's three young men, about fifteen years old, who've banded together to give Miss Arnell a hard time. She's been doing a pretty fair job managing 'em, but they're bigger than she is and I imagine somewhat intimidating. You're taller, larger than any of the three, and you'd give them pause before they start any trouble."

Mr. Walker's smile widened. "You have my permission to do anything. Outside of killing 'em." He adjusted his crutch underneath his arm. "In that classroom, Miss Arnell is the law. And I want to see a little more respect for the law." With that, he thumped out the door.

Nat lay back on the pillow. Speaking of the law—he still didn't have a handle on what had happened to his brother. That irked him, failing to get that thief on the half-moon. No. It was more than that. He was angry, angry deep down inside. He'd just been too plumb sick to notice until now.

His thoughts went back to the school. Those three bullies. Might be some sport there. Suddenly, he wasn't thinking about his shoulder, hardly noticed it. He was looking forward to visiting that classroom after the roundup.

22

Nat decided to walk the mile to school the first day. The prairie stretched before him brown and gray, fall in full force. After the recent roundup, anyone meaning to get some learning would be in school.

Margaret had agreed he should arrive late, quietly, so most of the students wouldn't notice. It would give him a chance to see everyone acting naturally. After all, part of his reason for being in the classroom was to take care of *the boys*.

He figured he'd not have much trouble with them, he was just about back to his old self. This was all working out so he could help Margaret. And it gave him an opportunity to learn. Who would have thought an injury would lead to this?

Mrs. Walker said God works in mysterious ways. Could this be it? She added, "Sometimes His ways involve a little pain on our part, but that's just the way it is. We live in a world that's broken. Sinful." She'd smiled at him in an understanding way, and added, "Why should we be immune from experiencing both its ups and downs? Especially when we're out there rubbing shoulders with it?"

Speaking of the "downs," he still smarted over that rustler on the half-moon horse. He'd kept his exasperation down inside.

Hadn't talked about it with anyone. Not even Mrs. Walker.

But whenever she saw him scowling, she reminded him what the Bible said "to think on these things...whatsoever things are true, whatsoever things are honest..." He couldn't remember the rest on the list—but that one, "whatsoever things are *lovely*"...made him think of Margaret.

From the first, she'd treated him fine, even though she was way more educated. They'd had those nice times when he escorted her on rides. And discussed *Ivanhoe*. Though he didn't have her education, they could talk about that. He could tell they both enjoyed it. Maybe there was more to him than he thought. He smiled.

But Margaret was so genteel, he wondered if he could ever be worthy of her. Seeing her sit ladylike at the table—down at the opposite end—a pleasant feeling would spring up inside him.

He couldn't help remembering that trip up the canyon when they'd been near each other. How he'd caught her before she fell on the rocks, helped her spot the eaglets through the field glass, and then huddled with her underneath his slicker during that downpour.

He felt a little embarrassed about the time he'd barged into her room without knocking, but not much. It was worth seeing that white shoulder. And that other part of her. He smiled again.

He'd tried to keep his thoughts respectful. Months ago, Mrs. Walker had challenged him that he was now a "new man." He could choose higher thoughts.

Dang, sometimes he didn't want to. Especially when he was angry. Mad at Colburn. Or that rustler. He felt himself go back into his old skin. It wasn't a good feeling. At first, yes, it felt good to let go, but not in the long run. He ended up feeling guilty and dark inside.

Now, if Margaret was his wife—he could let himself go thinking whatever he liked about her. But now, sometimes he wasn't sure where that "line" was.

It was a sure thing, though, God had made man and woman for each other. Especially the physical part. Mrs. Walker had said something about that, and added the mental, emotional bits were part of His plan, too. The whole shebang.

She said love between a man and a woman was meant to be a picture of God's love for us. It was all-encompassing....

Well, he tried to keep his thoughts about Margaret respectful. But just remembering her near him while he recovered in bed, wanted to make him raise his good arm, rope her in and bring her on down.

He kicked a rock. *Now, how had he got off on that?* Walking like this gave him too much time to think. He needed a ride on a good, rambunctious horse to keep his thoughts in line.

Like that wild mustang he'd started on. Jason had got into the corral just when the horse started calming down. He'd had to shoo the boy out—the horse wasn't that tame yet.

Mr. Walker had a good stable of horses. Nat dreamed of having something like that someday on a ranch of his own. Good horses and a few cows.

A deep sigh escaped him. There didn't seem much hope. That would take time to build up. And on his salary, a *long* time.

Margaret. Was there even a chance she would marry him when he was only a cowboy? Heck, he was lucky to make $40 a month. And Mr. Walker was generous. On some ranches cowboys made only $30.

It was durn hard to support a wife on $40 a month. Besides, that was no life for Margaret. He remembered her and Mrs. Walker talking about the fine house she came from back in Chicago. He'd been sitting nearby and been all ears. Been interested in her way back then. Of course, he hadn't admitted it. Told himself he wanted to know what building was like back in Chicago, her father in construction and all, and himself interested in building. Margaret hadn't gone on and on describing her home, but he could put two and two together. He had enough brains for that.

A gust of wind whipped up dust. Nat stopped and turned up the collar of his coat. This Wyoming wind was downright brisk. Hopefully, the first snow should be off a way. Yet, some years they'd already had it. He hunched his shoulders. School would be over that next rise, still some distance away, but clear enough to see with just brush spotting the terrain.

He started walking again. He'd worked hard these last years, paid little attention to rain, sleet or snow. Broke the rough horses, ate roundup dust, and drove cattle to the pens in Cheyenne. All the time learning about range conditions, the different kinds of grass or forage. He'd asked Mr. Walker questions. Colburn, too. Anyone who seemed to know something.

No, he wouldn't give up on his dream. But could he get it together soon enough for Margaret? She was a right pretty woman. No, she was beautiful. Any time he thought about that banker claiming her, it made him all crazy inside.

Nat arrived at school an hour after it started. Onto the main room, he'd built an entry hall where coats could be hung. It also provided dead space so that cold winter air wouldn't enter direct into the classroom. Of course, Miss Arnell had lived through Chicago winters. But he bet—nothing like here in Wyoming.

She had left the door slightly open to the classroom, so he could peek in without the students knowing he'd arrived.

Part of his plan was to give her time to get into her stride. Give the *boys* an opportunity to cook up some mischief. Then nip it good.

He peered into the classroom. A place had been saved for him at the back of the room. The students might have wondered what the empty seat was for. In a little while, they would know.

Miss Arnell had her back turned, writing on the blackboard. One of the big boys, probably one of the three troublemakers, rose in his seat and shot something at a little girl in front. Her hand flew up to her neck. She didn't say anything but spun around. The big boy sat down before she turned.

The boy had shaggy dark hair.

Nat made a note of him, but decided to do nothing yet. He wasn't particularly worried about the students. His concern was the teacher. It was only reasonable she'd want to run her own classroom. But there was times when a little help might be appreciated. He'd let her run the show until he judged she needed him.

Till then he decided to learn something. He stepped into the room.

A couple days passed, and Margaret enjoyed having Nat in school. Things had calmed down with her problem boys, and she was glad for the reprieve. It had come to the place where she had almost dreaded going to school each morning. She'd pour water from the pitcher into the basin, wake herself up, then immediately pray.

She quoted Joshua 1:9 to bring her courage. "Have I not commanded thee? Be strong and of good courage. Be thou not dismayed for the Lord is with thee withersoever thou goest."

It was a distinct provision from the Lord that Nat had been sent to the classroom. Of course, she knew it could not last long, but she was grateful for whatever she was given. Before this, she had never doubted her ability to run a class. But after that last week, when those boys had defied her, she had had to muster up all the authority she could in her voice and person to take command of the situation. After that, each night during the week she'd become more and more tired.

She never told the whole story to Mrs. Walker. Had Jason said something? Margaret didn't want Mrs. Walker to think she was incompetent, because she knew she wasn't. It was that each day there was a new challenge, something upsetting she hadn't expected.

After recess, Margaret stood aside as the children entered the classroom. Nat stopped at her side. "Keep an eye on that oldest boy with the shaggy hair. He brought something in a sack and the older boys snickered."

Well, forewarned is forearmed.

Margaret stood in front of her desk and took up the history book she'd placed there before recess. They'd read up to the signing of the Declaration of Independence. She found it rewarding, reading how these brave men had put themselves up against the British Crown. Today, most in the United States didn't realize the peril these men had brought into their own lives by this act. She hoped she would have been as brave.

She didn't read long, because the attention span of the younger children was short. But a little each day would build up the story of their country in their minds.

She closed the book and walked around the desk to sit down. Pulling out her chair, she jerked back, stifling a scream.

A snake! Draped over the seat! Her hands and feet started tingling. But within moments she noticed the snake wasn't moving, its head had been cut off.

But it was a rattler. She recognized the diamond markings along its length.

Only seconds had passed, and she doubted most in the class had even noticed anything wrong. She made herself breathe deeply in and out, forcing herself to regain her calm.

Snickers came from the back of the room. Those boys. The oldest one had put this dead rattler on her seat during recess. But he'd never confess.

She stood for a few seconds, perplexed as to what to do. Then suddenly, it came to her.

"I'm going to trade seats with someone. He can sit in my seat. Robert! Come forward.

And, Robert, when you come, why don't you bring that gunnysack?"

As the boy walked to the front, Margaret glanced at Nat. He was sitting quietly, but he was all attention. As of yet, most of the class didn't know about the snake, but Nat knew something was amiss. When Robert reached her, she bent down and whispered in his ear. "Put the snake in the sack without anyone seeing. Place it on my chair and sit on it until I give you permission to get up."

She stayed long enough to see him obey, then calmly started down the side of the room. "Now, class, if you will get out your slates, we'll have our spelling lesson." As she reached the back of the room, Nat reached out and caught her wrist and drew her down.

He whispered in her ear. "You all right?"

"I'm fine. I'll tell you about it later." If she told him now, he might take the matter into his own hands.

He gave her wrist a squeeze, then let go.

After the spelling lesson, she walked up to Robert and instructed him to return to his seat. He grabbed the bag, taking it with him.

When he reached his seat, Nat jerked his head, motioned Robert over to him. Nat took the bag, glanced briefly inside, tied it and dropped it beside him.

Margaret knew that would end the mischief.

Nat looked up and winked.

A little shot of pleasure ran through her. He approved of her handling of the situation. But she quickly sat down. Her knees had given out.

A week later, Nat stabled his horse in the lean-to just before the children exited the schoolhouse for morning recess. He'd done a few extra chores before school this morning.

He remained inside the lean-to, in the shadow, wanting to observe without being noticed. He'd seen firsthand that the older boys had set themselves to be troublemakers. But also that his presence was something of a deterrent. Now, he wanted to see what they'd do if they thought he wasn't around.

Seeing the children's enthusiasm as they ran out the door, he was sure recess was a favorite part of school, at least, for many of them. Almost immediately, he saw Robert leave his buddies and walk up to a young girl. She turned away.

"Hey you, don't walk away like that. It's rude." He lifted his leg. "Here! I'll learn you a lesson," and he kicked her backside. She yelped and thrust her hand to the injured spot. Tears welled up in her eyes as she staggered off.

Nat knew how it felt to be kicked in the tailbone. Growing up, he'd been kicked there by a bully. Pain had shot through him, and it hurt for days.

Nat strode out of the lean-to and grabbed Robert by the shoulder. "What you doin' kickin' someone like that?"

The boy stared, his eyes defiant.

Overwhelming anger rose up in Nat. He grabbed the boy's wrist, swung the arm back and under, forcing it up his back. The boy winced, trying to draw away. Nat jerked the arm higher. The boy cried out, his eyes began to water. For a long moment, Nat held the arm up in a fierce grip. He wanted to yank it even higher.

He'd seen it done in his brother's gang, the wrist pushed up the back, then with brute force, snapped up to the shoulder. He remembered hearing the crack as the bone broke. The man screamed in pain. Afterward the arm hung limply at his side.

The sharp memory stopped Nat.

He let the boy's arm down slowly, his voice rough with

emotion. "If I see you doin' that again, you'll be asking for a repeat. Next time, I won't be so easy on you."

The boy looked up, apprehension in his eyes.

Nat turned and glared at the other boys who had kept their distance. "The same goes for any of you. You make me sick, pickin' on someone smaller. A girl to boot. Now, git!"

That boy deserved a thrashing, but because of his shoulder injury Nat grabbed his arm instead. He was so angry, he'd a hard time controlling himself.

But what had he been thinking, almost breaking the boy's arm?

He wasn't sure. But he knew one thing—he still had a terrible burr in his saddle. Was it about that rustler? Remembering he'd been shot and whacked on the head still made him see red.

23

Margaret turned from the desk after neatly stacking her few textbooks. She looked up at the man waiting for her.

"Well, my last day...." Nat stood quietly, gazing at her.

"Yes. You've done wonders quieting those older boys. I hope it lasts."

His mouth quirked into a grin. "Last night I talked with Mrs. Walker. Because I won't be here after this, I told her somethin' needs to be done. She agreed, so we're drivin' out to Robert's homestead and speak to his parents. Lay down the law. If Robert can't behave—doesn't want to learn—he can't come back."

"Oh!" Margaret was at a loss for words. "I appreciate your offer to visit Robert's family...but shouldn't I be the one to do that?"

"Mrs. Walker and I talked that over. This is her school, and she's the final boss. What she says, goes. So that's the end of it."

Nat turned his hat round and round in his hands. "We both thought you didn't need to be in on this particular visit. Parents and students need to know you've got a backup, and word will get around. Everyone knows Mrs. Walker and respects her. Let her do this. And I'll be there as witness." He chuckled. "I might even take that old snake and gunnysack with me."

"Oh my!" Margaret laughed. "That would be the finishing touch. Well...thank you. I wondered how this would all pan out." Margaret wanted to reach out her hand to touch him, to thank him in a warmer, more tangible way. But she stopped herself.

"We're goin' to ride over there in the next day or two. That way you'll start out next week brand new."

"Thank you." She smiled. "One other thing. I know you've been an astute observer of the classroom—and of my teaching methods. Have you any advice to give?"

Nat chucked. "Now, that beats all—askin' me, who was never much of a student." But his eyes narrowed, as if he was considering. "You're different from the teachers I remember. They had us do a lot of memorizin'. We memorized everythin', seemed like. There wasn't much in the way of books. Somehow learnin' wasn't as interestin'. Of course, you're a lot prettier than they were." Suddenly, heat rose up his face.

She waited a little, then repeated her question. "So, did you have any suggestions for me?"

"Sorry, Miss Arnell. Just thinkin' of somethin'—"

"I'm glad you're thinking," she said in a teasing voice. Apparently he was embarrassed...the way he was looking at her. She should lighten the mood. It would be good if they could joke a little.

He cleared his throat. "Well, take arithmetic. That was somethin' I was never good at. I like the way you handled the beginner students. Instead of just sayin' the numbers and expectin' them to understand, you made it like a story. You talked 'bout puttin' four horses in a corral, then bringin' in three more. How many horses would that be, you asked. They could *see* it. We all could see those seven horses together in that corral. You made addin' easy."

He smiled. "Course those are easy numbers. But you did the same with harder ones. I could always see those horses or cows bunched together."

She was pleased he'd noticed her methods.

"Now, 'bout memorizin'. There's one thing I *was* glad of. You picked parts of *Hiawatha* for the class to memorize." Nat chuckled. "And you assigned me the part I'd already recited to you on horseback that first time we went out."

In a sing-tone he recited:

On the shores of Gitche Gumee,
Of the shining Big-Sea-Water,
Stood Nokomis, the old woman,
Pointing with her finger westward....

"Yes!" she said, laughing. "The other students were amazed how quickly you memorized your section of the poem."

"Got me respect. I appreciated that. Didn't want them thinkin' I was some dumb cowboy." His eyes glinted his amusement. "But that was a good idea each student memorize a different section of the poem—that it told the story. I liked the part where Hiawatha killed Megissogwon, the evil magician who'd killed Nokomis' father."

"I had a feeling you liked that part. Well, as you know, it's a very long poem. We couldn't memorize it all, so I had to choose parts carefully in order to weave it together as a tale. I've thought about using it in our program at the end of the year."

She ventured, "Would you participate, recite your part of the poem?"

A sheepish look suddenly appeared. "I'll have to think about *that*."

"Well, you can decide later." Her smile widened. If she had anything to say about it, he would. She'd like to see him back in school for the program. It had been good to have Nat here. She'd begun to look forward to each school day....

For a quiet moment, they just looked at each other. They

were seldom alone like this. The ranch and this classroom always had people milling around. He stepped closer. Suddenly, she felt the intimacy of the moment. And felt uncertain. She wondered if this might jeopardize the casual relationship she was trying to maintain.

She took a step back. "I really appreciated your being here. Like I said, those big boys have quieted down wonderfully." But she continued to look up at him, and his hand reached out to her. Her heart quickened.

Just then Jason burst into the room. "Someone's riding up, Miss Arnell."

"Who is it?"

"That banker. Probably wants to see you."

Margaret didn't know if she was disappointed or relieved. She'd thought, of course, that Nat and she would ride home together...with Jason maybe out ahead. Now....

Her eyes went from Jason to Nat. His demeanor had changed.

Anger flared up inside Nat. He didn't need to ask what Mr. Banker had come for. He knew he looked angry, but he couldn't help it. He'd counted on seeing the teacher home.

The change in him had been so sudden. How could he feel soft and gentle one moment, and just the opposite the next?

Before the banker entered the room, Nat sidled away from the teacher to stand beside Jason. His old buddy. He'd ride home with him.

But his jaw remained tight, he could hardly believe he was so angry.

Well, that showed him now, didn't it? He'd begun to think of Margaret as his. This time together in school...he'd felt the specialness of it. It had been the two of them against the world.

Well, those older boys, anyway. And it'd felt good. Good to be protecting her.

Those days here…waiting for her eyes to seek out his. They'd shared something…it was hard to put into words. But it was there, a sure thing. He hadn't felt this way about anyone else.

He stood watching her now, getting ready to leave with the banker. He made small talk with Jason. He could've already left, but he wanted to make sure that man didn't try anything while alone in the classroom with Margaret.

The banker put his hand on Margaret's elbow. To help her down the schoolhouse steps, Nat supposed. Why hadn't he ever thought to do that?

He motioned Jason to follow him to their horses.

Now, standing next to his mount, Nat looked over the saddle. He watched the banker help Margaret up onto her horse.

That should have been his job…his privilege.

All afternoon during school, he'd imagined arriving back at the ranch and helping her down from her mount. He'd feel his hands on her waist. Hold her up in the air just a little before swooping her down—something they'd often done together. She liked it, too. Well, that wouldn't happen now.

The banker motioned their two horses to start toward the ranch.

Why had he been so stupid to allow that fancy Dan to accompany her home on his last day here? Couldn't he have done *something* to prevent it?

Suddenly, he felt like fierce Hiawatha. He saw himself lifting a hatchet, Hiawatha's tomahawk. He hurled it at Banker Megissogwon.

His aim was true. The ax blade embedded itself between Megissogwon's shoulders.

Too bad Megissogwon still rode beside Indian Princess. Somehow, Indian Princess had to understand evil Megissogwon must no longer ride at her side. That was Indian brave Nat—

Nathanial's place. A thing of honor done for the Walker tribe!

"Nat!" Jason gazed up at him. "What did you throw?" His eyes had confused look. "I didn't see anything in your hand."

Nat stared. He'd been feeling so intensely—had seen it all so clearly in his mind's eye—had he actually swung his arm? "Nothin', Jason. I was just dreamin'."

"You don't like that banker, do you?"

"Not when he takes Miss Arnell."

"But she's ours, isn't she?"

"You're right." He grasped the boy's shoulder. They were comrades in arms.

"When are we leaving?"

"In a minute. We'll first water our horses at the stream." He needed some space from that fancy Dan.

Mrs. Walker heard raised voices in her husband's office. She was working in the sitting room, but it was difficult when that firebrand, Major Wolcott, was riding his favorite hobbyhorse. The homesteaders were getting under his skin again. She wondered where it would all end.

Earlier, her husband had called Colburn into the office to iron out some things about the ranch. Major Wolcott was now doing most of the talking while the other two listened.

"...no more homesteaders at our round-ups. I've said this before," Wolcott shouted.

Her husband responded more moderately, but the big rancher wouldn't listen. The more Josephine heard what was going on, the more it seemed this whole problem wouldn't end peaceably. Some of these big ranchers refused to compromise, or admit another side of the issue existed.

A chair scraped the floor. "That's all I've got to say, George Walker. You mark my words. Something decisive must be done

one of these days. You and your foreman talk it over."

Josephine heard more movement in the office and the out-side door open. She crossed the room to look out the window, standing to the side where she couldn't be seen.

Major Wolcott mounted his horse and rode off. Colburn and her husband stood on the porch watching him go.

Out of the corner of her eye, she saw Sally approach from the kitchen side of the house. She evidently wanted to speak to one of the men. But she stopped at the edge of the porch, waiting.

"Did you want something, Sally?" Mr. Walker asked.

"Only if you're done with Mr. Colburn. I'd like to see him a minute."

"Well, I think we're finished for the time being. Colburn, after you've thought over my plans for the ranch, we'll talk again."

Her husband turned and entered the office.

Mrs. Walker knew Colburn liked Sally, had liked her for a good while. Yet, Sally had always shown a preference for Nat. And then she'd gone off with that salesman. Where was the man, by the way? Had he ever made an honest woman of her? The baby had weighed with Josephine. She'd taken the kinder route of letting Sally stay at the ranch until things got sorted out. At least, that's what she hoped. Now, she wasn't so sure she'd made the right decision. She was curious what Sally wanted with Colburn, so remained hidden beside the window.

She had a good view of Sally's face. Right now, a coquettish smile appeared. She asked Colburn if he might help her with something. Her head cocked to one side, and her lips held a flirty little curve.

Colburn quickly agreed to whatever she proposed, and the two of them walked toward the barn. Sally stumbled a little and Colburn was quick to place a hand on her elbow, steadying her. He kept it there. Josephine watched them until they were out of sight.

Sally was supposedly married to that salesman, but since she'd been back, she'd been going after Nat. And now she seemed to be making up to Colburn.

"Lord, give me wisdom," Josephine prayed quietly.

She was about to turn from the window when she saw two horses in the distance approaching the ranch. It didn't take long to identify the riders as Margaret and Mr. Norland. She'd thought, this being Nat's last day at school, that he would escort Margaret home.

Another place would have to be set at the supper table. She must tell cook, and ask her to whip up a special dessert, but she stood some moments longer at the window. What were Margaret's intentions toward the banker anyway? She tried to see something of the answer in the way Margaret responded to her riding partner.

Just then, two more riders came over the rise following at a distance, one tall and the other short. Nat and her grandson.

Nat. She knew he wanted to be where the banker was, beside Margaret. Josephine noted the way he sat in his saddle, not the relaxed, controlled manner she was accustomed to seeing.

Now his carriage had an unaccustomed stiffness. Taut.

Lord, have mercy!

24

Nat looked down the long supper table, his glance going again and again to Margaret. She and the banker sat on either side of Mrs. Walker. Nat couldn't see the banker well, but whenever Nat looked that way, he saw Margaret act all interested-like talking with the man.

Nat shifted restlessly in his chair. He felt like a tinderbox ready to blow, the least provocation would set him off.

For the first time in his life he recognized a fierce jealousy. But something else, too. Hopelessness. It'd grown in him this afternoon when the banker showed up. Margaret had *naturally* ridden back to the ranch with him. She hadn't had to say anything. Nat could hear her the first time this had happened: *Oh! he's come all this way from Buffalo. You don't mind, do you?*

Of course, he minded. He'd figured on riding home with her. Had wanted it desperately—after all the time they'd spent together in school.

To be honest, he hadn't asked her in so many words. But what the heck! Naturally she would go with him. It was a foregone conclusion.

Nat stuffed some beef into his mouth. He chewed fiercely, staring at nothing in front of him.

Just then someone leaned over his shoulder. Sally's mouth was close to his ear. "Nat, I need to speak with you tonight," she whispered. "Can you meet me in the barn after supper—when no one's around?"

He glanced up at her and nodded. She placed a dish on the table then left for the kitchen. He settled back in his chair. Now. what in tarnation did she want to speak to him about, all private-like? But just the fact she wanted to talk, needed him in some way, took some of the edge off his anger. He didn't feel quite so much like dynamite, only like a six-shooter loaded and cocked.

Soon after supper, Margaret accompanied Mr. Norland to his horse. She had suggested as much—he would have a long ride back to Buffalo. All during the meal, he'd talked about the bank and how it was coming along.

"Now, both of you ladies and Mr. Walker, of course, will be invited when it's dedicated—as special friends of mine. He had looked at Margaret in a significant manner.

When he eyed her like that, inwardly she wanted to pull away.

Paradoxically, at the schoolhouse she'd felt almost relieved when Jason had announced the banker's arrival. At that moment, Nat close to her, the feeling so intimate, it had scared her how she was reacting. She had wanted him to touch her...she remembered the kiss he'd given her before riding out after the rustlers. In a rush, she'd wanted the same caress this afternoon.

But hadn't she wanted to keep their relationship purely on a friendship level? Surely, what she was feeling for Nat must be only temporary. An infatuation.

Margaret brought her thoughts back to the present situation. Mr. Norland stood next to his horse, waiting for her to say goodbye.

Truthfully, she wanted to say goodbye for good. When she'd glanced down the table, her eyes had met Nat's and the *look* in them cut her to the quick. She knew he had figured on riding home with her this afternoon. But she'd taken the chicken's way out. When the banker entered the classroom, she'd meekly gone with him, instead of saying....

She didn't know what she could have said, but it should have been *something*.

So now, she mustered her courage.

"Before you leave, Mr. Norland," she began, "I feel I must be honest about something." She forced herself to look straight up at him. "You have been most kind in escorting me on rides from time to time. This afternoon you appeared suddenly at school to do the same."

She paused.

He looked at her expectantly. "It was a pleasure, Miss Arnell." He reached out to take hold of her arm. "May I call you Margaret? It seems we've become good enough friends to call each other by our Christian names."

She saw where he was leading, and now knew for sure the air needed clearing.

"Yes, one would think that would be so," she began, "but I have come to realize something important, that while we can be acquaintances, maybe friends—"

She was trying to soften this; she didn't know if she wanted to be even friends.

"—we can be nothing more. Your kind escorts are something that cannot continue. I would be leading you on to think our friendship will develop into something deeper. And that is not the case."

Again, she rushed to add something to soften her words.

"Of course, you would be welcome to visit the ranch, but only to call on Mr. and Mrs. Walker. I would be here, but it would be no more than a friendly visit. It would be best to have no more rides together."

She said this last as firmly as she could while still keeping a friendly tone to her voice.

"This is sudden. I hardly understand…" He looked over her shoulder, in the direction of the barn, and a hard glint sprung up in his eyes.

"This afternoon—if it's that cowboy who's caught your fancy—Miss Arnell, I want to warn you." His voice took on an edge. "Oh yes, I saw him hanging around you when I arrived at school today. He didn't want me there, and he stayed in the room until we left. He was angry, angry I was there to carry you off, so to speak.

"Miss Arnell, I don't apologize for what I'm going to say. These cowboys know little more than cows and how to herd them. Why, he's no match for you. You are so completely above him—I can hardly say. You need to be free from the likes of him."

His hand tightened on her arm. "You should not be considering him, not encouraging him in any way." He took a deep breath. "And, of course, it would be a disgrace for you to marry him. Your family would be distressed."

His hand moved down her arm, to her wrist, as if to draw her closer. "Let me tell you something else." His voice strengthened. "We, the leaders of Buffalo, are asking the cowboys and the soldiers from the fort, to remain on the west side of Main Street. We want to keep the wildness and such away from civilized society. This cowboy would not even be allowed to escort you on our side.

"You have no idea, Miss Arnell, what goes on in Buffalo, especially on a Saturday night when the cowboys come into town, when soldiers ride in from the fort, and others too, real rowdies whom I expect are rustlers. These last, I've noticed their horses are the finest." His lips curled into a grim smile. "Of course, they need to be, in order to escape the law."

211

His gaze went toward the barn again. Margaret couldn't help turning to look.

Nat. How long had he been standing there? He probably wondered at this long goodbye—and was disgusted. He suddenly turned to enter the barn.

"As I was telling you—"

"Mr. Norland," she interrupted. "Please, say no more. You've made yourself abundantly clear. I'm sure you're right about Saturday nights in town. Yet, some of these cowboys are dear friends of mine, and I won't have them belittled. Or disparaged in any way. Mr. and Mrs. Walker require their hands to be respectful, to be gentlemen while in town. You aren't talking about *our* cowboys."

She stepped back, forcing his hand to drop from her.

"And you would be surprised how educated some of them are. Why, this afternoon we were discussing the poem, *Hiawatha*, before you arrived. It might surprise you what these cowboys read."

She took another step back.

"So goodnight, Mr. Norland. I hope I have made myself clear."

He stared at her as if hardly believing what she'd said.

She returned his look with a firm, clear gaze, meaning for him to see she knew her own mind and wouldn't change.

He took up the reins.

"I think you will regret this decision." Disapproval showed in his eyes. "Well, I'm a busy man. Unless there is business of some sort with Mr. Walker, I won't be calling at the ranch again." He lifted himself onto his horse.

Stiff in the saddle, he rode off.

She turned away, relieved. *He was gone, and would not come back.*

She must speak to Nat—soon—and tell him how sorry she was they hadn't ridden home together. He would still be in the barn with his beloved horses. But first, she needed a few minutes to collect herself. Dealing with the banker had been more of an ordeal than she'd anticipated.

She took a seat on a porch chair and spread out her skirt. Sitting quietly, she suddenly saw it all so clearly. What had she and the banker ever talked about? Anything literary or poetic? Hardly. She thought back to *Hiawatha* and smiled. So, now, who was the more educated? More sensitive to the finer things in life? Surely not the banker.

Nat had put off entering the barn, wanting to keep track of Margaret and that banker. Well, now he knew. He'd seen the banker's hand grasp her arm like he owned her. Nat had wanted to charge over there and knock his hand off.

Then hit him squarely on the jaw.

He stopped his charge before he even got started. Margaret hadn't drawn away from the banker. Nat tried not to let hurt and anger burn inside him. But it wasn't possible. He'd known all along he wasn't really good enough for her, but just wouldn't listen to his own common sense.

He turned, entered the barn and headed to where his favorite mare was stalled. He picked up a currycomb, but first went to the horse's head and rubbed her fondly. She was his girl. He stepped to her side and swept his arm up and down in the familiar movements of grooming.

"Nat." Sally's soft voice broke the silence.

His jaw tightened. He'd promised to talk with her, but didn't feel like dealing with anyone right now. He continued stroking the mare.

"Nat!" Sally whispered, teary.

He could hear the misery in her voice. Here was someone who was hurt, crying. His heart went out to a fellow sufferer.

"Over here, Sally. Wait. I'll come out. There's not enough room in this stall for three of us."

Sally stood in the open area of the barn, having squeezed through the large front entrance left ajar.

"Three of us!" Sally smiled weakly. "You always did love your horse. Almost as much as a woman, I reckon."

He brushed his hands down his pants legs, sweeping off any dust. "So, Sally, what's the trouble?"

"It's something important, Nat. I wonder…if you could help me." Her eyelashes swept her cheeks, then she looked up. "I've been thinkin' a lot lately…about when I went off with the salesman…"

There was a long pause. Nat wondered what was coming.

Finally, she said, "I've been feelin' bad about it. Particularly this last month. He said he'd be here by now. In fact, I'd told Mrs. Walker it would only be a month or two at most. And look how long it's been. Fact is, I don't know if I'll ever see him again."

"Oh, boy," Nat muttered.

"He could have written. Tellin' me he was delayed…or somethin'." She sighed.

"Did he know the ranch's address? How to get in contact with you?"

"He's been to this ranch a bunch of times. But that doesn't make any difference. I made sure he had the address before he left me in Cheyenne. He promised to write. And he hasn't once."

"Doesn't he come up to the ranch 'bout this time of the year?"

"Yes. Actually, he should've been here last month. But never came." She shook her head a little angrily. "What really got me was when I heard he'd been to see our neighbors, the Reids—and never showed up here—" Sally kicked a clod of dirt near her shoe. "I don't think he's ever comin', Nat. I can feel it in my bones."

"But Sally, you're married to each other."

"That's just it. I didn't want to say anythin' before this...but we didn't get a...license or anythin'. We just made promises to each other on a bluff overlookin' the Big Horns. It was beautiful. It really was. He said that's all we needed for now. We both loved each other and could get a regular license anytime. And then we—well, he didn't want to wait for Cheyenne for us to be together."

Her eyes took on a wistful look. "Once we got to Cheyenne, we had a good time. I'll give him that. He spent some kind'a money on me. We were so busy, we never got 'round to gettin' that license. Then he ran out of money, I guess. Early one mornin', I woke up to find him packin'. He said not to worry. He was goin' to get some money for us, and he'd be back."

"So you were never really married?"

"He said we were as good as married...we'd made our promises. He called it a 'common law' marriage."

"But Sally, don't you have to live together a certain number of years for that to be true?"

There was silence. "Oh, Nat, is that right?"

He nodded.

She stared at him. "I feel such a fool!" Her eyes teared, and she stepped near him. Then she was against his chest.

What could he do but try to comfort her, so he put his arms around her.

"Oh, Nat. Can you help me?"

He felt helpless. So he just held her.

She cried a little, and her face nuzzled into him.

Holding Sally like this, old feelings started coming up in him. Like before she'd gone away with that salesman. Nat had seriously considered asking her to marry him. Had been getting up the nerve when she ran away with that man. Boy, that had hurt.

But it touched him she'd come to him in her trouble. He

held her a little tighter.

Sally looked up, her face close to his. Her lips parted, inviting him...and he felt the temptation.

At that moment he thought of Margaret. But with Margaret he wanted more, expected more. Mrs. Walker had planted something in him. And he'd seen it even more clearly those days in the classroom.

He wouldn't give up that time with Margaret for anything. She stimulated him. And not just physically, like what was happening now with Sally. His mind...something deep within him was excited, deeply satisfied with Margaret.

No. Even though it didn't look like he'd ever have Margaret, he couldn't settle for just this with Sally. The realization flashed through his mind in a matter of seconds. Sally stirred, restless. She lifted her lips a little nearer.

A sound at the barn door startled Nat. He looked over his shoulder. The door was open a little, but no one was there. He glanced over at his horse; its head had turned, ears pricked up. The mare had sensed something.

Mentally, he kicked himself. He should have gone over and closed that door all the way. But he never anticipated this with Sally.

He loosened his arms, but Sally clung to him. She looked up with a teary smile. "Oh, Nat. You're such a comfort."

He stirred, knew he'd held her too long.

"Nat...do you think...we've meant so much to each other..." She held onto him. "And Davy needs a father. Do you think we might go back to what we were...before my foolishness?"

He stiffened, more restless than ever.

"I'm still your little Sally. I love you, Nat. I've never really stopped. I don't know what got into me with that salesman. Maybe because he promised me a life away from this ranch..." She was trying to look up into his eyes. "You used to talk about gettin' a spread of your own someday. Horses. I know you *do* like horses." A smile came into her voice. "And I'm sure I could come to like them almost as much."

Her arms slid up around his neck. "Nat, Mrs. Walker thinks the world of you. If she knew you were settlin' down—and I've noticed you haven't been spendin' your money in town—I think she might help you get started with your own spread."

Sally's voice became more assured. "Gracious, the Walkers own enough land. They could give you a piece, it wouldn't take much. Horses don't take as much pasture as cows. You could— we could start our own little spread."

Inside, Nat winced. *Once Sally got started, it seemed she couldn't stop.*

"You built that beautiful schoolhouse. The boys here could all pitch in and build our cabin. And I know my aunt would give us extra things from the kitchen to start with. Mrs. Walker lets her do what she thinks best—"

"Sally!" Nat grasped her wrists and took them from around his neck. "You're thinkin' way beyond where my mind is goin'."

How could he say this without hurting her? "I've changed. I could never be a husband for you. Or a father to little Davy. I just couldn't."

Abruptly, she said, "It's that teacher. I know. She spoils everything."

"No! It's not Miss Arnell. Or at least," he tried to be truthful, "I don't think she'd ever consider anythin' serious with me. She's just too fine and educated. One of these days she'll probably go back to Chicago and settle down to a good life there. Or maybe here in Wyoming, if there's someone to her likin'." He didn't even want to name the banker.

"Oh, Nat! Are you sure—sure we couldn't make it? I still love you." Her arms encircled his waist.

"I'm sorry, Sally. No." He reached back to take her arms from around him, then grasped one of them and led her to the barn door. "Now, you go back to the house. Look after little Davy. You might not be a wife, but you are a mother. Be the best you can."

———————————◦◦◦◦———————————

Josephine stepped onto the porch, clutching her shawl tightly around her shoulders; the air was brisk, and the sky dark. Margaret had seen Mr. Norland to his horse some time ago.

Standing at the rail, she breathed in deeply. The spicy scent of fall was in the air. But autumns here were short—when would the first snow arrive? The children always got excited, and Jason would love it. Afterward, however, a glorious Indian summer would descend and surprise them back into warm, mild weather. *That* was what she loved.

Her eyes roamed the ranch. A dim figure approached from the barn. Margaret. Her slim, lithe figure was easily recognizable, but tautness now governed her usually free and easy gait.

A glow emanated from the open barn door. Was someone else there? She wondered if she should go see about that light. But no, one of the cowboys or her husband would extinguish it.

Margaret neared her, but didn't see her at first.

"My dear, aren't you cold? You have only that light shawl around your shoulders."

Startled, Margaret stood still. "Oh! Mrs. Walker! No, I'm fine."

Josephine could hear the strain in her voice. Had Mr. Norland upset her? But she'd come from the barn.

"I need to tell you," Josephine began, "that we'll be leaving for Buffalo late morning, right after Nat and I return from your favorite student's house."

Margaret looked confused.

"Robert. Your troublesome fifteen-year-old."

"Oh, yes! Thank you. Do you think I should accompany you?"

"Not this time. Just be ready before noon to leave for town. We'll have a quick bite to eat beforehand."

"Thank you. I'll be ready." Margaret hesitated, adding, "If you don't mind, I'm going to turn in now."

"Certainly, dear. Have a good night's sleep."

Josephine watched Margaret enter the house. While she would ordinarily have followed her, she sensed Margaret wanted to be alone. Besides, she wanted to enjoy solitude on the porch a little longer. Yes, she and Nat would take care of the Robert business, then she'd ask him to accompany them to Buffalo. Or maybe her husband would go. She'd get all her ducks lined up tonight.

She stood at the rail, relishing the quiet. Off in the distance she could hear faint voices from the bunkhouse. But their cowboys were good hands. She was grateful for them.

Just then Sally pushed out of the barn door. Had Sally and Margaret been talking? If so, that might be enough to explain Margaret's distracted manner. Josephine watched quietly. Sally halted between the barn and the bunkhouse. The door to the bunkhouse opened, and in the doorway's dim glow, Josephine recognized Colburn. He stepped out and stood for a minute, apparently not aware of Sally.

But Sally saw him. In a low voice, she called his name. He immediately strode toward her. As soon as he was close enough, she reached out and took his arm, motioning him toward the back of the ranch house. As they disappeared from view, Josephine couldn't help but notice Sally's confiding attitude with the foreman. Like the last time she'd seen them together. Was she latching onto him now?

She looked back at the barn. The light was still on. She wouldn't wait for her husband or a cowboy to extinguish it.

She strode across the yard and opened the barn door a little wider.

Nat was bending near a horse.

Suddenly, Josephine knew she needed to talk with Sally. She didn't know what had happened in the barn but had a feeling it was nothing good, not with Margaret coming out looking so disturbed.

Sally was a bad influence on the ranch. She was a married woman, but she didn't act like one. She would have to find another place to live. Maybe she could find work in Buffalo.

Josephine would talk with Cook. They would help her get established somewhere else. She thought, again, of the baby. She'd not throw the mother out on her ear with nothing. But Sally's days on the ranch were numbered.

25

Margaret and Mrs. Walker rode in the back seat of the wagon with Mr. Walker driving. Shorty sat beside him. Margaret looked over the prairie grasses, taupe and fawn colored. In places, yellow and sere. The aspect would have been more cheerful if a blue sky were in evidence, but its pale gray matched her mood.

Nat had declined to come with them, said he might ride into town later. Margaret was both disappointed and terribly relieved he hadn't ridden with them, didn't know if she could bear his being so near. She would have had to look at Nat's back, seeing him tall and broad shouldered. And her heart would ache.

She could still see Sally's arms around his neck and his around her waist. Remembering it, her chest felt constricted. What a little fool she had been to think something special existed between Nat and herself.

To confirm it, this morning when she'd seen Nat briefly, he'd treated her with a distant, polite respect. *It's happened then. He and Sally are pledged in some secret way.* The traveling salesman hadn't shown up when expected last month; some speculated Sally would get a divorce or maybe she hadn't been married in the first place.

Colburn said as much this morning while Margaret rubbed down her horse in the barn. He hoped Sally would be free for good. Margaret had noticed his interest in Sally and her baby, but when Nat was around, Colburn suffered by comparison. Even though he was foreman, everyone knew Nat had the edge—on nearly everything. Margaret didn't know why he wasn't foreman.

She forced her mind to a different subject.

"You mentioned your talk went fine with my 'favorite' student's family," she said to Mrs. Walker, "but you haven't shared any details."

"Yes!" Mrs. Walker grinned, her eyes twinkling. "Like I told you, Nat and I rode over first thing this morning, wanted to catch both of Robert's parents, especially his father before he left the cabin. They invited us in, and we sat around the kitchen table, all friendly like. But I could tell Robert's mother, particularly, was nervous." Mrs. Walker leaned over confidentially. "It isn't often she has a visit from a prominent rancher's wife, no less one who's founded the school."

"I can well imagine," Margaret responded. She knew the respect Mrs. Walker engendered among her neighbors.

"I insisted Robert be present, to give him a chance to hear what we thought of his conduct. His mother was mortified to learn he'd kicked that little girl in her tailbone. And believe you me, his father had a scowl on his face.

"Now, the best part—Nat had insisted on bringing that gunny sack with its occupant. I didn't want the old thing along, but Nat threatened to stay home if he couldn't take it." Mrs. Walker grimaced. "I declare, Nat can be as bad as Robert. I guess it takes one to know one."

Margaret smiled involuntarily.

"You should have seen Robert's parents when Nat told the prank their son had played, and then dumped that snake on the floor. The mother screamed, jerked away, and turned white as a sheet. His father shouted, 'That's the final straw!'

"He said that he'd see his son would act more respectful in school, or he'd know the reason why. His face was so fierce, I almost felt sorry for Robert—but not quite." Mrs. Walker laughed, enjoying her own story. "That boy has been such a thorn in your side, Margaret, something had to be settled. And, after all was said and done, I was glad Nat brought that sack. It did the trick!"

Nat walked down Buffalo's Main Street toward the Occidental Saloon. He wanted to know what was happening, the latest news. As he approached the hitching rail, hackles suddenly rose on the back of his neck.

Tethered to the railing, stood the appaloosa with the half-moon. Right away, his mind went back to the fight with the rustler who'd been stealing Walker cattle.

He stepped up to the saloon door, took a deep breath, and swung it open. Quickly, he assessed the occupants. His glance told him the men at tables were those he'd seen around town. The horse wouldn't belong to them. His eyes fixed on two strangers at the bar.

He made himself saunter up to the counter. The man nearest him turned, and Nat looked into a familiar face. "That appaloosa with the half-moon on its rump, that yours?"

The man's companion muttered, "Told you that bronc was trouble."

Nat looked squarely at the rustler next to him. "You claim it?"

"Why?" The man's tone was surly.

"That's my brother's horse."

"Like h— it is!"

"Someone would've had to kill him to git that horse."

"I didn't kill him, but should have. He all but maimed my best friend—for life."

"Where's my brother?"

"How in this god-forsaken earth should I know?" He took a swig from his glass. "We let him know he wasn't welcome. And if we ever saw him again, we'd kill him." The man smirked. "But first, I gave him a taste of his own medicine."

Maimed his brother? "I'm askin' for the last time, where's my brother?"

"Off in California, Timbuctoo—who cares?"

"I do—" Nat just got out the words when without warning, the man threw a wicked punch to Nat's jaw.

Instinctively, Nat's right fist balled up and hit the man hard in the belly. With his left Nat struck him again, backing him against the counter.

The other rustler bolted around his friend, and jammed a blow to Nat's head.

The bartender caught up a shotgun from underneath the bar. "Hey! Let those two alone. It's a fair fight!"

The blow stunned Nat. Before he could react, his opponent struck him again, so hard it brought stars to his eyes. Nat stepped back, but then a cold fury took hold of him. He blocked the rustler's next swing, went for his face, then the stomach. The thief tried to sidestep the blow to his head but caught the one to his mid-section. After that, both men hit each other furiously, veering toward the saloon's entrance.

"Open the door!" yelled the bartender.

Nat got in another hard blow and knocked his opponent through the doorway.

The man fell, but sprang up and, as Nat lifted his hand to swing, the rustler smashed a wild punch to Nat's stomach.

For a moment, the blow stopped Nat, but then he hit his opponent again and again, backing him up to the hitching rail. In retaliation the thief swung a wide haymaker to Nat's head, and knocked him sideways.

A woman cried out and Nat glanced right. *Margaret?* Mr. and Mrs. Walker and Shorty? The moment he looked, his opponent ducked under the rail and grabbed for his horse.

Nat rushed him and dragged him off, both landing in the dusty street. Locked together, the two rolled over and over in the dirt, slugging each other clumsily. When they stopped rolling, Nat lay underneath. The rustler seized Nat's throat and squeezed hard, pushing his thumbs into his neck. For agonizing moments Nat felt a terrible, constricting hold on his throat. He couldn't breathe. Frantically, he jerked his two arms up inside the rustler's arms and threw them apart, away from his neck.

The rustler was the first to scramble up, and aimed a vicious kick at Nat's head. Nat saw the boot coming and twisted out of the way, then grabbed the man's ankle, giving it a heave and a twist. The thief fell heavily to the ground.

Both lunged up like drunken men, but before his opponent could get set, Nat grabbed the man's wrist. No longer aware of the crowd, all he thought about was this man maiming his brother. Swinging his opponent's arm back and under, Nat pushed it upward.

Higher, he thrust the rustler's right wrist up his back, forcing it to the right shoulder. The man gave out an agonizing groan, his face white. He tried to twist to relieve the pressure, but Nat blocked him, and suddenly with brute force, Nat heaved upward with all his strength.

***

The bone broke with a crack. The man screamed.

Margaret's stomach lurched. For a moment, she stared at the two men, dirty, exhausted, one slumped over in pain. Turning, she pushed her way through the crowd. Tears stung her eyes.

Her hope, her faith in Nat shattered.

She rushed up the steps to the hotel. Opening the door, she saw no one in the lobby; they'd all gone into the street to watch the fight. Even the desk clerk.

Thankful for the quiet, she stumbled to a chair in the corner, her chest tight. Wanting to cry, but couldn't.

Nat!

Her hands went up to her face and covered it, hard. How she hated violence!

Mr. Norland was right. These cowboys were different, she couldn't understand them. Why had she ever allowed herself to become involved with Nat? Helping him further his education. He'd probably *used* her, used her to further his schooling, and had a little fun with her in the process.

Her lips pressed tightly together. How could she have let him develop such influence over her, so many thoughts centering around him? How had she allowed it? She wanted to weep she was so angry. Angry at him. Angry at herself.

Even now, the man wrapped around her. Maybe not physically, but surely emotionally. His actions, his personality, had bound themselves around her like a vise. At this moment, she felt helpless to get away, even though she'd distanced herself physically from him.

Outside the hotel, she'd seen him slump in the aftermath of the fight, and now wondered if he all right. Oh! She was angry at herself for even worrying about him.

The clerk entered the lobby. Others walked in who had watched the struggle in front of the saloon.

"Boy! That was the best fight I've seen lately.

"Yeah, a humdinger! Did you hear that bone break?"

"I thought that kick to Nat's head would've done him in— but wasn't that a great twist and heave of his?" They continued calling out and laughing, discussing the fight.

The clerk noticed Margaret in the corner. "Gentlemen, keep it down for the lady."

The men quieted.

Margaret could still hear the crack of the bone, see the man's arm hang limp and useless. She felt heartsick.

Nat should have let the law handle this. But no, he had to exact his own form of justice.

She looked at the men talking quietly now. No one seemed upset. Was there some kind of justice, western justice she didn't understand?

But it was *animal* justice.

Pictures of that terrible grappling, hitting and kicking remained in her mind in a kind of horror. She didn't know men fought like that. Nothing seemed off-limits.

She started trembling. This wild west brand of justice—it was too raw, too violent.

Coming west, she'd had a sense of adventure, but now saw her desire had been for a much tamer variety.

She wanted life to have a sense of order and beauty.

She'd stubbornly held onto the idea Nat could change. That he was different, so far above the average ranch hand that she had considered…what *had* she considered? Marriage?

What had she been thinking?

Yes, the banker had been right. But she would never tell him. She had *that* much pride. Pride was a hateful thing in the eyes of God, but in this case….

And with this upset, she'd almost forgotten what she'd witnessed last night…that tender scene between Nat and Sally.

She hated being lied to, feeling his care, his attraction, then seeing him turn to another woman. Sally, of all people. Oh! She was angry.

And she felt the fool.

Her hands clenched tightly on her lap. Her thoughts were in turmoil. Could she even think about going back to the ranch tonight and seeing Nat?

She dreaded it, absolutely dreaded it. She didn't even want to look at him. The hurt, embarrassment, and anger were too much.

If she could just cry. Get out all this terrible emotion.

At that moment, Mrs. Walker entered the lobby, and looked in her direction.

"Margaret!"

Mrs. Walker hurried to her. Her brows were knit, worry in her eyes.

Seeing such loving sympathy, Margaret burst into tears.

26

Josephine held Margaret hard against her, letting her cry it out. She could feel the dreadful ache in the girl's heart. However, some of it was unwarranted, or at least it would be for a Western woman. But Margaret had so much of the Easterner in her, it was understandable.

How she wanted this girl to mature into a woman needed in Wyoming. Of course, she herself had had to grow into life on the frontier. Living on these plains was not easy. Nevertheless, goodness and beauty existed here in the shadow of the Big Horns.

Finally, Margaret's sobs subsided.

"Are you beginning to feel better?" Josephine ran her hand down the back of Margaret's hair, comforting her. "A good cry is sometimes best. Women are tender-hearted and emotional, and that needs to come out, at times in full force. Then, we can begin to think more clearly."

Margaret slowly drew away.

"I've had my share of crying fits in years past." Josephine chuckled. "But I assure you, 'this too shall pass.'"

Margaret sat, her head bowed, her eyes on her hands in her lap.

"I love my home here in Wyoming," the older woman continued. "But when its difficulties threaten to overcome me, I know my heavenly home is waiting. All my loved ones who know the Lord will be there, and we'll all be together. This helps put life and its troubles in perspective."

She spoke gently. "Margaret, I want to comfort you, but maybe what I'm saying is too general. Do you need sympathy and guidance on something more specific?" She looked at the girl lovingly. "Is this about Nat?"

"Ye-e-s, I suppose it is."

"You know, Nat is suffering, too."

"That's unlikely," Margaret burst out, and started sobbing again. She groped in her satchel for a handkerchief and buried her face in it. Josephine was glad it wasn't one of those little scraps most Eastern women carried.

"Oh, I think he is, my dear. Men don't show it the way women do. Especially in this rough territory. They've got to be tough, tough in a demanding land. And, Nat, more than most, had hard years growing up. He's had to be strong to survive."

Margaret looked up.

"But the way he broke that man's arm. Without mercy. I saw that terrible look on his face. It was angry, bitter—hateful!"

"Well, he'd been holding it in a long time, that anxiety about his brother. Once he saw his brother's horse ridden by someone else, it plagued him. Even though he'd said a final farewell to his brother when he turned his back on robbery, Nat began to feel he was his brother's keeper. It started coming on him after he came to know the Lord. Nat didn't say much, only a word here and there, but I put two and two together. With that rustler business at the Big Horns, his getting injured, and not being able to get to the bottom of what had happened to his brother—his concern became more and more weighty."

Josephine considered if she should say more, then went ahead. "Nat takes care of anyone he loves, his is a strong, protective nature. Remember that first time we traveled to Buffalo, shortly after your arrival? Well, my husband chose Nat to accompany us. He knew Nat could be relied on to protect us."

Margaret seemed to consider Josephine's words, but then she shuddered. "I still don't know if I could be around a man who exhibits such violence."

"I've said enough, I think." Mrs. Walker leaned over and gave Margaret a long hug. "Why don't you stay here at the Occidental for the night and tomorrow as well. Give yourself time to think about what I've said." She took the girl's arm and led her toward the desk. "I'll pay for tonight. You can get along without some of the necessities. Pretend you're playing 'pioneer.'" She smiled. "I've had to do it in my day. But, at the desk, I'll make sure they look out for you."

<hr />

Nat straightened up his things in the bunkhouse. Mrs. Walker had told him about seeing Margaret in the hotel after the fight, why she stayed in Buffalo that first night, then moved to a neighboring ranch giving her time to sort things out. She'd added that Margaret rode to school from that ranch, the two young girls living there thrilled to have "Teacher" as guest.

Well, that had been a week ago. It hadn't occurred to him Margaret would be so upset by the fight. But after Mrs. Walker explained things a bit, he began to see. "After all, Nat, she's an Easterner, born and bred. Adjusting to western life, especially on the frontier, is a big change."

But that fight couldn't be helped. The rustler had gone for him without warning, that first brutal punch decided the issue. He probably wanted to kill Nat, particularly after the fight at the Big Horns. Nat could still feel the man's hands clamped around his throat, squeezing the life out of him.

No, he wouldn't have done anything differently. Actually,

he'd wanted to kill the man himself. That renegade got off easy, particularly after maiming his brother.

Of course, Nat had cooled down now. He walked to the door of the bunkhouse and stood at its opening.

How could he bring Margaret around to his thinking, understand how things needed to be done out west? Sure, the law was important. But with only one sheriff and maybe a deputy to look after the whole county—and Johnson County was big—sometimes a person had to take care of things on the spot. Particularly, to save his own neck.

But boy, that fight had felt good. It'd put him back in fighting form.

And now he'd fight for Margaret, especially with that banker. He wanted Margaret as his wife. After their time in the classroom, he'd come to see her as his. Sure, they were different, but he'd seen what they had in common, too.

His gaze went off in the direction of the schoolhouse. It was there, over that rise. When he'd built it, he'd done it for her.

That time in school…how he'd liked to watch her. Every move was graceful. When she wanted the students to remember something particular, she made a strong gesture to catch their attention. Like an actress onstage.

She never just stood in front of the classroom all day. As she talked to the class, she moved from one side of the room to the other, then walked down to its back. Once she'd been so close to him, her skirt brushed his outstretched leg. From then on, he'd made sure his leg was outstretched every time she walked near. It'd happened only once more. But he'd liked that "once more."

He stepped back into the bunkroom. He'd left his gloves somewhere near his bunk. Boy, he was getting absentminded, thinking about her.

Looking down at the place where he slept, before he'd nod off at night, she'd barge into his thoughts. He had to watch himself or else he'd have her right there with him, snuggling close.

A few times, he'd kept her there.

But more and more he tried to honor her. Even in his thoughts. Kept her out of the bunkroom and, instead, make himself think about the ranch he'd have someday. The ranch *they'd* have someday.

Before he could ask her to marry him, though, he'd need more than he had right now. There was that banker, too. What was Margaret going to do about him? Couldn't she see he was a stuffed shirt? Would things ever work out between him and Margaret? He grabbed his pillow and slammed it down.

Suddenly, he felt sheepish. Good none of the boys saw that. They'd think he'd gone plumb loco. He made quick work of straightening the pillow, grabbed his gloves off the floor and strode to the door.

Closing it, he looked over the ranch, noting the new stallion running around the corral near the barn. Along with the other horses on the ranch, its coat had grown a good inch, and would grow another before the harsh winter set in.

His eyes drifted to the ranch house with smoke drifting up from the kitchen chimney.

Man! He didn't even know if Margaret could cook. That would be important on a spread of their own. Life would be pretty basic. Just him and Margaret on the ranch.

He liked to think of that, *them alone*—

What was that word she used in school to describe colts?

Frolic. Yeah, frolicking colts. He grinned suddenly. When he and Margaret were alone, there'd be some frolicking. Bathing in the stream. In bed. He was up for some of that.

There he went again. He would honor her, as he hadn't done, by a long shot, with Sally. *Lord, help me to be pure with Margaret. I'd sure appreciate it, if You could get her back here to the ranch. Then make her my wife.*

He walked over to the barn. Of course, there'd be hard work on their ranch. Lots of it. But before he'd see her out there, he'd have things shaped up. Get the boys here to help.

Once inside the barn, he took up a lasso looped over a peg. Might as well get started breaking in that bronc. Mr. Walker had bought some beauties from those wranglers who'd passed through from up north.

He stepped outside and approached the stallion in the corral. That horse had spirit, too good to geld. Maybe Mr. Walker would sell him to Nat, along with a couple of mares for starters. The boss only wanted one stallion anyway. A welcome thought crossed Nat's mind. Maybe the boss would remember their last conversation when Nat had talked about starting a spread of his own.

If he knew anything about Mrs. Walker, she'd help Margaret. She knew what eastern girls needed to adjust to life on a small ranch.

And Margaret was a worker. He'd seen that in school. Her father had worked hard to help build Chicago after that fire. Hard work ran in her family. After all, she'd come West when she could've lived an easy life in Chicago. Said herself she'd come for some adventure. He smiled. Maybe the adventure got a little raw with that fight the other day.

But something like that fight probably wouldn't happen again. More and more, the law was coming to these parts, even if the big ranchers still thought they ran the roost.

Now that was something to think on. If he started a small spread, where would he stand in the clash between the big ranchers and homesteaders? Wouldn't he be considered a homesteader?

Well, he'd worry about that later. Right now, he'd deal with this stallion.

Nearing the corral, he saw Jason run out the kitchen door. "What you going to do with that rope, Nat?"

"Tame this bronc."

"Can I watch?

"Sure."

"Can I help you?"
"We'll see."

———————◆———————

Josephine watched her grandson from the kitchen window. What a handsome lad he was growing up to be. She was so proud, but, more than that, she just loved him. Her husband did, too. At times, they liked to talk about Jason as they cuddled in bed. Her husband, particularly, thought of Jason as part of himself, his legacy to the world. They were both getting older, and one thought about such things.

As she watched her grandson, she saw Nat leave the stallion and exit the corral. Apparently, he needed something else from the barn. He waved to Jason, probably told him to stay put, the horse was rough yet. Nat hadn't put in much time with him. She'd seen that horse kick with his hind legs. Even Nat was wary.

Jason was sitting on top of the corral bars, but now climbed down and walked outside the corral toward the horse. He looked for some moments at the stallion, then reached out his hand to pet its nose. The horse took a step closer, and Jason could just touch it.

Good. The horse was reacting in a docile manner. He was a beautiful stallion. No wonder Jason wanted to get near.

Then Josephine saw her grandson climb the bars and swing his leg over the top. What was that boy doing?

He stepped down a rung.

Josephine made for the kitchen door. If he so much as put a foot into that corral, she'd have his hide. Exiting the house, she saw Jason already standing inside the fence, patting the horse's side, moving his hand near its rump.

"Jason! Get out of there!" She gathered up her skirts and ran.

From her peripheral vision she saw Nat exit the barn.

It all happened too fast. The horse kicked. At its sudden

235

move, Jason fell into the dust.

"Help! Help!" Josephine cried.

Nat jumped the corral bars, slapped at the horse's rump, and quickly bent down to help the boy get out of the way. Suddenly, the horse kicked wildly, his iron shoes hitting Nat. He fell into the dust, his arms circling Jason to protect him.

Josephine rushed to the gate and was swinging it open when her husband and a couple of cowboys came running—from the barn, from the bunkhouse—she couldn't say from where.

The stallion kicked wildly. He hit Nat again.

Her husband pushed past her. "Stay put!"

One cowboy bounded over the bars into the corral. Another grabbed at the rope dangling from the horse's neck.

"Get him over there!" her husband shouted. He pushed and slapped the stallion away from the two on the ground. He and the two cowboys strong-armed the bronc to the other side of the corral, then he ran to Nat and his grandson.

Josephine rushed to her husband who had bent over the two on the ground.

Their grandson slithered from underneath Nat. Josephine cried out in relief and took him into her arms. Then she looked at her husband examining Nat. Letting Jason go, she bent down near Nat. He lay perfectly still. Too still. He was breathing, but there was a gash on his head, and dust covered his shoulders and back.

Josephine insides sickened.

Several other cowboys came running.

"Need your help, boys!" her husband said. "Nat's been hurt, don't know how bad."

Josephine continued to gaze at Nat, white, his breathing shallow. "George!" she addressed her husband, "We need a doctor."

"Gus, you ride into Buffalo and bring back Doc Watkins. And, if he's out, get Dr. Lott at the fort. Fast as you can." Her husband turned to the other cowhands. "Boys, Mrs. Walker and I will look after Nat, but we need to get him inside."

"Hank! Get a blanket," Josephine called. "He'll be getting cold. And tell Cook to heat some water. We need to clean that gash on his head."

27

Josephine gently removed the bandage the doctor had wrapped over Nat's head wound. Doc had said to keep the wound clean. Of course. She quietly bathed his face, gentle as a mother with her child, and looked for signs of consciousness. Nat had come to for a short while this morning, but had slept on and off for most of the day. His one side had been pretty badly hurt as well. Thankfully, it was the opposite side from his previous shoulder injury. Right now, he had the use of one good arm. She looked down at him fondly. What were they going to do with this boy?

Her heart went out to him, especially after he'd saved her grandson's life. She didn't want to think what could have happened to Jason under that horse's hooves. Right now, she'd do anything for this man who lay so silently.

Her husband entered the room.

"How's he doing?"

"About the same. I think he could hear me talking, once earlier. He seemed to respond a little."

"Can I sit down?" her husband asked. As soon as Josephine gave up her seat, he leaned near the invalid.

"Nat. This is your boss. Listen carefully." He cleared his

throat. "I want you up and around as soon as possible. You're needed on this ranch. Especially with those new mustangs I got from the wranglers. I count on you to tame those horses. You're the best. In fact, I've been thinking it wouldn't be too long before you'd want your own spread with a few good horses."

He paused. Josephine saw him look intently for any sign of response.

"My wife and I are more than grateful—what you did for our grandson. So we'd like to make you a present of some acres, that northwest parcel by the Big Horns. There's a nice little stream where you could build your cabin." He took Nat's good hand that lay inert across the blanket. "We'll shake on it. Soon as you get better, let's start working on that."

He stood up and took Josephine's arm and led her toward the door.

"His eyelids moved," he whispered. "I'm sure he heard me. I want to put some gumption in that boy to get better."

Josephine looked up proudly at her husband and drew his head down. "This is to seal the deal," she said and kissed him.

He kissed her back. Hard.

"That's a double seal, woman. You're my woman, you know."

"I know." Josephine saw his smile, warmth crept up from deep inside.

He pinched her cheek and stepped out the door.

She looked at his retreating back. She loved it when her rough and tumble husband showed a little romance.

Josephine turned to her patient. He was perfectly still. Leaning over him, she gently placed the new bandage around his head. She tenderly pressed her hand over his good arm.

Nat's lips moved.

She couldn't make sense of what he was saying.

She leaned closer. His words came a little clearer. They had a rhythm to them.

"Minnehaha, Laughing Water,
Handsomest… of all the women…"
He stopped, took a shallow breath, and continued.
"Give me… as my wife this maiden,
Minnehaha, Laughing Water,
Loveliest…"
He stopped and groaned softly.

Josephine looked at him, perplexed. *Hiawatha?* Why would he be murmuring, reciting that poem? Was he delirious?

She thought back, remembering what she'd learned as a youth. Minnehaha was the lovely Indian maiden Hiawatha wanted for his wife. He traveled many miles through meadow and forest to claim her, to make peace between their two peoples who had warred with each other.

Nat's face contorted. "Margaret!" he cried out.

Josephine's heart wrenched to hear such yearning in his voice. Minnehaha…Margaret. Her breath caught. As soon as she could leave Nat, she would ride to the Springer homestead and have a talk…with that Margaret.

Josephine knocked at the Springer's door.

It opened. "Mrs. Walker! How nice to see you. Please come in." Mrs. Springer ushered

her inside. Two young girls hovered their mother.

"Thank you." Josephine stepped into the room furnished with a couch and a couple of

chairs, throws folded over their backs. Despite its sparseness, it felt homey. This had been a good place for Margaret to get away for a while. But now—

"Won't you sit down?"

"I really came to talk with Miss Arnell. Is she here?"

"Yes, she's in the back room at present. I'll send one of

the girls."

Moments later, Margaret entered.

"Mrs. Walker!" She held out her hands in welcome, but Josephine could see the wariness in her eyes. "So good to see you. What brings you?"

Mrs. Springer and her two girls stood near, listening. Much of what Josephine wanted to say to Margaret must be private, but what had happened to Nat would be common knowledge in a few days anyway, so she went ahead with her news.

"Nat has been injured."

Margaret startled.

"He had begun breaking in a new stallion when my grandson fell on the ground nearby. Nat moved to protect Jason, but the horse kicked him. And kicked him good. Nat suffered a gash on the head and injuries to his arm and body. He's been unconscious or asleep most of the time since yesterday when it happened. My husband and I can't thank Nat enough for protecting our grandson at such cost to himself."

Margaret sat quietly while Mrs. Springer asked about the chances of Nat's recovery.

"Oh, I just hate to hear that," Mrs. Springer said. "He's such an able man. So handsome and considerate of others. Of course, we heard about the fight he had with that rustler in town. Served the man right to get a broken arm. I hate to think what he did to Nat's brother. That rustler's in jail now, I hear. The good citizens of Buffalo will bring him to trial. But I don't want to think what that man would have done to Nat if Nat hadn't been stronger and a better fighter."

Josephine was glad Margaret heard all this. It would give her a better idea of Western perspective. It was certainly different from that of Chicago society, although she'd heard they had problems with crime, too. But law was more firmly established, unlike the West.

"Yes, we're terribly grateful to Nat," Mrs. Walker said. "And it's about that which I've come to see Miss Arnell." She looked at Margaret. "Could we talk privately, my dear?"

"Why don't we go to the back room," Margaret suggested.

"I'll see you're not disturbed," Mrs. Springer said. "Would you like some coffee or something else to drink?"

"I'm fine for now. Maybe later." Josephine followed Margaret and stood a moment while Margaret closed the door.

"Please sit on this chair. I'll use the bed," Margaret said.

"Thank you." Josephine took the offered seat and considered the young woman before her. Pain showed in Margaret's eyes. She seemed terribly upset, yet she arranged herself gracefully on what must be an awkward seat. She was truly lovely; no wonder Nat was taken with her. Josephine's mind went back to Nat covering her grandson, protecting him from the blows of the horse's hooves. She decided to get right to the point.

"I don't want to stay long. I left Nat with Cook, and need to get back soon. He's that bad off. In fact, we're not sure how seriously injured he is." She looked Margaret straight in the eye. "I've come to ask you to return with me."

Margaret sat silently, staring ahead. Finally she said, "I don't know what to say. This has been a difficult week." She sighed. "Truly difficult."

"Margaret, Nat wants you. He needs you. True, he didn't come right out and say it—he was conscious for so short a time— but it's as clear as the nose on my face." She then related what Nat had mumbled about Hiawatha. The Indian's love for Minnehaha. How Nat had said *Margaret*.

Margaret's eyes widened. "But what about Sally? I saw them together in the barn…" she choked on the words, "in an intimate…."

Josephine quickly countered. "I don't know what happened in the barn between them, but afterwards I saw her cozy up to Colburn. That girl has more than one iron in the fire."

"Oh!" Margaret clenched her hands. "I wish they'd all go

to the—"

"To the devil?" Josephine smiled inside, sympathizing with the girl. "I can understand that. It's only natural."

She reached for the girl's arm and held it, comfortingly, for some moments. "But I think that should tell you, right there, the depth of your feelings.

"Yes," Josephine went on, "Nat cared for Sally at one time. Or thought he did. But he's seen the difference between the two of you. What he felt for Sally was mainly physical. He's drawn to you in that way as well, but there's so much more.

"An intellectual bond exists between you. He saw that particularly after his time in school. And there's the spiritual as well. I don't know how much you've shared about this most important area, but you do have that in common." She held Margaret's eyes. "Be sure to make the most of that."

Josephine shifted in her chair, giving herself time to consider how much more to say. Some of what she knew in her heart, she had little direct evidence for. But then she thought of Nat lying unconscious.

"That night in the barn, with Sally all but throwing herself at Nat—of that I can be sure—he had to make a difficult choice. Especially after seeing you with Mr. Norland that same night and believing, I think, that you were choosing the banker."

Margaret interrupted. "That's all over. When I said goodbye to Mr. Norland, I told him I would no longer welcome his attentions."

"Does Nat know that?"

Josephine's hand once again closed over Margaret's arm. She shook it gently to emphasize her next words.

"I want you to understand something, Margaret. That night in the barn, let me repeat, Nat had to make a choice. Was he going to choose Sally who represented an easy way—the way 'of the flesh' as Christians say? Or would he choose the harder, but ultimately more rewarding way 'of the spirit'? You represent this last, my dear. Even though he thought you were deciding for Mr. Norland, I believe he chose the harder way and said no to Sally. When I saw her walk out of the barn and cozy up to Colburn so quickly, it's what I assumed. Wouldn't you draw the same conclusion?"

She searched Margaret's face. Was she making herself understood?

"Nat has grown so much into the man I hoped him to be—after I almost kicked him off the ranch when he first arrived, believing him to be trouble." She shook her head at herself. "However, God saw fit to use me in Nat's life. I became like a mother to him. Nat's thankful for that, having had so little time with his own mother. But now he needs more.

"When Nat was half-conscious and recited Hiawatha, he revealed his heart. He wants *you*, Margaret. He's a red-blooded male who has come to the point of needing the woman he loves. Like I said, he not only loves you, but needs you, now."

"Oh!" Margaret tried to stifle her cry. Her face strained, her shoulders suddenly shuddered. "But I still don't know if I could marry a man who could be so violent."

"I know this requires a big shift in your thinking, in your conviction of what life should be. After all, you are still in many ways an Easterner. But this is the West—with a vengeance. Your decision regarding Nat involves more than just deciding in favor of a man. It involves deciding on a way of life. And it is not easy living here," she added, smiling, "particularly in the winter."

She took the girl's hand. Squeezed it. "But I want to give you hope for your future. The West is changing. In time, law will be available wherever needed.

"Also, Mr. Walker and I promise to be there for both you and Nat. Helping you. Of course, we will do so from a distance. You need to make your own way."

Josephine felt such fondness for this young woman, yet she knew she would need old-fashioned grit and determination to live in Wyoming, and to make it a worthwhile life, a beautiful one. At the present moment, Josephine would not coddle her too much. "Now, I'm taking up Mrs. Springer's offer of that coffee before I leave. When I'm ready to go, I hope you'll return with me."

28

Margaret entered the room quietly and closed the door behind her. She looked at the figure on the bed. A single lamp burned low on a table nearby. The room was dim, but she could see Nat's strong, active figure inordinately still. On the ride to the Walker ranch, she remembered that first time she'd seen Nat on the prairie, swinging that axe to make a new axle for the stagecoach. Even then she'd gloried in the strength of him, in his skill. Little did she know she'd come to love him as well.

He hardly breathed. For a minute, she was afraid to approach him, fearful of what she might see in his face. Would it be drawn and pinched from pain? He had endured a lot, kicked by that wild mustang to save Jason.

Her heart went out to him, as it had done when Mrs. Walker told of his heroism. After Mrs. Walker left the room for Mrs. Springer's coffee, Margaret had flung clothes into her suitcase, wanting to leave as soon as possible.

Did she need this accident to wake her up, act as a catalyst to strip away non-essentials? Now she realized she'd let other things and people become too important to her.

She stood a minute longer at the door, afraid to approach him. Yet, she was eager to go to his side, to once again see his eyes, those eyes that had embarrassed her on more than one occasion with their intensity. She hadn't understood at first what his look meant. Now she knew, and trembled. He had hungered for her then, yet, except for that one brief, startling kiss, had all but kept his distance. She had thought it was her silly imagination, making more of the kiss than he'd meant. But now....

She glided forward. She'd heard it was his left side that was badly hurt, so she stepped to his right. There, the light would shine on his face so she could judge for herself how he looked, his state of mind—if he awoke. But she would not purposely wake him. Rest was his friend, his healer.

Standing at the side of the bed, she looked down at him. Suddenly, his face winced in pain, or was it a bad dream?

She waited. If a dream, should she gently wake him enough to get him out of a nightmare? She could not bear to think him in distress of any sort. She wanted him well and strong again.

But that might never be. Mrs. Walker had indicated her doubts as to the outcome of his injury. "But if anyone would be a tonic for Nat, it'd be you," she'd said. She had taken Margaret's hat and coat, and sent her into the room alone. "I'll be in later," she said. "Let's keep it to a single visitor for now."

Nat groaned and his face screwed up again. Margaret felt torn as to what to do. She looked back at the door. Should she get Mrs. Walker?

"Oh—h!" the figure on the bed suddenly cried out.

Margaret promptly decided to nudge his good side, wake him just enough to get him out of his nightmare. She gently shoved against him. "Hmm..." She hoped the noncommittal sound would help rouse him without giving away her presence.

After a few light shoves, he seemed to quiet. She bent over him to ascertain how he was doing, when suddenly his eyes opened. A crease formed between his brows, his eyes squinted in the dim light. He looked as though he was trying to see clearer. "What?" he whispered.

Margaret didn't know if he knew it was she hovering over him. But now he was obviously awake, if in a haze. She gently touched his shoulder. "Go back to sleep," she whispered. "Everything is all right."

His eyes remained open, their look intensified. Trying to focus. Margaret held her breath.

The room was very quiet.

"Margaret?"

To hear his voice, even weak, was a pleasure. "Yes, it's me."

He gazed at her. "You've come back." He looked as if he wondered if it could be true. Then he asked, "For how long?"

That was a good question. She'd come so precipitously, she hadn't made any plans. What should she say?

Then it came to her. "For as long as I'm needed." She couldn't say, for as long as *you* need me. He'd said her name to Mrs. Walker in delirium, and Mrs. Walker had interpreted it that Nat had wanted Margaret, but…she wasn't sure how necessary she was to his recovery.

He closed his eyes.

Was he going back to sleep?

He took in a deep breath. It seemed a long, satisfying, life-giving breath.

She moved away, her dress catching the bed clothes.

His eyes opened suddenly. "Don't leave." He said it with such vehemence, for a man who moments ago had seemed about to go back to sleep, that it startled her.

"I was just drawing up a chair." She noticed a pitcher on the night stand. "Would you like some water?"

"Yes."

She poured a little in a glass and helped lift his head to drink.

He sank back onto the pillow, his eyes closing.

The fingers of her hand pressed together, remembering the feel of his thick hair under her fingers. Another pleasure, mixed with the pain of seeing him suffer.

He murmured, "I'd been dreamin' of you. Dreamed you were leavin', and...."

"I'm right here." Then suddenly, she blurted out, "I won't leave if you don't want me to." Now, that was a confession.

Suddenly, his lips slid into a half smile. "You'll stay, then?"

"That depends...I need to finish the year here as a teacher, but I would have better students back East...."

He gazed at her for some moments. "Margaret, I can't talk...with you way off like that. Would you kneel down by the bed?"

She slipped to her knees.

"That banker...what's he to you?"

"He's nothing more than a good acquaintance. I told him I wanted no more special attention, that night after he'd escorted me home from school."

Nat took in a long breath, as if he'd been holding it. "Good."

That one word told her he'd been worrying. Well, let him worry no more. But she had something to ask as well. "And Sally? What's she to you?"

"She's the past. You mean so much more."

He paused. "After you get married...you can't be a teacher. Only single women allowed." His mouth suddenly drew up into a crooked smile. "Unless...you want to teach me?"

She looked at him. "What do you mean?"

"Teach me—readin' together. After we're married."

"Oh!" The single word burst from her mouth. She hadn't expected a proposal.

He seemed to gather steam and barreled ahead. "I love you, Margaret. Marry me?"

Sudden warmth rose in her. He *did* love her. The relief, and wonder of it. After all the tears of the past week.

And somewhere riding back to the ranch with Mrs. Walker, she'd decided Nat was not a violent man. He would act so only to protect those he loved, like Mrs. Walker said.

"Margaret. What'd you say?" He had that *look* in his eyes. "I can't stand…to wait much longer."

"Yes, Nat! The answer is yes." She smiled at him.

His voice strengthened. "Come up here."

What was he asking?

"On the bed. I can't stand up and hold you, so you have to come up here."

He winced in pain, trying to shift to the other side of the bed.

"Don't move, Nat." She looked at the space at his side. *What would Mrs. Walker think if she walked in?*

It was as if he read her thoughts. "Hang it, Margaret!" His voice roughened. "I don't care what Mrs. Walker thinks. I need you up here beside me. Besides, you don't know Mrs. W the way I do." A smile quirked at the corner of his mouth. "She'll give lots of leeway, after what I did for Jason."

Margaret knew this was true, and her lips widened slightly. Nat always was impetuous. She got up on the bed and lay beside him. He encircled her with his good arm and held her against him. She was surprised at his strength, there was nothing wrong with this arm.

His face was near hers, and she moved closer. His hand reached up to the back of her neck and gently pressed her face, her mouth to his. His kiss was tender. Then searching, as if exploring a new-found love.

She never knew a kiss could be so sweet and good. And exciting.

"That clinches my proposal," he murmured with satisfaction.

His lips hunted hers again. Long moments later, he drew away. Then he burst out, "You 'bout take my breath away. Thought you were a prim little school teacher…where'd you learn to kiss like that? Not from the banker?"

"No! No! I've no experience. Just that one kiss you gave me." She felt momentarily confused. "I kissed…what came naturally."

Nat laughed softly. "I got myself a virgin kisser!"

"Oh Nat!" She laughed softly. "What a thing to say. But it's one of the things that drew me to you, how you express yourself. You're not the usual cowboy."

He held her closer. "Can't wait till we get married."

She looked into his insistent eyes. Something in them jerked Margaret awake. She drew away and slid down to kneel at the side of the bed.

"Where you goin'?"

"You need to rest."

"Like heck I do! Here, take my good hand." He grasped hers warmly. "Soon I'll get the use of my other arm. You're not marryin' a one-armed cowboy...or rancher."

"Rancher?"

"Yes. Gettin' my own spread. Land from Mr. Walker." His voice was stronger in his excitement. "To raise horses and graze a few cows to keep us in beef." His eyes probed hers. "You're goin' to marry a rancher."

"That's wonderful, Nat."

"We'll establish a ranch, the two of us—with a little help from our friends, of course. But seein' as you and I are doing this together, this calls for a contract." His mouth twitched. "And we're signing this contract with another kiss." He squeezed her hand. "Get up on this bed."

"Nat!"

"You can keep your clothes on," he whispered teasingly.

"No. I'm staying right here." But she lifted her face close to his.

The kiss was long. Long and....

She could tell that now Nat was awake, he was *fully* awake.

She drew her face away. "I can see I'll need to take a lesson from Jane Eyre."

"What's that mean?"

"Before she and Mr. Rochester married, she wouldn't allow

more than the ordinary courtesies between themselves, no more than they would show anyone."

"Don't want to hear that," he protested. "This is the West. We're freer here."

Just then the door opened. "Oh! I see you two are getting reacquainted." Margaret turned and saw Mrs. Walker smile knowingly. "I came to offer lunch, but I can postpone it a little while."

"Lunch is just what we need," Margaret said on rising. "I've hardly been able to eat this last day. Now I find I'm hungry."

"How about you, Nat?" Mrs. Walker asked. "I've had Cook make her usual gruel for you. But maybe you're ready for something a little more hardy?"

"Yes. Somethin' solid. Margaret can bring it after she's eaten." He looked meaningfully at Margaret. "And she can bring a little sugar, too. Forget Jane!"

"Sugar? Jane?" Mrs. Walker asked.

"An allusion to Jane Eyre and Mr. Rochester—" Margaret started to say.

"Don't worry, Mrs. Walker," Nat said, "Margaret and I understand each other."

Glad for his interruption, because Margaret wasn't up to explaining, she followed Mrs. Walker out the door. She glanced back. Nat's eyes had that same look of intensity. A little feeling of excitement welled up in her. She didn't know if he'd be as amenable as Mr. Rochester at keeping his distance.

Yet, she was a teacher and accustomed to keeping students in line.

But when his look held hers like that, she remembered in the classroom he was the one who'd had the upper hand with the older boys.

"Margaret." Nat's voice cut through her musing. "Come back here." She hesitated, and he added, "Close the door. This is private."

She gave him a long look, then decided to comply with his request. She shut the door and walked to the bed and knelt beside it.

"Sorry I got carried away with that last kiss," he said resolutely. "The Lord just talked to me about it."

Her breathing slowed and her eyes teared up. "Thank you, Nat. Thank you for speaking about the Lord. Mrs. Walker encouraged me not to neglect this most important part of our relationship. I want what Christ means to us—to be something we always talk about."

"I know. I haven't spent this much time around Mrs. Walker without knowin' that. It's what I want, too."

"Nat! I love you!" She leaned forward and gave him a quick peck on his cheek.

"Hey, what kind of a kiss is that?" He reached for her hand. "I'm tellin' you right now, this waitin' to get married will be hard. You're goin' to have to help me some."

"Oh, Nat—"

"What I mean is, I want to honor you, not take advantage…." He squeezed her hand. "I can be pretty impulsive. And, once I get goin', I get goin'."

"I know."

"You might have to say 'no' once in a while." He shook her hand slightly for emphasis. "But, after we're married, we won't say 'no.' You agree?"

"Yes."

"That's my girl."

He caressed her hand. "I'm glad we can touch. 'Cause I think somehow God's in that, too, the physical part."

He was quiet some moments. "This physical part…somethin' Mrs. Walker said made me think. She said, 'The pleasure in marriage can be an earthly picture…of the love between us and the Lord'." He smiled, but looked serious. "I'm not sure what that all means, but she said that the intimate, physical part—

ne—is something beautiful God created for two
ple. And somehow, it also shows God's love for us
way. The Bible says it's a mystery. I guess we'll find
that out as we go along."

"Nat, I can't believe you're saying that. If we can talk like
this, we'll have…a rich marriage." She gazed at him. "This is all
rather new to me. I came here to be a teacher, not to get married,
you know.

She held his hand a little tighter, loved its firmness, even
its roughness. "Being out there alone on our ranch—practically
speaking, I will need mental stimulation. After I give up
teaching…."

"That's why I said we'd read together. Your parents can send
us more books from Chicago. We'll build a library in our home."

"Oh Nat!"

"Another of my…ideas. But that's way in the future. For
now, it's just us…" His eyes gleamed. "It looks to me because
we're makin' all these agreements, we should finalize them.
With another kiss, Miss Arnell."

She smiled and started to lean forward.

"Oh no! Come on up here. All these special plans and promises need somethin' extra."

"Nat," she warned.

"Margaret, we're not saying 'no' just yet." His eyes had that
look.

She laughed. "I think you're getting better fast. I don't
think—" Then she remembered all this injured man had done
for the Walker family. And if she were honest, how much she
wanted to be near him, too.

She rose from her knees and slid up alongside him. "All
right then."

AFTERWORD

THE JOHNSON COUNTY CATTLE WAR

This was a plan to scare smaller ranchers into leaving Wyoming. In April of 1892, tensions that had mounted for years between the cattle barons and small homesteaders erupted. The Wyoming Stock Growers Association (WSGA) took action against the small ranchers suspected of "rustling," hiring 23 gunmen from Texas plus some of their own members to embark on an expedition into Johnson County where they were to "shoot or hang" some 70 county residents and officials named on a list compiled by the stock organization. They were under the command of Major Frank Wolcott; Tom Smith, who recruited the Texans; and Frank Canton, former sheriff of Johnson County. Second in command was to have been Fred Hesse, former foreman of Moreton Frewen's ranch.

From the first, the expedition went awry with two homestead cowboys murdered, and the Invaders (as they were called) ended up surrounded at the TA ranch by a posse of 200 from Buffalo. After three days, the Invaders were "rescued" by order of President Harrison, who sent three troupes of cavalry to escort them away. Incarcerated at Cheyenne, the Invaders never saw trial as Johnson County was not stable enough financially to thoroughly pursue charges. The Invaders were released without punishment, bringing an anticlimactic end to one of the most monumental battles of the Old West. Over the years, many movies used this conflict as a basis for their stories.

'S "CASTLE"

͞ present-day Kaycee, Frewen's home was dubbed by
astle" because of its size and opulence as a ranch. (The
great central hall was 40 feet wide by 40 feet long. Buffalo robes,
horns and trophies from Moreton Frewen's many hunts adorned
the room. There was an upper mezzanine for musicians and as
many as 20 guests could dine comfortably at the large dining
table.) Visiting the Occidental Hotel, I discovered an old map
that had Frewen's Castle notated on it. The house is no longer
standing, but its logs make up a homestead now housed at the
Hoofprints of the Past Museum in Kaycee, and its rosewood
staircase (shipped from England) was transferred to a house in
Sussex, Wyoming.

HOLE-IN-THE-WALL

Located in the Big Horn Mountains of Johnson County in
northern Wyoming, the site was used from the late 1860s to
around 1910, by various gangs of outlaws as their base of opera-
tions and a place to lay up during the harsh Wyoming winters.
It contained a corral, livery stable and one or two cabins for each
gang. The area was remote and secluded, easily defended because
of its narrow entry passes. No lawmen ever successfully entered
it to capture outlaws. Butch Cassidy's Wild Bunch (with the
Sundance Kid) were among the cattle rustlers and other outlaws
which used it as a hideout.

OCCIDENTAL HOTEL

Built in 1880, it hosted most of the major political, social,
and cultural gatherings of Johnson County. In 1890 rooms were
$2.50 a day and meals were served around the clock. Many
original features remain such as the embossed tin ceilings
along with the 23 bullet holes in the saloon. It hosted many

famous guests over the years including Butch Cassidy and the Hole-in-the-Wall Gang, Calamity Jane, Buffalo Bill Cody, General Phil Sheridan, Tom Horn, Ernest Hemingway, and Presidents Teddy Roosevelt and Herbert Hoover. Owen Wister, author of *The Virginian* spent many happy hours in the Occidental lobby and saloon, and based characters in his celebrated novel on cowboys and gunslingers he observed there.

CUSSION QUESTIONS

1. Which characters come to mind in the title: *The Rugged and the Refined*?

2. How does the "half-moon" horse help drive the plot?

3. How is Mrs. Walker a mentor to both Nat and Margaret?

4. Contrast Margaret and Sally. How do these women high-light—in Nat—the struggle of the "flesh" versus the "spirit?"

5. What was the trouble between the homesteaders and the cattle barons?

6. How do the historical figures Lord Moreton Frewen and Major Frank Wolcott give a preview of the future trouble coming to Johnson County, Wyoming?

7. What does the book highlight about education? How do the characters of Nat and Margaret illustrate this?

8. What do you believe is the main theme of this novel?

9. Do you detect any subthemes?

10. Share a favorite scene in the story.

Rode in a stagecoach.
And, yes, it was rough!

If you enjoyed this story,
I invite you to leave a review on the book's Amazon page.
Thank you!

Visit my website:
ruthtrippy.com

Write me via email:
ruth.trippy@yahoo.com

Made in the USA
Las Vegas, NV
21 December 2021

39166604R00154